TAP OUT

by ERIC DEVINE

ISBN 978-0-7624-4569-1

Library of Congress Control Number: 2012934247

E-book ISBN 978-0-7624-4700-8

9   8   7   6   5   4   3   2   1
Digit on the right indicates the number of this printing

Cover and interior design by Ryan Hayes
Edited by Lisa Cheng
Typography: ITC Century Book, Gotham
Cover image: Honza Krej / Shutterstock.com, Warren Goldswain / Shutterstock.com, ilolab / Shutterstock.com, Darryl Brooks / Shutterstock.com, David Arts / Shutterstock.com, Evok20 / Shutterstock.com, StockLib / istockphoto.com

Published by Running Press Teens
An Imprint of Running Press Book Publishers
A Member of the Perseus Books Group
2300 Chestnut Street
Philadelphia, PA 19103–4371

Visit us on the web!
www.runningpress.com

TAP OUT

by ERIC DEVINE

RP|TEENS
PHILADELPHIA • LONDON

For everyone who has wanted to tap out,
but found the will to keep fighting.

1

I am a pussy. I know this, and not much else.

A wet smack sounds in the next room. My mother cries in pain. "Please, Cameron, I didn't mean anything." He hits her again, twice, dense flesh on flesh.

"The fuck you didn't," Cameron, my mother's boyfriend, slurs. She must have made some joke that he was too drunk to understand. Again.

So he's kicking the shit out of her. Again.

I'm sitting on the corner of my bed, listening, but not doing anything, even though I want to. My muscles are all coiled, tight, like I'm ready to roll, but I won't. Cameron is wiry, works construction, and could toss me across the fucking room. At least that's what I tell myself about him, *this* boyfriend. I've had excuses for all the others as well, and an entire list of reasons for my father.

He hits her again, a dull thud, the sound of his fist hitting her head. "You gonna apologize or what?"

"I'm sorry. I'm sorry. I didn't mean anything."

Another blow, and she hits the wall. The house vibrates. "Damn straight, you dumb bitch." The door squeals as he pounds down the hall and the fridge opens. He's grabbing a beer, or two. The can clicks and pops, followed by the sound of him falling into the recliner. The volume on the TV goes up: lots of screaming and yelling.

Fuck, maybe it's over. I grab the back of my head and bury my face into the crooks of my elbows. I want to block out the sound of him and forget what I just heard, but my mom's crying seeps through the paper-thin walls. I hate the noise, but more, I hate how common it is. How many times has she been like this? It's impossible to keep track, there's been so many.

Her cry lifts and then is muffled. She must be using her pillow. I hope so, because if he hears her . . . hopefully she'll be able to calm herself and then sit, red-faced and swollen, and wait for Cam to get a sleepy buzz. Then, like always, she can ice or shower, depending on how bad it is. Once it started, it only took them three months to find this pattern. Not a record, but pretty fast.

Wonder how long it took for her and my dad?

He's the reason I'm such a little bitch now, hiding out instead of stepping up. As a kid I never once went after him, just daydreamed about taking him out. In the end I didn't have to; he just left. As have all the rest. But Cameron's still hanging around, and this time I see myself stepping into her bedroom when he's wailing on her. I grab his arm midswing and twist him around. He sees me and his eyes go wide, but then he gets that sneer like he always does. But before he can do anything, I head-butt him. He collapses to his knees, grabbing his face as the blood pumps out. I ignore it and put my fist into his jaw. No, through it. My mom screams, but I ignore her and enjoy his pain. He goes to speak but realizes that his jaw is shattered and I laugh, because I know in that moment I could kill him. I may not be big, but you don't get beat your entire life without hardening.

I *could* take him out. I have the capacity, and that is enough for me, because I don't want to actually do it and be like him, or the others. In my fantasy I help my mother up and walk her out of the room, away from the oozing mass in the corner. We step into a cleaner version of our life, where we're not confined to our prison of a trailer and no one sees us as white trash.

It's never gonna happen though, so there's no point in wishing for it. I stand up and walk to the bathroom and the trailer wobbles. Or it could be I'm still amped and it feels that way. Or the fucking thing may really be falling apart. Why wouldn't it? Everything else is.

I piss and brush my teeth. The TV blares and I listen: an announcer's voice. Fuck. I peer down the hall. He's watching a cage match. Two guys hop around a mat. One is all tatted up and has blood leaking out of his nose. The other is so thin that his abs look like individual plates. I don't know how they can even be in the same weight class, but they throw jabs back and forth and then the tatted one kicks. The skinny one catches it, and the tatted guy's eyes go wide. He knows what's coming, and sure as shit the skinny dude latches on to the tatted guy's leg like a monkey to a tree and takes him to the mat. The skinny guy squeezes on the tatted guy's leg and arches his own back, every muscle popping. The ref hovers over them, wearing the same black latex gloves we wear at Vo-Tec, and the tatted guy screams as the blood pumps faster. He looks up, grinds his teeth, and then taps the mat. Fight's over.

"Fucking leg bar." Cameron tosses an empty can to the floor and then pops open another.

I head back to my room and have to shake away the fantasy rising again. I'll stay awake all night if I don't put it out of my mind. I sit on my bed and can hear my mom still crying. I lie back and pull a pillow over my head, but it doesn't help. Her tears still seep through, and the sound of another fight beginning on the TV punches in.

2

I'm standing out by the Pleasant Meadows park sign, waiting for the bus. There's not one thing pleasant about this place and no meadow that I've ever seen. Feet scuffle down the lane and the girls giggle, while Rob's laugh echoes.

"There's my little bitch." Rob wraps an arm around my neck and squeezes. My head throbs as he pulls me down. "You ready to suck it? Huh?" His crotch is inches from my face, and I go limp, just hang as dead weight in his arms. "Man." He lets go. "No fucking fun if you don't fight back."

"Leave Tony alone. His house was on fire last night." Amy kicks Rob in the ass. I stand and tuck my hands into my pockets, happy to be out of the hold, but not if I have to talk about this. "Cameron?" She takes a drag off her cigarette and closes an eye when she exhales.

"Yeah." There's no point in denying it. Everyone knows everybody's business around here, and sadly, mine is real fucking common. I kick the loose stone at our feet.

"Fucking temper. But hot as a motherfucker. I'd do him." Amy licks her lips.

"You'd do your fucking dog, you whore." Charity lights a cigarette and juts her chin.

"If his dick were big enough. Holla!"

The girls laugh, and Rob shakes his head.

"For real, man. You need to get ready for when he turns on you. I'll show you some moves." Rob pops into stance, like the fighters on TV from last night, and paws at the back of my neck. He's wearing his MMA gym's hoodie today. Like every day. But he's got a point about Cameron, just like I was thinking last night. Sooner or later they all turn on me: all her boyfriends, and my dad, too. But Cameron just doesn't seem to be going anywhere. He doesn't have the ability to be disgusted with us, or himself. But fuck Rob and his karate-ass shit. There's no ring at my house.

"Yeah. I wanna grapple with you. So we can get *real close* to each other."

Rob's eyes draw together. "Yo, it's not like that."

"Really? You just wanted me to suck your dick."

The girls laugh.

"Fuck you, Tone. I'll kick your ass right here. No grappling." He pops his stance again and weaves around me. I used to be able to take him back in middle school, and even freshman year. But now? Maybe. He is bigger, but that doesn't always matter.

Brakes hiss behind us, and the bus door wrenches open. "Put them cigarettes out!" Hack-Face, the bus driver, leans over her seat. She looks like someone once went over her with a cleaver. Every inch of her skin is wrinkled and red.

The girls take long drags, and then step on the butts and mount the stairs. They exhale as they pass Hack-Face. Rob's still in his stance and I shake my head and turn my back on him.

I sit alone because I don't feel like talking to Rob. He'll just want to go on and on about fighting and the gym, and with last night still swirling in my head, it's about the last topic I want to deal with. He's been trying to get me to join ever since he started last year, but it's not like I've got the money. All the guys who go there wear the same hoodie with the gym's logo on the front—two figures, one standing, the other lying on the mat—and some quote on the back. Either that or it's those ugly fucking TAPOUT shirts or the ones with images of fighters on them. It's like they're in fifth grade again, busting a nut over some A-Rod or McGwire jersey. No, I really don't want to be one of them, either.

I spin the dial on my locker and then check the schedule taped inside. It's Thursday, but I don't have a clue what day in the rotation it is. A girl nearby closes her locker. "Hey, what's today?"

She looks at me, squints, and her mouth forms a wiggly line, like she wants to say something, but can't find the words. It's always like this. Kids know I'm trash from who I hang with, but not from the way I look. I keep myself clean, ironing board in the bedroom and everything pressed. I do my own laundry and make damn sure my kicks stay spotless, so if I'm on my own, they have to guess. "Thursday." She presses her books close to her chest.

I shake my head. "No. What day?" I point at my schedule.

"Oh." She straightens. "C-Day."

"Thanks." She's got her back to me before I speak, but at least she spoke. Shit, C-day blows. Bio, then PE, then English. Afternoons are always Vo-Tec, but it doesn't make up for the three long hours I'm here. The bell rings and kids look around, waiting for the first person to take off. Eventually, we all do.

I don't even know why I gotta take bio. Not like I'm

gonna be a fucking doctor or some shit. Mr. Bransfield starts writing notes on the board, and kids get out their binders or notebooks. I don't have a notebook or a pen. Not even a book bag. I look at the extra textbook he makes me use and listen. Period. If it sticks, it sticks. He's written something up there about the three layers of the skin. Who gives a shit? Skin's so thin, might as well all be one.

I skim the section we're supposed to read and catch words like "ruptured capillaries" and "trapped blood" and "trauma," but I know all this shit. A fucking bruise happens when something hits you. A hand, a belt, a shoe. Who gives a fuck what occurs beneath the surface?

Mrs. Myers gives us a quiz on the first chapter of this book, *Lord of the Flies*, I didn't read. Don't ever read. At least not since I was a kid. So I guess at the answers and probably fail. Mrs. Myers asks us to pass up the paper and then read Chapter Two for the rest of the class. I don't have a copy, and she doesn't hand out loaners like Bransfield, so I put my head on my desk and pop my hoodie over. Lights out.

The bell rings. I pull myself together, rub my face, and head to the main entrance. I could go to lunch, but none of the other Vo-Tec fucks do. It's the hassle of getting the shit for free. We all do, but have to give the ugly, old, hair-netted bitch who runs the register this special card. That's if we remember to bring it. Which is never. So the old hag has to yell to some other old hag to look up a "Free lunch." Asks our last name and yells that, too. That's a mistake I've only made once.

Somebody opens a bag of chips and passes it around.

Rob, Amy, and Charity chow down. The girls all go to become hairdressers or some nail salon shit. We go and work on cars. I grab a handful and think to take more. This is the first I've eaten today.

"Afternoon boys." Mr. Greyson wipes his hands on a rag, but they're still black when he finishes. I breathe in the greased air and love it. "As you can see, we've got a project for today." He throws a thumb at the pickup, a 250, new, black, and beautiful. "Just an oil change. But we'll do the filter and check the fluids and brakes, too."

Greyson's a hard ass, but he's the only one who can get away with it because he's the only one who actually teaches us something useful. He smacks the clipboard he pulls from his shop table. "Looks like Rob and Tony have the honors."

My stomach drops, but Rob pumps his fist. "Sweet!"

"Good, get to it. Remember the pan." Greyson whips the air with his hand. "The rest of you, follow me." The group walks to the pair of junkers that we learn from, these piece of shit cars, stripped down, like dead, open bodies for doctors. Rob and I grab the tools we need. We weren't allowed to touch anything our freshman year, just watch and memorize. Sophomore year, we could hand off tools. Junior year, we could touch. Now I know almost every tool and how to change oil, tires, and bulbs. I can monitor electrical systems, brake rotors, and on and on. It isn't a great living, but I could be a mechanic anywhere, and get the fuck out of here.

I check that the bay is clear and that the truck is secure, and then hit the switch on the lift and the truck rises. Rob moves under, pan in hand, already wearing latex gloves. I love that we're given the chance to keep our hands clean.

"You should at least come to one class." Rob unscrews the nut, and the oil drips.

"How many times do I need to tell you? I'm not into it."

"Till you change your mind." Rob turns his back to me. "Read this."

"Douche, I don't give a shit about your fucking sweat-shirt."

Rob spins and puts a thumb into my collarbone. I go to my knees; the pain is so sudden.

"Everything all right over there?" Greyson calls.

"Yup." Rob waves with his free hand.

So do I. "All right. Fucking quit."

Rob releases and turns his back, again. I wipe my neck with a clean rag, but nothing comes away. Still, I think about kicking out his legs and watching him fall into the pan of oil, but I just read his sweatshirt for the hundredth fucking time, because if I don't he'll keep asking: *The cage will reveal your true self. Whether you like it or not.* I shove him. "All right. Happy?"

"Not until you find out, fucker."

I stand and move to the lift control. "Well, that isn't hap-pening today." I shrug. "Screw that shit in before I crush you."

Rob stares at me for a moment, his typical bad-ass stance. They must teach this shit, and I feel like flipping him off, but that's not the point. I know what he's thinking, that he could take me out right here. Fuck, maybe he thinks he's so fast he could get to me before I hit the lift button? I don't like it, but his cockiness reminds me of Cameron, and I'm glad that he turns and does his job.

We finish and Greyson checks on us, gives a grunt, and says, "Nice work." After that we clean up and then hit up the bus for home. As soon as we're off Amy and Char light up.

"Tonight, Tone." Amy blows a ring. "You need to run and hide, come on over."

Everyone laughs, but Amy looks at me with her fuck-me eyes. She means it, but there's no way I'm putting my dick in her. She's been used so much, I bet the shit's like a baseball glove. I open my mouth to make the joke, but don't bother. I just don't have the energy. "Whatever." I wave them off, and Rob walks with me. He slaps my shoulder.

"You change your mind, I'll be rolling past round six." I shake my head, just because I don't feel like speaking, and am glad that he just lets it go. "All right, catch you tomorrow." He takes off, and I turn toward my house. I heard someone once say that all of us in the park live in sardine cans, and I guess that's true. My house is small, metal, and looks like it should be thrown away. The smell is pretty rancid as well. But I don't have anything else, so I head in.

Mom's not home and the place is a fucking mess. Cameron's cans are spilling out of the garbage, or lying next to the chair. Dishes and food containers from my mom's work spill across the counter. It looks like spaghetti, but I turn away from it. I'm not *that* hungry, and I'm not cleaning up their shit, even though I'll get bitched at later. Whenever she fucking gets home from the diner. Fuck her. She had time to clean.

I go to my room and close the accordion door. Unlike the rest of this heap, my room's clean. Everything has a place and is put there. I take off my shoes and line them alongside my other pair, beneath my bed. It squeaks when I hop on it, but is damn comfortable. I lie back and stare at the ceiling. Brown water stains dot the corner. The last time it rained heavy I woke up wet. Cameron said he'll fix it, but I think he's just grunt labor, doesn't know how to do a damn thing for himself.

My stomach growls so I roll to my side and pull my knees up to my chest. Hope my mom brings home leftovers or I may have to eat that spaghetti. I grab the blanket from the foot of my bed and pull it over me. Cover everything. The only thing to do is sleep and wait for whatever's next.

"Whad'ya mean I can't come in?"

I sit up. It's dark and Cam's voice is worming in from outside. She must be blocking the door. I get into position to roll.

"Not tonight. I'm not in the mood."

"You're always in the mood, baby. Can't resist this." Cameron laughs. It's throaty, sounding like he's working up a hawker, and I'd like to strangle that noise inside him, not out of him. I want him to hear the way he sounds to me.

"Cam, fuck off! I ain't having this shit tonight. It's been a long fucking . . ." The slap sounds as if he's hit her flush in the cheek, wet and fleshy. She doesn't finish.

"I don't give a fuck! Boo fucking hoo. You had to work. I did, too. Now let me in."

I roll my legs over the side of the bed and slide my feet into my sneakers. I don't know why. I'm not going anywhere, especially not outside. I'd only *like* to strangle him, not actually do it.

"Go away."

"What, you got someone else in there?"

I stand and push back my door. It's like I'm in someone else's body, because this is not me. Ever since the first time I can remember my dad going after her, pulling her hair down to the floor, where she became eye-level with me, I've frozen. Then, I just couldn't understand why he'd want her in that position. Now, after seven years with him and a dozen or so of her boyfriends, I understand all too well.

"No, no one else is in here. Just Tony, and he's sleeping."

"Sleepin'? That little bitch is taking a nap. Let me wake his ass up."

My insides tighten, and I grab the doorframe. What the fuck am I doing? I look into the hall. My mom's standing in the doorway, and her face is drawn, eyes puffy. She's spent. This fucker needs to leave because she doesn't have anything left to fight with. But between her and my pussy ass, what can we do? She holds up her hands. "Cameron, go home. Enough."

"Yeah, yeah. Same ol' shit, 'Yer nuthin' but a drunk.' Save it. Cuz you'll be callin', crying to me about how sorry you are."

I step into the hall and lock my jaw, grinding my teeth. He's right, that's exactly what she does, but it doesn't mean she has to, again.

"Just go." Her voice is a whisper.

"All right." His feet crunch outside, and I relax. Fuck, maybe he's got more sense than I thought. Or is just too loaded to continue. I lean against the wall, and the sound of him hitting her, like someone slapping down beer cans, brings me back to standing. His hands fly through the open door, and my mom grabs the frame to keep from falling. He catches her square in the eye with a fist, and she goes down on her side. I'm down the hall in five steps. She's trying to stand, and he's on the steps grabbing her legs.

"No!" I can't stop myself. Here I am, out of my room, not fantasizing, but about to enter the mix.

Both of them freeze and look at me, my mother's eyes wide, her mouth bleeding and hanging open. Cameron's forehead knots, but then he smiles. That fucking smirk pulls across his face. "Woo hoo. Big man steppin' up. All right!"

I look at my mother, her bloody face, spit and snot dribbling out her mouth and nose. I've seen this image so many times that it's left me numb. I know it's wrong, but she looks pathetic to me, lying on the ground again, helpless. Cameron laughs, and I look up, into his eyes. They're sinister, like something from a nightmare, and I feel again. First fear and then panic. My mother's not helpless, he's just fucking evil, and now that I'm standing up to him, for her, I can't go down as easily.

I rush to the door, and he slips, trying to react. I pull my mother's legs inside and then slam the door in place. I lock it just as he grabs the handle, but the door is secure, so he pounds on the thin metal.

"You fucking pussy. Get yer ass out here. I'll fuck you up real good. Then I'll fuck yer mother." He laughs again and pounds some more.

Again, I want to strangle his words in his throat. I help my mother up and move her to the couch. Cameron's still pounding and screaming. This is nothing like my fantasy. My head spins, but I go to the bathroom and wet a washcloth. I bring it back and hand it to my mom.

"Thank you." Her voice is low, and she does not look at me. I sit next to her, and she cleans her face, and we both seem to tune out whatever the fuck he's screaming out there, something about his dick. "I thought he was different, honey. Really."

I open my mouth to speak because I can't imagine what she saw in him that was any different from the others. He's a fucking loser with a dead-end job, who drinks until he passes out, and when he feels like it, beats the shit out of her. But I keep my comments to myself. She's still wearing her work uniform. He must have followed her or have been waiting.

Maybe it's not her fault—this time.

She looks at me out of the corner of her eye. "At least I know who you are."

I nod but not because I'm agreeing. I don't know what else to do because I don't know that who I am is as solid as she thinks. Up until five minutes ago, I never once stood up to any of the men in her life. It's not as if she has ever asked me to, but with what she just said, it makes me feel as if she's been waiting. Unreal. Even my own mother thought I was a pussy. But maybe, just maybe, I'm not.

3

I pop up and sit in bed. All is quiet, which is good, because I tried to stay on guard all night, listening for Cameron outside. His voice came and went, but he didn't do anything, so I drifted off around 2:00. Hope that was enough.

I climb out of bed, and my head crackles with the lack of sleep. I'm used to it, though, and know I can just catch up in school. It's early, 5:45, which means there's still time to drag the garbage out, since I couldn't last night. I slide into my shoes and goose bumps rise along my arms because of the chill in the air, but from something else, too. The echo of his voice saying my name.

The shit hole is the same, disheveled. I head down the hall, past my mother's room and into the kitchen, where I tie up the bag, then hesitate before unlocking the door. Did I really stand up to him last night? Lock him out? Fuck, I did. Shit, what the fuck was I thinking? This is gonna get ugly. But if I want something better, something more than this, maybe it has to get ugly first?

Outside is damp and cool. I shiver and walk around back to the can. A fly darts off my ear and I swipe at him. Then another. The fuck? The bag bounces off my calf, and the stench hits me. "Shit!" I toss the bag to the ground, and it joins the shredded mess. The can's been dumped and the bags ripped. Cameron's stomped on the contents, so wrappers and food are half buried in the ground or mashed to a pulp. Flies pour out of a Styrofoam carton. I step away and slip on something black and greasy. The stench overwhelms me, and I head back inside.

The door slams behind me, and a moan comes from my mom's room. I don't give a fuck if I've woken her up. I first wipe off my sneaker on the doormat and then grab the dustpan and another garbage bag from the cabinet. When I turn she's leaning on her doorframe.

"What's up?" She pulls on the ends of her extra long T-shirt. Her hair's a tangle and looks unwashed, and the greased pattern it falls into does not cover the bruises from last night. They're as bad as ever, and I feel ashamed for being pissed with her.

"Nuthin'. Taking out the trash."

"Oh." She looks away, as if somewhere far. Like we've got a double-wide or some shit.

"Yeah. Cam fucked it up out there. Needs to be cleaned." I don't know if I expect her to do something because I've said this or that I wish she *had done* something differently so that I wouldn't have to take care of this, but either way, I'm still pissed. "*Somebody's* gotta do it." My voice doesn't seem to register with her. She just keeps staring.

"Oh. Okay," she finally says and turns back into her room and snaps the door in place.

"Stupid bitch." I say it low, to my chest, and it makes my face hot. I know Cam did this, not her, but in a way she's responsible. She brought him onto the scene. I know I wasn't just talking about cleaning up this mess. There's so much that needs to be done, but who's going to do it? Fuck, I can't go there right now. I head out the door and set to work.

I dry heave once, but manage to get the shit into the bag, and then the can out to the road. Cameron did this once over the summer. It was the first sign that things were turning between them. June was a scorcher, hot and humid, so by the time I got to the garbage, maggots were crawling everywhere, and I did hurl, and then had to clean that up. At least this isn't as bad.

I head back in and go right to the shower. The water takes a while to heat, so I sit on the toilet and wait. Six months. She's been with this douche for half a year, which means she'll go back and forth for another three months before she dumps him. Or he puts her in the hospital. Same as with Karl. And Steve. And Jake. And all the rest whose names I can't remember. Or just won't. Oh yeah, and Number One himself, Tony Senior. I wish she could just . . . fuck, there's just too much I wish she'd do.

I shower, scrub until it hurts and my skin is red, but I don't mind the pain. It's only superficial. I dress in a plain gray tee and my black jeans, cuffed at the ends because they're too long. I slide my sneakers back on, making sure all of whatever the fuck I stepped in is gone, and then throw on my hoodie. Amy keeps my hair close-cropped with the clippers she's got from Vo-Tec, so I slide a hand over my dome and dry the remaining water. Then I rummage for food. Never did eat dinner last night, and there's nothing in the house except some crusty bread and fruit punch. Mom must have eaten that spaghetti. I drink a glass of the red liquid and take off.

"That motherfucker never quits." Amy's already smoking, sitting on her steps. She stands and I turn away. "Seriously, Tone. He was out here till like one, two?" I shrug, but she doesn't seem to notice that I don't want to talk about this bullshit and catches up with me. "You shoulda called the cops."

"Wouldn't have helped." The pigs don't like to come inside the park, so unless someone's getting murdered, they don't do shit.

She takes a drag and exhales. "Maybe. I don't know. But you gotta do somethin'."

I look at her out the corner of my eye. It's like she was reading my mind, and I don't like the feeling. She's short with big tits and nice hair, but already going old. Like her mom. Some parts young and hot, but the face, it's like a Halloween mask. What the fuck does she know? She's never been in my shoes. Not exactly. "Why? Why do *I* have to do somethin'? Why can't *she*?"

"Your mom? Cuz it's Cameron you stupid shit. She can't do nuthin'. That whole family is fucked up. And besides, this is her thing, isn't it?" Amy laughs and ashes her cigarette.

I spit and kick a large stone. It sucks that my life is this obvious. Is it because we live in this shit hole, all on top of each other? What if we lived in town, or better, the suburbs? Would it be the same? Wish I knew. We walk on and Charity pops off her steps, joining us. She doesn't say shit, though, and looks as pale as a crackhead. She bums a smoke off Amy. Her hair's still wet and she's been chewing her fingers. One's bleeding. We reach the bus stop and Rob is already there. The girls split off and speak in whispers.

"'Sup?" Rob looks at the girls.

"Char's a mess."

"Her fucking dad, I bet." Rob frowns.

We've all got our shit. Rob with his mom that stays home all day while his dad works a thousand shifts to make ends meet. Amy's mom doesn't work either. My mom's used up. But Charity, her problem's her dad. He's one bad-ass fuck.

Harleys, heroin, and a gang. Whenever he rumbles through somebody ends up busted, in jail, or dead. He's always recruiting, though. Never seems to have a problem finding guys, either. It's the money, I guess. Or something else, I don't know. I steer clear.

I look over at Rob's sweatshirt. Same one as yesterday. He sees me and watches, but doesn't say anything. I take in the image: one guy standing, the other flat out. Amy's words run through my head, as do all the images from last night, and my mother's face, this morning. "So I can just drop by a class or some shit? Or do I need to come with you and wear like special gear?"

Rob tilts his head. "Fuck you just say?"

"You heard me."

"Know I did." He pumps his fist and laughs. "Nah, man. You don't need any special gear. This ain't fucking tae kwon do. It's fighting. But you should roll with me."

I don't respond, but look away, back at the girls. Char's crying now, her face red and puffy. She's telling some story, pointing back at her place and shrugging her shoulders. Both girls are veiled in a cloud of smoke.

"Cameron up to his shit again?" Rob's voice has dropped.

I nod.

"How bad?"

"Been worse."

"But now you're thinking about if it goes that way, what are you gonna do?"

The fantasy swirls inside me, but in the light of this morning I consider Cameron: a rope-muscled construction worker and former safety on the football team who used to jack shit up. Still does, just off the field. And me? I'm everything besides. "I don't know. Just want to check it out. All right?"

"You know it is." Rob smiles, and in the distance the bus's brakes squeal. My stomach growls, and Charity weeps.

Today I've only got two classes, history and math. Study hall third block and then back to Vo-Tec. I chill at my locker until the bell rings, not talking to anyone, and no one looking to. They're all checking texts and have earbuds hanging from their ears. I throw up my hoodie and pretend I'm alone because I want to be. And am.

The bell rings, and I head to Mr. Lance's. He's a fucking dick. Has us take notes for the whole class, but I just doodle. I turn the corner and Dave Jensen swivels and looks directly at me. My body clenches in fear when he smiles.

"My man, Tone." He clears the distance between us.

I only know Dave because he's fucking insane. Pissed in a garbage can in front of the class one year. Threw a teacher off him when he tried to break up a fight. This might be his fifth or sixth year here. He's also a fighter, like Rob. "What's up?" I say and look around, wondering if Rob's part of this. Told Dave I'm a new recruit or something.

Dave snorts. "Heard you've been giving my uncle shit."

My mind spins and I look away, but then it stops when I remember what Amy said about Cam's family. Fuck, no. I stop looking around and stare at Dave. His forehead's wrinkled, and his nose twitches. He's got his tongue pressed behind his top lip, just like Cameron.

"That true?" He leans closer.

My throat tightens, and my body tenses. I shift my weight back. Even though I know, I gotta bluff. "No, I . . . I mean. I don't know what you're talking about. Who's your uncle?"

Kids pass by and look over. They see Dave and look away, and he licks his lips. "Dude who's been boning your mom for the past few months." He laughs, and it's ugly and evil and makes me feel dirty. More than that, I want to hit this fuck, almost as bad as I wanted to hit Cameron last night. But if Cameron is tough, Dave is unbreakable. Everything from my throat to my nuts clenches, and I open my mouth to speak, but nothing comes. Dave grips my shoulder. His hand's a fucking vice, and he increases the pressure. "You fuck with my uncle, and if he don't kick your ass, I will." He licks his lips, again. "Clear?"

I nod but he grips my shoulder a bit more fiercely before turning away. The bell rings, and I look up the hall. Mr. Lance stands in his doorway, sees me, and taps his watch. Really? Is he fucking blind? Every teacher in this school knows Jensen. This douche can't pretend that he didn't just see our encounter. But he waves, a little, pathetic, underhanded move, and I walk up the hall and stumble into class. He says something, but I don't hear it. The sound of Dave licking his lips, followed by what he said fills my head. There's no fucking way I'm going anywhere with Rob.

"Pop quiz. Take out a sheet of paper."

The entire room groans. I score a sheet from the kid behind me. Still don't know his name, but it's not like we do any group work or shit in here.

I write answers to the questions on the board: *Don't know. Don't care. He felt like it. His third birthday. Your mom.* Lance'll probably give me detention for that last one, but that's fine. Actually, that would help me avoid Rob without having to make up some bullshit excuse he'll just bust my balls about. Like he's done for the past year. Shit, but Lance won't read these until later. I need something, today, now. Not here, though. Next block. I have a plan.

4

'm set. I played the scene in my head while in Lance's. But even though I know I'm set, I can't look at Mrs. Sagehorn. This is going to fuck her shit up, big time. She loves math. I think she gets off on the way "Geometry is everywhere around us." But she has no idea what I see in my world. I raise my hand to volunteer.

"Tony?" She blinks and tilts her head. "Really? You'd like to plot the points on the axis?"

"Yeah."

"Please, go ahead." A smile breaks across her face, and I slide out of my seat. Kids watch me go, no doubt wondering what the fuck is up. I don't answer questions in class, don't speak unless spoken to, and even then may not reply. It's sad because I actually used to love school.

The board has this built-in grid, like a giant piece of graph paper, and next to it she's written all sorts of letters and numbers. I grab a piece of chalk and glance at them like I actually know what they mean.

"Class, while Tony plots the points, do the same on your own paper. We'll compare when he's done."

My head throbs and my stomach knots when she says this. But it doesn't matter. I have to get an excuse for bailing on Rob. I need detention. I stay tight to the board so she can't peek. Sagehorn's hovering over kids' desks, giving help. I add the last touches and set the chalk on the lip. My heart pounds, vibrating my throat. Maybe I should erase it? Clean the board and make up an excuse? But Dave's words echo. I'd just have to figure something else out.

"Tony, are you finished?"

I jump at the question and turn around, now keeping my back tight to the board. Sagehorn's smile has faded. "May we see your work?"

I look around the room. They're all waiting, some with eager faces like Sagehorn. Others have smirks. They know, and I feel awful. I take a step to the left, toward the door and look down at my shoes. I examine them for smudges while the class absorbs the naked woman spreading her legs. There's a group gasp, a few laughs, and then Sagehorn screams, "No!" She runs to the board and erases the image with her palms, looks at them like they're covered in shit, and then turns to me. "To the office! Now!"

I nod and step out of her room. The hallway is quiet, but behind me the room is bursting with noise. My pounding heart lowers into my stomach. I was hungry, but now I feel like I might hurl. I rinse my mouth in a nearby fountain and then walk into Principal Ostrander's office.

His secretary is on the phone. She eyes me, and I have a seat. We've danced this dance before. "Yes, he's with us now. I'll let John know." The phone clicks as she hangs up, and a long sigh follows. Sounds like my mom's.

The secretary walks into Ostrander's office and closes the door. A minute later it opens, and he's standing in the doorway, red-faced and sweating. His gut balloons in front of him. Fucking dough-boy in a suit. "Get in here!"

The Big O smells like Old Spice and sweat. Tangy. I sink

into a chair while he shuts the door and grumbles. "What in the hell is wrong with you?"

I don't answer. He doesn't really want me to.

"Drawing filth like that, in Mrs. Sagehorn's class of all places." He moves to the side of his desk and stares at me, face hanging limp around his neck. "I expect shit like that from . . ." His voice drops, like he's talking more to himself than me. Pisses me off though, how he doesn't finish. He's always doing that, at least with me.

"From who?" I sit up and lean on my elbows.

His eyebrows dart together. "Watch yourself with me. Understand?" He straightens, smoothes his tie. "From someone with no *direction*." He says the last part as if he was searching for another way to say *white trash*, but with less sting.

"What's that supposed to mean?" I ask, only because I want him to elaborate. To see if he can.

He smiles and ignores my tone this time. "Oh, I think you know. Lot smarter than the rest." He watches me, waiting for my reaction. I know exactly what the fuck he's talking about. My scores on those tests years ago. He brings them up whenever he can, as if their existence will somehow change something. Everyone thought the same years ago, and look at me now. Here I am because I drew something nasty and now must be punished. He's trying to get me riled, but fuck the Big O. I'm not losing it. I just want my detention.

He clears his throat. "Smarter than the rest, but you love that Vo-Tec."

I shift in my seat. Something's different, and I don't like it.

"It's fine with me if you want to be a grease monkey when you're smart enough to go to college. Just not on my dime." He waits. He wants me to look at him, show that respect. Just like all my mom's former boyfriends. And current. Fuck that. He sits in his chair, and the thing wheezes from the strain. "Pull shit like that again and you can kiss the program good-bye."

I look up now and open my mouth for air, feeling like I'm in a choke hold. The fuck did he just say? No more Vo-Tec? Can he do that?

"What? What?" He's almost laughing. "Think I can't? Watch me. It's not like this is your first offense." He leans forward. "Remember the pot last year. You and Tuckerson all red-eyed in the bathroom?" He leans back and looks up at the ceiling, and the anger has started to boil within me. "Or the fight after homecoming? You know we have footage."

Fuck this motherfucker. I bite the inside of my cheek and press my palms into my knees to keep my legs from bouncing. None of this has anything to do with anything. Fuckwad has no clue about who I am, but he sure can paint a picture. He watches me, and I concentrate on breathing. I just wanted detention. Not all this. If I blow, it'll get worse, and I refuse to get suspended. My mom would probably let Cameron give me a good once over if I did.

"So do we understand the situation?"

I nod because it's what he wants.

"Good. Because one more mistake and that's it." He leans across his desk and looks through some papers. "You've got study hall next, right?"

I don't respond because he's staring at my fucking schedule.

"Normally I'd give you after-school detention, but with the bussing and all . . . and since you just sleep through study hall according to Mr. Stevens, I think a different arrangement is in order."

My body snaps upright, but Big O doesn't seem to notice.

Fuck, he can't be serious. What the hell am I gonna do instead of detention? My body goes limp, and I let out a sigh. I'm fucking past angry.

"Cleaning duty every study hall until Christmas." He slaps the paper.

Shit. I've seen kids doing this, pushing a broom and taking out trash. Fuck me. I look at my schedule, scan the empty spaces that represent my free time and do the math. Something like thirty hours of sweeping and mopping for three minutes of drawing. I fucking hate the corners I get backed into. If I'm so smart why can't I see one or two moves ahead?

"One more thing."

What else does he want to grind into this punishment?

"I know you're friends with Rob O'Connell and that he's been working with Dan Rayburn. Coach Dan. He used to go here."

I'm already fucked up from holding my shit together, so I don't know how I'm supposed to feel about this.

"Well," Big O sits back and takes a breath. "Coach and I are working together to help out Rob, give him a future."

Rob hasn't said anything about this. I almost blurt that he's going to be a mechanic, like me, but don't. I can tell there's more. Why else would he be telling me?

"Antioch, I think he and I need to bring you into that plan. I'm worried about you. I don't really want to take away Vo-Tec; I'd rather help."

Why'd he have to pull this 180? I went from pissed to blushing. It sucks, but I can't hide it. Big O's gone from giving me hell to offering me help? *No one* offers me help. The fuck is going on?

"What I'd like to see is you join the gym. It will give you

somewhere to go. Keep you out of trouble. And help you with things at home."

My head snaps up at the last part. How could he possibly know? "I can't. I can't afford that." The words tumble out and my face beats hotter.

"I'm not asking you to. I'm asking you to stay out of trouble, and this is a way." Big O leans across his desk. "Antioch, look at me."

I don't want to, but I do. There's something in his voice I only have a vague notion of. Compassion, I think.

"You do this, and you'll both have a shot. Rob's got a good head, but you two are tight, and I don't want to see him brought down by whatever you're sinking in."

My thoughts start connecting again, and the heat burns again from anger. "But what's in this for me? So I'm out of trouble for a few months? Rob gets some future? What do I get?"

Big O's eyes glitter for a second, like he's ready to strike out, but then he sits back. "Don't worry, I've got plans for you, too. But first, you need to clean up your act. Any more crap in class, any fights, anything, you can forget this conversation and all that comes with it."

If I was confused before, now I'm bewildered. So Big O may still take away Vo-Tec, but is going to pay for me to go learn how to fight? But he wants me to do so to help Rob and so that I stay out of trouble? This makes no sense. But, if I do, then he'll hook me up? But how? What the fuck just happened?

"Now," Big O slams his meaty hand on the desk, snapping me back to the moment, "go report to the janitor's station. It's right behind the cafeteria."

I grip the chair's handles and try to think of something to say. Nothing comes. He looks up, as if wondering if I've heard him. In his face I see a question, and for a moment I wonder if Big O is wrong about this, about believing in me, or if this fat fuck is one hundred percent right.

Two janitors sit around a busted up table, drinking coffee and watching TV, some fucking game show. No wonder this school looks worse than my house. I knock on the open door. One turns, looks at me, and blinks, like maybe he was expecting someone else, but he doesn't speak, just pushes his lips into a knot.

"I'm supposed to come here for cleaning duty?"

The blinking one blinks. The other one keeps watching TV. I look around for someone else. Just mops and brooms and cleaning solution.

"What do you want me to do?"

Neither answers. This is fucking bullshit. Big O must have known the retard crew was working and sent me down to be tortured. What's he gonna do if I bolt? Like these guys'll know whether I'm here or not?

"Behind you is a sweeper. Let's start with that." The voice comes from my left, outside the office. I turn and a giant in a tight blue T-shirt is watching me. His eyes dance. I look for the tool and then step to it.

"This one?"

He nods.

I grab the handle and lift the head, which is heavier than I thought.

"You know where the science wing is?"

I look up. "Yeah. I'm not stupid."

He crosses his arms over his chest and veins pop along his forearms. "Yeah, maybe." He waits a moment, then continues. "I want you to sweep both sides. Go up one way and down the other. Clack that thing out when you're finished. I'll show you." He extends his arm, and I hand it over. "Here." He grabs the pole like a hockey stick and smacks the wall. Wrappers and dust fall out. He grunts. "Grab a dustpan and clean up the piles. Toss 'em in the can." He hands me the pole. "Do the English hall after. Then come back here."

Fuck me. This is gonna blow, but I don't have any questions and I don't feel like hanging around this freak, so I drag the sweeper behind me, grab a dustpan, and head out.

The halls are still quiet as I hit the science wing. It smells of formaldehyde. I drop the dustpan, and the clatter echoes. Fuck, I started my morning cleaning up a mess, and now I'm stuck doing *this*. But, then there's the other shit Big O was talking about. I have to talk to Rob, see if he can get me straight on this. The anger that was rising simmers, and I put my head down and start walking.

There isn't much to this. I just direct the head at shit lying around, and it picks it up, like a mini street sweeper. In a way, I enjoy the result. I finish one side, head up the other and a pile of filth rolls before me. A door opens, and a kid pops out. I stop and put my chin to my chest. No way am I going to let him see my face. He unwraps a stick of gum and puts it in his mouth. My stomach growls. He heads my way and slows down, tosses his wrapper into the pile, and laughs. He continues past, real close, his shoulder just touching mine. I go hot and choke the shit out of the handle, but he keeps going, busting his heels hard on the floor, and I bite my cheek and don't say a word. I just start pushing again.

I don't see anyone in the English wing, just hear teachers blabbing away. I sweep up the pile, toss it, and then head back to the office. The two idiots are gone, but the big motherfucker is there, marking a pile of florescent bulbs. He looks up. "All set?"

I nod.

"Good. I'll tell Ostrander." He squares to me, his chest sticking out as far as Big O's fucking gut. "You'll be back on Monday."

Funny, he doesn't say it like a question. "Yeah. I guess."

"You guess or you will?"

Fucking shit, for a janitor he thinks he's a fucking bad-ass. "Like I've got a choice?"

"Always have a choice."

Who is this douche, the fucking philosopher of janitors? "Then I guess we'll see." I turn away, and if he was going to say anything, the bell cuts him off.

Rob and the rest are hanging at the front door. No one's got any food though. "There he is. Fucking Picasso." Rob rolls out and slaps my back. "The fuck, man? Didn't know you were an artist?"

"How'd you hear?"

"Some dude got a text during bio. Started losing it. Then like eight other kids got the same. The guy next to me let me see his phone."

"What was it?"

"Picture of your naked lady. Nice job. Bald pussy and all. What you get?"

I shake my head. We can't have the conversation we need to here. "Fucking cleaning duty."

"You're a fucking janitor? No detention?"

Why is he surprised? Or did he already know? Shit, how connected is he with Big O? Is that how the big man knows all about me? I should have just lied. "Nah. Just sweeping."

"Nice, so you can still come tonight."

I wrinkle my forehead, trying to appear clueless.

"You know? Practice." He takes his stance. Damn he's good at playing the part.

"Right, right. Yeah. Why not?"

He smiles and pulls a pamphlet out of his pocket and hands it to me. "I snagged one, just so you could check it out, you know, since you don't have a computer and all."

I feel like cracking on him, making a joke how he's like those holy rollers passing out their shit, but I'm not sure if he knows what I know about what Big O's up to. Also, I'm drawn in by the team picture on the back. Rob is in the last row, all tall and goofy, but Dave's in the front, smiling like the devil.

"Jensen rolls with you?"

Rob looks down at the picture. "Yeah. Coach doesn't like him that much, but Dave's legal and can be on the cards. And he's fucking nuts."

I swallow. I don't want to ask, but I have to. "You know he's Cameron's nephew?" I'm still looking at the picture, even though there's no reason I should. I feel Rob behind me shift and open his mouth, but then he closes it and crosses his arms over his chest. He gets it. I tuck the pamphlet into my back pocket. Maybe now he'll give me an out.

"The fuck does that matter? Maybe Cam will back off if he knows you're fighting." Rob's words sound as hollow as I feel. He knows better. That's something Big O doesn't understand.

I turn and tell him about what happened with Jensen this morning. Rob listens and then looks me square in the eye. "Tone, you got no choice then. You gotta go. Can't be a pussy."

I've been thinking the same thing, but being or not being a pussy isn't so black and white. I'm not so sure it's just something I can decide not to be. Kind of like being smart

the way I am. What has come of it? Nothing. Because someone else is always steering my life, and they don't give a fuck
about what I want.

We pile off the bus and Amy and Charity light up. Char's eyes
are bugged out. I forgot about how much of a mess she was
and am surprised that she's still out of it. Amy exhales. "Just
stay at my place."

Charity takes a long drag. "Maybe." She looks over at her
house, and her eyes look just like I imagine my own do. I
stare at the ground and Rob speaks.

"You need some help? Something you'd like us to do?"

There's a long pause. I want Char to speak. She may be
loud and obnoxious, but we've always had each other's back.
Whatever's up, we'll be there for her.

Instead, Amy answers. "Not now."

I get that too and nod. We walk away, and Rob jabs me in
the kidney before darting out of reach. "See you around six?"

I ignore the pain. "Yeah. Six."

He runs off before I have a chance to ask him about Big
O. I'll get to it later. Fuck, I can't believe I'm going.

I head up the stairs and into my trailer. It's dark and cool,
like a cave. Still filthy and reeking, though. I head directly to
my room, take off my shoes, and lie on my bed. The pamphlet crinkles in my back pocket. No doubt Cameron will be
back tonight, and maybe by then I'll have picked up a move
or two. But Dave will be there, and then Cameron will know,
and before I've really learned anything, he'll kick the shit out
of me for trying. Story of my fucking life. I gotta get out.
Before I'm stuck. But how?

5

Rob told me we'd be barefoot at the gym, so I need to take care of my toenails. They're way too long and yellow. I head to the bathroom and rifle through the drawers and behind the mirror. Nothing. I go to my mom's room and stand at the threshold. I hate going in. There's clothes everywhere, dirty dishes on the nightstand, dresser, and floor. And it always smells like ass. But I step in and move around the shit on top of the dresser, then knock over a half-finished beer can but don't bother to clean it up. Not like she would.

Her nightstand's got only her alarm clock and a bottle of aspirin. I pop open the drawer, and there's a big ass nail file next to a lighter, but no clippers. I reach in and my fingers brush against something cold. I grab it and the file. It's a pipe. I run a finger through the center of the scoop, and it's sticky with residue. "The fuck?" I look around as if something in this room will we give me the answer.

Fuck, is this hers or Cam's? Either way, I need to know what's been cooked. I use the file to move around the rest of the shit in the drawer but don't find a bag, so I sit on the bed. It sags.

This isn't the first time. Two years ago she detoxed for a month. She needed to. Started getting the sores from picking. Least she didn't get the mouth, because she'd never be able to work again. No one tips a toothless waitress. She told the CPS people that I was with my dad. Gave 'em some bullshit number. I hid out whenever they came around. One of the women she worked with hooked me up with food. It was like I was some embarrassing pet.

Fuck this. I'll kick her ass before I go through that again. Wonder when she started back up? There's no money, and no one around here slings meth . . . except . . . motherfucker. Charity's dad. I toss the pipe back in the drawer, slam it, and head to the bathroom. I hover over the toilet, but nothing comes.

I sit on the floor with my back to the tub. What the fuck am I gonna do? I can't have her fucking nodding off with Cameron in the house. I'm sure he's the one paying, and he'll be back, like all the rest, and he'll be able to do whatever he wants. Like all the rest. I punch the cabinet in front of me and a flat echo returns. I pinch my head between my knees and close my eyes, breathe slow, and enjoy the sensation around my temples.

I can't remember during which boyfriend it was when I found this position, but it's the only good thing any one of them's given me. He was the first one that hit her for hours. I was used to a few slaps and a punch, but this one liked to torture her, and I was too scared to tell him to stop, could only focus on drowning out the sound. The pillow over my head worked at first, but if she screamed, I still heard it. She screamed more often and that's when I tried my knees. Breathing adds a constant noise, and the sensation soothes me. Like now. I think I'm okay. I release my head and open my eyes. My feet come into focus, the nails stretched over my toes. I see myself, from above, crouched like a rat in its cage. I'm holding the file just as hard as I'm trying to hold on to my emotions. I take a deep breath, grab my foot, and start chiseling away.

Rob rolls up, and I open the door before he can knock. "I'm ready." I step out and he looks surprised, but turns and we head down the steps.

"All right. You look good to go."

I am. After I took care of my toenails I found a jar of peanut butter and a roll and made a sandwich. I threw on my cleanest gear and left my mom a note. Told her I was out. That's all. Don't need to provide all the details. Not if Cam might have a chance to read them. Not if she's gonna be passed out.

We hit the main road and turn toward town. I have no clue where the gym is, but Rob leads the way and is light on his feet, bouncing every so often. "So, I'll basically be paired up with you. Show you the ropes. It's Friday so we're working on takedowns from the clinch."

I nod like I understand.

"We're not punching or kicking, just working on getting to the ground fight, gaining leverage."

Beyond the fights Cameron watches, I've seen some of this shit on TV. Liddell, Penn, Lesnar. I think I know what he means, the slow part where they roll around, looking like they're trying to fuck each other. This is gonna suck balls.

Rob draws up to me. "Fuck, you got a cup?"

I screw up my face. He cracks his knuckles off his junk. There's a hollow plastic sound. That kind of cup. I shake my head.

"Don't worry, I'll watch out, but you need one."

The way my life's headed, I need full body armor.

We come into downtown. There's a gas station and library and church, but I don't see a gym. Never have. There's a fitness something or other a few miles out, but that's all douche bags on treadmills and shit. Rob seems to read my mind. "It's right over there."

I follow to where he's pointing. "The burger hut?"

"No man. Next to it."

I look, but all I see are cars in the parking lot.

"Come on."

We dart across the street, past the restaurant, and to a small section of the larger building. I've never noticed a door here. It's glass and has EAST COAST BOXING AND MMA stenciled in thick black letters. The bottoms are red, like they're bleeding. Inside, guys sit on the floor, stretching. My throat tightens, but I have to ask Rob before we go in. "So how long you and Big O have this planned?"

Rob whips around. "What are you talking 'bout?"

He seems genuine, but I still don't know. "Come on. Enough with the bullshit. Big O told me about what Coach Dan has in store for you. What did you say to the big man to get me on board?"

Rob drops away from the door and gets real close to me. "Tone, what the fuck are you talking about?" His jaw sets, and his eyes don't leave mine.

Fuck, I've known Rob long enough. I know this clueless-ness. He doesn't know. "Shit. I thought . . . Fuck, I'm an asshole."

Rob stares and waits.

I shake my head at myself for doubting him and explain what Big O said to me.

Rob looks out in the distance for a moment but then back to me. "Big O and Coach have talked some about me being a trainer or some shit, but nothing serious. I had no idea he wanted you here and that he's all looking into your shit at home." He turns away. "Fuck, man, if you don't wanna do this, don't. It's fine. I had no idea about Big O and Coach. I just thought you'd like it, and it would help."

"Help with what?" I ask even though I don't need to.

"You know." He looks me dead in the eye again.

I'm embarrassed and wonder why he hasn't given up on me. Like everyone else. I put up my fist. "I got this. Because *I* want to. All right?"

Rob cocks his head. "For real?"

I nod and he reaches up and pounds my knuckles, and I almost believe my own words. He didn't know, and now here I am because of Big O. Where the fuck am I headed?

Rob turns and opens the door.

A chime sounds, and most look over. I scan quickly. Good, no Dave. "Big Rob!" A man steps out from the back and crosses over the mat. He's short and bald and thick around the neck, chest, and legs. He smiles and looks at me. "This the new recruit?"

Rob nods.

The man stops short of us both and looks me over. "Tony, right?"

Now I nod and Rob gives me a look.

"Good to have you. Rob will take care of you tonight. We'll take it slow, but don't be afraid to ask questions." He places a hand on my shoulder. I stop myself from brushing it off and nod. He claps his hands and turns to the room. "Keep stretching, we'll get cracking in ten."

The guys on the floor resume their postures, mostly

lying on the ground or stretched out over a leg. "That's Coach Dan," Rob says and we walk over to the only piece of furniture in the room, a small wooden bench. Shoes and gym bags are scattered beneath and around it. We pull off our shoes and then take a place on the mat, which takes up all but the space in front of the door. It's like the wrestling room at school. The same blue padding covers the lower half of the walls. Above is an American flag, and next to it is the Marine's. One of my mom's boyfriends was a Marine. That flag and "Semper Fi" are all I can remember of him. Well, those and his booming voice.

I look over and mirror Rob, stick my legs out in front of me and press my nose to my knees. The mat smells like feet and sweat and feels wet. Kind of like my house.

"'Sup Rob?" The guy who speaks is built like a mother-fucker. Wide shoulders and sweet biceps. I feel even smaller than usual.

"Not bad. Bit sore."

The guy laughs. "Same way every day."

Another guy juts his chin toward us while the first nods. He's light-skinned, maybe Latino, and he extends a hand to me. "I'm Amir."

I take Amir's hand. "Tony."

"Nice to meet you."

"Yeah."

The first guy does the same. "Shit, sorry man, sorry. I'm Phil." I shake his hand and he waves toward the room. "You'll meet the rest as we go. Don't sweat it. We were all new once." He pops over to a wall and stretches against it.

Fear rises up as I look around the room. I'm not the smallest in here, but I sure as shit am not the biggest. No one else looks like me though. They're all calm. It's fucked up.

They're all about to fight each other, but no one seems to give a shit.

Coach Dan steps to the middle of the mat. "All right, tonight we're focusing on takedowns, and I'd like you to work on these three." Everyone is still, no more stretching, just intense focus. "Amir?"

Amir pops up and moves to the center with Coach. "Remember, it's all about leverage. So when I'm in the clinch, I want to force my opponent off his." He wraps an arm around Amir's back and grabs his bicep with the other. "Remember your base. Feet just outside shoulders." Coach Dan positions himself as he speaks. "Now you push." He thrusts Amir away from his body. "He'll react and push back." Amir does. "Once he moves into you, pull, then move your feet between his and roll him off to the side." Coach pulls Amir like a doll and then rolls him onto the floor. He slides across his chest in the same movement. I wince at the *thwap* they make. No one else does.

"Let me show you again." Coach and Amir demonstrate the move three more times and then Coach Dan pats Amir's shoulder. "All right, partner up."

Rob stands. I get up next to him but feel like running. "Just relax." He grabs me like Coach just did Amir, pushes, pulls, and in a flash, I'm flat on my fucking back. The air in my chest pinches and my teeth rattle.

"Shit." I sit up.

Rob's smiling. "Make sure you extend an arm when you go down. It'll cushion your fall."

"*Now* you tell me."

Rob laughs. "Sorry." He helps me up. "Your turn."

We get into position, but I forget where the fuck to put my hands, so Rob shows me. "Widen your feet." I do and Rob laughs. "Hold up." We separate. "Put your feet together."

"The fuck you doing?"

"Just do it."

Guys behind us turn to watch. Fuck. This better not make me look fucking stupid. I put my feet together, and Rob takes a step and shoves me hard in the chest. I fall to the fucking ground. My ass burns, and now I'm pissed. People are laughing. "The fuck was that?" Rob just smiles. I feel like wiping it off his face, but he extends a hand.

"Come on, I'll show you." He helps me up. It takes all I can not to pull his fucking face to the floor. "You need to keep your feet wide so you have a solid base. Too narrow and you'll get knocked down like you just did. Too wide and you'll get your leg kicked out."

Coach Dan appears but doesn't speak. The partners who stopped to look have resumed with slamming each other all over the fucking place. "So what do I do?"

"Jump. Like you're getting a rebound."

I'm about to say something but Coach nods. I jump.

"Again."

I do.

"Again."

The fuck? But I jump.

"Now, look at your feet."

They're under my hips.

"Move them out about one width of your foot."

If it were anyone else but Rob, I'd tell 'em to suck it, but I slide my feet and look up.

"Bend your knees."

I do and Rob charges me like before. His hand rocks into my chest, and I step back, but do not fall down. Coach smiles and so does Rob. "That's the way." Coach Dan slaps Rob's shoulder and walks over to another pair.

Rob's face is beaming, and I understand why he wants me here. He's good at this shit. He wants me to see him. But I already do, in Vo-Tec. He rocks that class. Huh, I wonder what it would be like to be so talented?

We get in the clinch again, and I get the feel. I roll Rob and we repeat the same steps a few times. It's awkward, but Rob tells me I'm doing all right.

Coach Dan shows us two variations on the move, and we pair up again and practice. It's fucked up. Guys around the room are holding on to each other like a bunch of drunk fucks learning how to dance. I'm sweating and breathing a little heavy, but I don't see how any of this would help me against Cam.

"All right, fighters to the middle."

"That's me," Rob says and darts to the center of the mat. I join all but Rob, Amir, and some other guy against the wall.

"Three lines, and don't worry, you'll rotate through all of them." Coach looks toward the group, and Phil shows me the way. We form lines off each fighter, four to a line. I'm in Amir's.

"Now, these guys are up in a month, so give them hell. Take them down. Make them work." He turns to the three. "Ready?" They pop into their stances, and I examine the pose: lowered hips, extended arms, bent at the elbows, hands open. "Go!"

The first guys in line move so fucking fast I don't know what the fuck's what. I watch Rob. The kid against him stabs with one arm, reaching for a wrist. With the other, he tries to get around Rob's head. I'd punch a fuck if this were real, trying that shit, but I guess there's none of that tonight. Shit, why aren't they wearing gloves?

Rob slips and slides and counters the kid's moves until

he manages to grab a leg and take the guy to the ground. They end up in a heap on the floor but pop up, slap hands, and the next guy in line bolts out.

The process repeats, and now it's my turn with Amir. He's sweating, breathing heavy, red around his face like he's been slapped, and looking pissed. I freeze. He's twice my size, easy, just fucking jacked. Rob and the other guy are already tangling with their opponents.

"Go on, Tony. Take it slow. He's tired. Make him work." Coach Dan nudges me from the side. I step out. Amir lowers his stance. I do the same. The guys behind me yell. "Come on, Tony." "Get into him." I don't know what the fuck I'm doing, so I go low and try to get in the clinch like we practiced before. Amir gets my neck, and I can't breathe. The ceiling comes into view, and then I'm on my back, just like before. But gently. Not like with Rob. Amir just laid me down. Didn't slam me. No shit? This fuck could have fucking broken my spine. I stand up with Amir's help and the crew claps.

"Nice job, Tony."

"Way to get at it."

I didn't do shit, so why are they clapping? Maybe on my first night it's all right. I move to the end of the line for the next dude and pay real close fucking attention. I watch how the guys tease each other, trying to get the other to grab an arm, lose his balance, and then end up on the floor. Or the way they get a hold of the neck and then don't fucking let go. Pull and push until they pop and drive the fucker down.

I get my turn with the second dude, Mike. "Dildo" they call him. He's like a fucking broomstick, but he can reach me standing against the back wall. I approach, get low, and keep my base. He reaches and grabs, and I slap his hand away. I watched him while I was waiting, saw how he's got nothing with his left, only his right. I reach toward the tucked-up arm, and he stretches out over me for my neck. His long-ass arm is an inch from my face. I grab the bicep, push it to his side and tuck down, and get the back of his waist and roll.

He's on the ground! Holy Shit! He looks up at me, fucking lost. Behind me all the guys inhale. "No shit?" someone says. "Muthafucka." Then they rip into applause. Somebody slaps my back, and Dildo stands up. He's pissed, but then he smiles. "All right newb. I'll take you serious from now on." He slaps hands with me, and I feel good. In fact, I haven't felt this way in, shit, I don't know how long. Yeah, Rob's onto something. Maybe Big O, too?

The door chime sounds, and everyone looks over. My stomach drops.

"Sorry I'm late. Got caught up at the gym talking to this bitch." Dave pulls off his sweatshirt and pants. He's sweating and wearing the same gear as everyone else, but way fucking nicer. His TAPOUT shorts look brand new, and his Under Armour is just that, the real deal, not the knock-off shit everyone else has on. "What I miss?"

Coach Dan steps forward. "Takedowns. You warm enough to demonstrate?"

"Fuck yeah." Dave bounces onto the mat.

"Rob?"

Rob steps forward. Dave squares to him, and the rest of us step back. This is totally fucked. I don't know how I did, but I forgot all about this douche. And now? Fuck, I should just leave. But, I can't. This is part of my deal with the big man. I've got to stay, if only for Rob. He deserves that much.

"Go!" They do, and I stick right where I am. Dave's fast as fuck, but Rob keeps countering. Dave gets insanely low and reaches out. Rob backs up, but it's too late, Dave's got him around the knees. Rob pitches back and, fuck, he's on the ground. But, shit, Dave's twitching like crazy. Rob's got a leg looped around Dave's neck, and the douche's face is turning red. He's flailing but getting nowhere. Rob's locked his feet at his ankles. Coach Dan moves to them. "Tap out, Dave."

Dave keeps squirming.

Behind me the guys are murmuring. "Squeeze, Rob."

"Take his fucking head off."

"Dave, tap!" Coach is now lying on the mat next to him. Rob doesn't let up, but looks back at his coach. Dan nods. Rob's face goes still for a second, like he just remembered some shit he had to do. Then he loosens his hold and slides away from Dave. Dave wriggles up and gets back into position like nothing happened.

"Dave, you're done. I told Rob to release."

"What the fuck, Coach? I didn't tap!" Spit flies from his mouth.

"You should have. You would have passed out in another five seconds." Coach Dan doesn't blink. He doesn't look anywhere else but at Dave's face. But Dave won't look him in the eye.

"You don't know that."

Coach Dan's face goes hard. "Yes. I do." He waits a moment and then turns to Rob. "Nice job."

The room claps for Rob, but I watch Dave. His eyes dart around the room and find me. He looks me over and steps forward. "Thought I heard you were coming." Dave grips my shoulder and squeezes. I wince. "Now I get to see how soon your pussy ass taps. My uncle will love hearing about that."

I don't look at him. Don't want to give him the satisfaction of seeing the fear on my face. I turn to Coach Dan instead. "Are we still rotating lines?"

He smiles and claps his hands. "Tony's right. Fighters, back into position. Dave, hop in."

I step away from Dave and move to Rob's line. Motherfucker, I was feeling all right, but now? Shit, *this* is exactly what I didn't want. I look over my shoulder at him, trying to chat up the guys, but most look like they'd rather be in a choke hold. They may not feel as I do, but at least they don't seem to like him.

Coach claps his hands. "Ready?" The group nods. "Go!" The guy in front of me takes on Rob and gets laid out in two seconds. Fuck, now it's my turn. My head's not right for this, but I approach.

Rob's breathing heavy, covered in sweat, and he's bright red from the neck up. I get low, then lower. He doesn't bend though, just stands tall, feet close together. Fuck, I don't need any moves for this. I rush him, and he steps back, stumbles. I get a hand around his neck and pull his head into my body. I'm about to Atomic Bomb his ass when he brings an arm up through and rips an elbow off my temple. I jump away. My head stings, and the room's blurry, but I see Rob coming at me. I slap away one hand, but he grabs my wrist with the other.

"All right, Tony!"

"Come on!"

"Turn away from him!"

I take the advice. Rob's palms are sweaty, so I slip from his grip, but he kicks out my legs and we're on the mat. Rob hops on top like he's trying to mount me. It's fucked up. He grabs my wrists and pins them to my stomach, looks down at me, and smiles. Like this is some joke. Fuck him. I didn't come here to look like a fucking tool. Especially not with that douche watching.

I pop my hips off the ground, and Rob pitches, lets go of one hand. I spring on top of him. I don't have a fucking clue what I'm doing, but I'm acting like I do, pulling his arm up toward his face and wrapping my legs around it. I've seen this move before. Trap the arm. I tuck my feet into his shoulder and hold on to his arm like it's the one thing in the world that might save me.

"Lean back!"

"Open the hips!"

"A fucking arm bar? He's got him! Fucking-A!"

I do what they tell me and feel Rob's muscles tighten and twist, but then go slack. He grunts and taps the mat twice.

The room fucking erupts. Hands slap my back. Someone says, "That was fucking awesome!" They help up Rob and give him props. I step to him.

"Nice job." He laughs.

Why the fuck's he laughing? I just beat his ass. Day one. Shit, did he? Did he *let* me?

"Tony, excellent job, and not just for your first time." Coach grips my shoulder and smiles. "You sure you haven't done this before?"

I shake my head, still thinking about what Rob may or may not have done. Coach looks down at Rob.

"You all right?"

Rob stands and looks from me to Coach. "Knew he had it in him."

Coach's face tightens, as does his grip on my shoulder. He looks me over, again. Taps my chest. "I'm glad Ostrander sent you my way. Warrior spirit in there. I can feel it."

Something inside me flutters. I can't remember the last time someone said anything like that, and I don't know how to feel about this praise, especially if it isn't deserved. Coach releases me. "Get some water." Guys go to their bags, talking about what happened. Dave goes with them and shoots me a look. I turn to Rob.

"Thanks."

"For what?" He heads for his water. I didn't bring any, so I follow him like a fucking pet.

"You know."

He swallows and eyeballs me. "Sure. Whatever."

After class we step outside and walk back to the park, steam rising off our heads. I turn to Rob and ask the question that's gnawing at me. "Hey, did you let me take you down tonight?"

He gives me a hard look. The steam's no longer coming off his head, and his eyes are intense. "You heard what Coach said, 'bout the warrior spirit."

"That the same shit he says to everybody? You know, make 'em believe in themselves or some shit."

Rob stiffens. "Ain't like that with Coach. He don't talk shit or blow smoke. He's never said something like that to me, and I've been there over a year."

"So, what, I'm special?"

Rob looks out over the park. "I don't know. Maybe. All I know is that, no, I didn't let you take me down, and that Coach did say that shit to one other dude."

"Who?"

Rob licks his lips. "You won't like it."

In the park, someone coughs hard, like a lung coming up. "Just fucking tell me."

"Dave."

I don't say a word. What can I say? There's no way me

and that fuck-face are any way like each other. If Coach thinks otherwise, he's been cracked upside the head one too many times.

"Come on. We should check on Charity."

I think about what he's said as we walk to Amy's. I don't like the comparison to Dave, but everything else . . . well, that felt more like a family than I've ever known. In spite of the fighting and all. Or maybe because of it.

Amy's outside cranking a butt. "So you actually fucking manned up, pussy?"

I just shake my head. I don't want to get into it with her. No doubt she's pissed about whatever's up with Charity. I get that. But I'm no whipping boy. Least not here.

Rob slaps my back. "Take it easy on him. Tone did all right for his first time."

I'm glad he didn't say shit about what Coach said.

"Popped your cherry. We should celebrate." Amy inhales and the ember lights her face.

"Shouldn't we just go and check on Charity?" I ask.

"Why you gotta fucking just get right to the point? Can't we just chill for a bit?" Amy crosses her arms over her chest but looks over at Charity's. Two more bikes—one a bad-ass fucking chopper—are parked out front. The lights are on, and there's a lot of noise coming from inside.

Rob touches Amy's elbow. "Come on."

She sighs and flicks her cigarette, scowls at me, and then tramps over to Charity's. Amy gives the door two good raps. The aluminum sounds like gunshots, and the voices die down. Goose bumps pop along my arms and neck. My hoodie isn't thick like Rob's, and I've got nothing at all to hide my nerves.

A big fuck fills the doorway. "Yeah?" His voice is deep and

charred. His beard is braided into a tight rope that brushes his chest, which nearly touches both sides of the doorframe.

"Is Charity home?" Amy's voice is small, and she twists her foot back and forth.

The dude grumbles and then looks past her, at Rob and me. His face comes into the light from the house. It's Charity's dad. I've only seen him a handful of times; he comes and goes so much, but the scar is unmistakable. It runs from his temple to his bottom lip. Someone tried to take his ear off. He fought back and won. Took the other guy's. "She ain't home. Her and her mom went to her grandmother's." He says this flat, kind of like he's just remembering, or just figuring it out.

"You know when she'll be back?"

"Can't say. Sometime." He looks at her like a trick-or-treater with a pathetic costume, just begging for candy.

I know the look. He's waiting for a reason to make a move. And from what I know of him, he wouldn't hesitate to hurt Amy. "Thanks. We'll catch up with her when she gets back."

Charity's dad shifts his gaze off Amy, to me. I grow even colder inside. "Tony, right?" I nod. He offers a smirk and looks at Rob. "And I know you, Rob." His smile widens, and I'm instantly confused. He seems downright happy to see us, especially Rob.

"You boys feel like partying some? Got good times in here. Girls, too."

My mouth drops and fortunately Rob answers. "Maybe some other time. But thanks."

"Your call." He nods and shuts the door.

We move off the steps without looking back and don't speak until we're at Amy's.

"What the fuck was that all about?" Amy can barely get the words out she's so amped to light her cigarette.

"I don't have a clue."

We look at Rob.

He puts his palms up. "No idea. He was probably just high and being nice." He turns to Amy. "Char tell you she was goin' anywhere?"

"Fuck, no. And there ain't shit that she don't tell me."

I clear my throat. "What about yesterday, when she was crying?"

Amy takes a drag. "Yeah. That was just about her mom ragging on her about her weight."

"Nuthin' about her dad and what he's doing?"

Amy shakes her head, and we're quiet for a while before she speaks. "They'll be outta here soon. Guess we'll just have to wait. Maybe it's better that she's out of the way." She takes a long drag, squints at us. "You sure there ain't nothing going on? That was fucked up that he knew your names, invited you in and all."

I agree, but have no explanation. Rob shakes his head. "Like I said, probably just toasted."

Amy keeps smoking and doesn't say a word. We say good night to her and take off. We pause near my trailer. "Tomorrow, then? You coming?" Rob asks.

How could I say no, even if I wanted to? "Have to. You know?"

"But you liked it, right? Still your choice?"

"Yeah. Of course. I lumped you up, and hell, I'm a warrior." Rob laughs with me, and then I ask, "What you think is up?"

"With Char? Who knows?"

"Her dad?"

Rob looks away. "Chaz is always on the prowl. New recruits, you know? Must be our time."

"Oh fuck that!"

Rob nods but keeps looking away. I don't like that one bit, but there's no reason to get into it now. We pound fists, and he heads toward his trailer. I wait a second, take a breath, and then walk into my own.

The lights are off, except in my mom's room, and there's music playing low. People talking. "Mom?"

Sheets rustle and then she's at her door wearing a robe. "Tony? I thought you were out?"

"I was. Now I'm home. What's up?"

She leans on the doorframe. "Nothing . . . just Cameron's over."

Every muscle tightens. I knew this would happen. It always does. But shit, things seem calm. He's not flying through the door tying to take my head off. My skin crawls, though. Something's up. I step toward her, and she hides more of her body behind the wall. She's glass-eyed and her head bobs down, then jumps back up. I take another step, and she grips the metal. I look into her room, to her bed. Cameron's staring at the ceiling with a kind of smile on his face. Pot, I smell it. That tangy scent. It's not meth. I back out of the room. "You high?"

She smiles and nods, her hair falling around her. "Don't be mad."

The fuck? *Don't be mad.* Who's the parent here? "I'm not mad, it's just, after last time, why'd you let him back in?" I know the answer even as I ask the question.

It takes her a second to process. "He said he was sorry, and he had a bag, and I thought . . ." She trails off, but I don't need her to finish.

"I'm going to bed."

She reaches for me. I pull away, and she stumbles. "Good night."

I walk toward the bathroom. "Shut your door."

The accordion plastic snaps into place behind me. I take my shoes off, tuck them under my bed, and then walk across the hall. I ignore the music and the way I feel. Well, at least I stuff it down so it's not filling my head. I've learned enough to know that at this point there's nothing I can do but wait. Wait for it to turn ugly again. Wait for her to need help. Will I give it this time?

I sit on the toilet and wait for the water to heat. My body's sore all over, but in a good way. Like I've done something useful. I could do this MMA shit, not because Big O wants me to or because of what Coach said, or because of Rob, or even because it's smart with Cameron's ass around, but because I liked it. The entire time I was there, before Dave showed up, I wasn't thinking about this shit at home. It's like I was someone else, not this piece of trash kid from the park. Because that's all I am to everyone. And that's why Char's dad offered to let us party. He knows what we are. Our options are almost nonexistent.

But I can't get excited about this. I can't get wrapped up in another fantasy about how *this* could be a way out, like it may be for Rob. No, I can't go stupid, thinking like I do about fucking up Cameron. Coach Dan's running a business, and Big O's paying. I'm there to keep Rob from getting fucked over by me. In the end I'll owe somebody for the chance I've been given, even if I am being used. If I've learned anything, I know nothing in this world's for free. Except pain.

6

t's Monday. Mom's door is closed, and Cameron's whining snore is ripping on the other side. They got high and stayed high all fucking weekend. Must be nice.

The good thing about them getting lifted is that there's food in the house: a box of Ding Dongs, a bag of salt and vinegar chips, and in the fridge, some cheese slices and a gallon of milk. I eat two packs of Ding Dongs and every bite makes my body tingle. I can't remember when I ate last. I didn't dare eat Cameron's food with him around. Too risky. Mostly I just hung out with Rob and did jack shit.

I wash the cake down with two glasses of milk and for once I feel full. I slide into my ratty hoodie and head out the door.

Amy's not out, so I walk alone. I pass Charity's, and the bikes are still outside. I hope she is at her grandma's, unless it's like my own. A worse park than this.

The bell rings, and I snap awake, slumped on my desk. I push up and Lance's room is a blur. I blink my eyes, but can't seem to get right. I stagger out of the room. Lance watches me but doesn't say a word.

I head straight to the bathroom because I gotta piss so bad I've got a semi. I drain the captain, wash my hands, turn for a towel, and there's Dave, staring at me like a shit he just can't get to flush.

"'Sup, Tone?"

"'Sup, Dave?" My hands drip. All I want to do is dry them, but I let them hang at my sides.

"So you gonna throw down with us or was last night too much?"

My body tenses. "Don't know yet."

He laughs, exposing his pointy teeth. His breath is hot in my face and smells like cinnamon. He chews his gum with his mouth open, and I'd like to put an elbow through it. "Don't know? Huh. What's there to know, you fucking pussy?" He waits for my answer. Cocks his head. "That's what my uncle says you are."

I flash hot but then see Cameron lying on my mom's bed, stoned, staring at the ceiling like some roach on its back. I could have dropped him without trying. I don't say anything, though. Feeding Dave would only bring some back to Cameron.

"Good at staying quiet." Dave squints.

"We done?" This sounds tough as shit, but, really, I know that my legs can't take much more of this stare down, and if I buckle in front of him, I'm fucked.

He chomps on his gum. "Yeah. For now."

I step around him to the towels.

"Just do me a favor and keep tight about the business down in your shit hole."

I wipe my hands. "The fuck you talking about?"

"Don't act like you don't know. Rob already knows to stay quiet. So should you. That is if you're going to be one of us."

My head scrambles for an answer. The only "business" of any kind is with, Chaz, Charity's dad. Is that what he's talking about? And who said I wanted to be one of them? It's a fucking gym, not a cult. I want to ask him what he's talking about, but I know better.

Dave watches me for a moment and then laughs. "See you tonight, bitch." He throws a jab into a stall door before leaving. I lean against the sink and run through what he's just said. How the fuck does he know anything about the park? Who would willingly come in when everyone else is trying to get out?

I take my seat in math and kids watch me. I play it cool, check 'em out from the corners of my eyes. A few laugh and nod toward me. I fucking need this? Sagehorn's heels clack across the front of the room. The bell rings, and the class goes silent. Sagehorn looks at me, blushes, and then turns to the class. "Today . . ." Her voice catches. She clears it. "Today, we will be measuring the surface area of various objects. You'll need to memorize the equations." She moves to the board and grabs chalk, all by the book, not even a hint of a smile.

I hate that I've done this, put that quaver into her voice. Fuck, I can't remember how many of my mom's boyfriends have done that to me, made me feel that small. I am a dick, just like them. No, I can't think that. I'm different. I am.

"Open your notes."

Someone nearby says, "More like, *spread your legs*." A few kids chuckle. Fuck, they can't start this. Sagehorn whips around and flashes red. She holds her look over the class, but it's more haunted than angry. She's hanging on by a thread, and I just look away when she stares at me.

"We'll start with the triangle."

The same kids who chuckled before laugh out loud now, and part of me doesn't blame them. Really, why would she choose *that* shape? But I bite my cheek so I don't laugh. I'm fucking toast if I do.

Sagehorn drops the chalk. It lands on the floor and cracks into three pieces, but she doesn't pay any attention to it, just stands straight and eyes the class, her face glowing hot. She levels a dirty-ass stare on me, and I stop biting my cheek. I understand where she's coming from, but if she's going to try and pin everything in here on me, well, I'm not *that* much of a pussy.

She turns back to the board. "Like I was saying, the triangle is rather easy to finger. I mean, figure. *Figure.*"

There's a pause. Mouths behind me sound like stifled screams.

"Let me just, let me just lay out an example for you."

The screams burst, and five guys lose their shit. Each is red-faced, laughing his ass off. One starts coughing and can't catch his breath. Kids turn and look at me, and I feel a bolt turn inside.

"Out!"

Sagehorn's looking at me.

"Get! Out!"

I put up my hands. "But I didn't . . ."

"I don't care!" Her scream stops the laughter and my argument. She's wide-eyed, red-faced, straight-up pissed. I hate these fucks for doing this, but what can I do? There's nothing I can say that will change anything. I'll only look more guilty. It takes me a moment to get the momentum to get out of my seat, and some chuckles pop as I go. She watches me the entire time, like some deranged animal ready to fight a predator.

I step into the hall, close the door behind me, and breathe. "Shit."

I walk slowly to Big O's. He'll be expecting me.

The secretary is standing when I enter, a little smile tucked just under the bottom of her glasses. "Go right in."

I don't bother to give her a dirty look or play dumb. Big O's door is open and obviously meant for me. I walk through, and the big man is looking down, one hand on his forehead, the other stretched out before him. He doesn't look up.

"It wasn't me. I didn't do shit." I stop. "Sorry. Didn't do *anything*."

He looks up now, gives me a long stare, and I wonder how he was as a teenager, because he's one scary-looking fuck. Bet he messed shit up. "Explain."

I do and his fat ass actually listens, his big lips opening and closing like a fish. He leans back in his chair and sighs. I know what's coming and brace for the hit, just like always. "I told you, one more mistake, one more, and that was it."

I feel like I might hurl. What am I going to do without Vo-Tec? And now, the gym?

"But I'm not ready to say you've made that mistake yet. I'll speak with Mrs. Sagehorn and see what her version of the event is."

I'm able to take a small breath. "You believe me?"

"I didn't say that, so don't go putting words in my mouth."

I jam my hands under my armpits and contain myself.

"Go down, see Mr. Franks, make some use of your time. Help him spruce things up around here. Homecoming's around the corner and we need to look our best."

I nod because I can't believe that he's giving me another chance.

"And by the way . . ."

I knew it couldn't go this smoothly.

"Coach Dan said you did well last night. Good job." Big O's smile cuts across his face, and I feel more like I'm watching someone else's life than my own. I'm never on the receiving end of this.

"Thanks." I can't think to get anything else out.

"You're welcome. Now go."

I flash a grin at the secretary as I pass her desk, and she doesn't seem to know what to do with her own face.

The two douche janitors are watching TV. I don't bother to talk to them, just grab a sweeper and do like before. I finish up, happy to have had something to lean against as I walked. My legs feel a bit better, but there's still a half hour until the block's through. I don't want to overdo it. I bring the sweeper and pan back to the office. Mr. Franks snorts at me.

"Figured it out for yourself?"

"It isn't that hard."

He grunts. "No, it's not." He steps away from the pallet he was sorting through, grabs a spray bottle and a rag. "There's some graffiti down by the gym. Near the main doors. Go mix some elbow grease with this and see how much you can get rid of. Figure it's a good penance."

He says the last word all slow, and as I take the bottle, wonder if he thinks that I don't know what *penance* means. Fuck him. I know penance inside out. I've been paying for mistakes my entire life. Mostly my mother's. I grab the rag and head toward the hall.

"No argument?"

"What's the point? You've got me all figured out."

"You're learning already."

The graffiti is mostly a bunch of f-bombs and cocks. Why the fuck do guys draw so many cocks? I've never once seen a girl draw a cock. Or a twat. Guess that second one's my department. I laugh and spray the solution. It smells like orange but works real fucking well. I only have to dig in a couple of times and the wall is clean. I could use some of this shit at home.

A couple days later we spill off the bus and into Greyson's room. He's smiling, which is not a good sign. He's got something planned, some project. "Gentlemen, have a seat." We sit at these thick-ass wooden tables that are busted to hell.

"Still can't believe that shit with Sagehorn." Rob swivels on his stool.

"Sorry you're stuck on my twat. Should get some of your won. "

Rob opens his mouth to speak but shakes his head, instead.

"Anyway, if Big O believes whatever bullshit she tells him, this may be our last class together."

Rob stops swiveling. "Don't sweat it, Tone. It'll work out."

I feel like telling him he's an ass for saying something like that, but part of me wants to believe he's right, so I stay quiet.

"Your next project is going to combine research and hands-on application." Greyson turns and pulls a cart toward him. Looks like a portable tool unit. But he punches a code on the built-in lock and opens the doors. Laptops? He pulls one out. "Back when I started, you consulted manuals or called guys to find out how to fix things you'd never seen before.

Now," he taps the computer, "it's all here." He sets the laptop on the top of the cart. "If you want to cut it as a mechanic you need to know computers and cars. Therefore, you will be teaching the class about one of the major car systems."

The guys murmur. A lot of us don't have computers, and I rarely use the ones at school.

Greyson pats the air to calm us. "Don't worry, you're not on your own, and these laptops will be here for your use. I'll get you started." He crosses to his tool counter and grabs a bucket. "First things first, partner up."

I turn to Rob while the rest figure out who's with who. With these idiots, it could take awhile. "Hey, you know what Jensen's business is?"

Rob frowns. "Really, you don't know?"

"No, dick, or I wouldn't be asking. He was talking shit in the bathroom but then said something about staying out of his business. Keeping our mouths shut."

Rob's forehead wrinkles. "Why the fuck would I want to talk about slinging meth?"

I immediately think of my mother. Shit. "He deals?"

"Yeah. For the Front."

Everything goes still for a moment. The Front. I know the name, but can't remember why.

Rob must see my confusion. "That's Chaz's crew. The Agnostic Front."

A hole opens inside, and I feel everything pull toward it. Dave is Cameron's nephew, and if he's involved with the Front, then I'll bet Cam is, too. And if Cam's that close to meth or whatever else their selling, Mom doesn't have a chance. And neither do I.

Greyson steps to us. "Grab a slip." He pushes the bucket between us. I reach in, grab one, and open it.

"Cooling and Lubricating."

Greyson writes down our names and the system on a clipboard. "All yours." He moves on to the last group and then passes out a packet for the project. We go through page by page and write in the due dates.

It's a fuck lot like school, boring as hell, but it keeps me from having to think about what Rob just revealed. What I should have been aware of all along. I know those tests said I was smart. Even Big O seems to think so. But sometimes I miss the most obvious shit. I have to find some time to think, to figure this out. I get that Big O's offered me something sweet—even if I'm about to lose it—but if it means because of it I'm pulled closer to the source of my fucking problems, I have to walk away.

7

We spill off the bus and pass Charity's. The hogs are gone. "You see?" I point and Rob nods. "Could be a good sign, right?"

Rob lowers his head against the cold. "Could be."

Amy pops out of her trailer, face puffy and eyes red. She's wearing only jeans and a T-shirt, but she lights up and we wait for her. "They're gone." She points with her cigarette.

"Saw that." Rob steps closer, looking like he wants to hold her. "You seen Char? She call?"

"No. That's why I stayed home, in case she came back." She takes a long drag and shivers. "I don't know what the fuck's up."

I picture Char's dad from the other night. Nothing good is coming from him. But Char's at her grandma's. Well, so he says.

Rob moves to her and puts an arm around her back. She lowers her head, and I can hear her crying. "I fucking hate it here," she says.

Don't we all. Rob's looking at Amy's neck, and I can't tell what the fuck he's thinking, but Amy's right, this place is a nightmare. Guys like Charity's dad make it so. I wish Mom could have made it work with one of those guys. I mean, did she only pick complete assholes, or is that all I can remember? Why can't life just give us one? Something to make this shit easier? But knowing my luck, it'd be even worse in the suburbs. And I'd never have been friends with Rob.

I take off and Rob yells into my back. "Tonight, Tone." It's not a question.

I climb into the trailer. It's dark and I don't bother with the light. I don't want to see what kind of condition they've left it in.

I pull the fridge open and half a turkey club is sitting in an open take-out container. I haven't eaten since breakfast, so I take a bite. The bread's soggy from the pickle juice and the bacon's chewy, but it wouldn't matter if the thing were balled up and dripping, I'd eat it.

I pour a glass of milk and lean against the counter. We've been here seven or eight years and not one thing has changed. The ugly-ass striped couch we got at Goodwill still takes up way too much space in the living room. If you can really call it that. The La-Z-Boy still leans to the right. And the TV reception blows. We don't have end tables, just floor lamps. There's no kitchen table either. Not that there's room.

It's fucking depressing. My mother and I live a pathetic life. And there's nothing that says it's going to get any better. I'm going to be a mechanic instead of going to college. Guess all those fucking tests from back in the day that said I was smart were wrong. Mom, she's going to? Fuck, I don't know. Serve food the rest of her life. Get beat by her boyfriends. Smoke too much.

What if? What fucking if my dad hadn't been a drunk? What if she stood up to him? Or if I did? I had my chance. I was five, and he was passed out. Mom was crying in the bathroom. He was in a chair, head craned back, Adam's apple bobbing away. I had the knife from the drawer, and I was cutting out that bobbing apple. And I was smiling.

Mom came out of the bathroom then and called my name, snapped me back to reality. She asked me what I was doing, and I just started bawling. The way she asked, I felt like she knew. But what if I'd gone through with it? All this shit, this violent, dirty fucked-up life we live, could we have escaped it?

I set the glass in the sink and hesitate before going into her room. The bowl and some shake lie on the nightstand. I open the drawer. The pipe's still there, but I still don't see a bag. All right. Maybe I was worried over nothing. I mean, I don't give a shit if she passes a bowl or smokes a joint, so long as she keeps that fucking pipe out of her mouth.

I head down the hall and flop onto my bed. The crash causes the trailer to creak. I've outgrown this shit. My eyes close, and I haven't yet taken off my shoes.

"Tone. Hey, Tony!"

I snap up, wipe drool from my face and look at my clock. 6:15. Fuck!

"Tony, you in there?"

"Yeah. Hold up." Fuck, we have to boot. I grab a pair of shorts out of my hamper. I'll change at the gym.

Rob screws up his face when he sees me. "Damn. You just wake up? Face's got pillow lines and shit."

"Didn't know I had to look pretty for you."

"I like my bitches to be smoking." We both laugh, and Rob notices my jeans. "You got shorts underneath?" I hold up the pair I snagged.

"Change when I get there."

He nods. "That's good, cuz you'll need this." He extends

a jock strap and cup. I head down my steps.

"The fuck?"

"I'm serious. You need to wear one."

"Yeah. But that's yours."

He shoves the filthy thing at me. "But it ain't like you're going to buy one."

That hurts, even though he's right. We don't have money for food, and Mom's already bitching about oil prices. Fuck it'll be a cold winter. "You clean it?" Rob nods and I look the thing over. I've worn one before, back when I played football for a season. Fucking joke that was. "I just hope it isn't too small."

"Doubt that'll be a problem."

"Right, cuz all Micks are hung like porn stars."

Rob shakes his head. "Whatever. Tuck that shit away. If we go walking outta here with you dangling it, someone'll beat your ass. And I won't stop 'em."

Same scene at the gym as last time, guys looking like they're waking from the dead. They slap hands with me this time, though, and give me props for last class. Dave walks in, already sweating, biceps popping. He's the same, but I can't help but think of him differently now. How he ended up working for Chaz is beyond me and why Rob doesn't say anything to Coach Dan almost is. If it weren't for his future.

"Fucking douche." Phil lies on his back and tucks up. Then he sticks his feet out behind his body, past his face.

"Summer's Eve." Amir spreads his legs and stretches out over one.

I hit up the bathroom, slide out of my jeans, and work

the cup over my underwear. Not bad, maybe a little tight. I pull up my shorts and see myself in the mirror. Every stitch of my clothing is wrinkled and my face still has those fucking pillow lines. In spite of how I look, one thought runs through: *I want to be here.*

I step out. Coach Dan and Rob are talking. I walk over.

"There he is." Coach looks at me. "The warrior himself." He puts out his fist and I pound it. I will myself not to blush but can feel it creeping along my cheeks. He hasn't asked me to leave, so maybe all is good with Big O? At least for now.

"Stick with Rob, and my protégé will turn you into the best we've ever seen. All right?"

I shoot Rob a look, and he's doing the same as I was, tucking away the emotion. "No doubt. Thanks, Coach."

"You got it. Now go stretch. We roll in ten."

Rob and I drop our gear in the corner and I ask, "What was that about?"

"You know. His and Big O's plan."

"Yeah?"

"Yeah." He looks at me, and I know the conversation's over. "How's the cup?"

I adjust it. "Do you cry when you look at your cock?"

"Yeah, cuz I know how much damage it does."

"Your calluses don't count."

We walk over to Phil and Amir, and there's a fat fuck who wasn't here last class. I elbow Rob. "Who's that?"

"The big dude?"

"Yeah."

"The Blob. You should roll with him tonight. The fucking stench'll kill you."

I push away that image and stretch. Everything is sore and screaming for me to not beat it down.

"All right, gentlemen, since we're rolling again, let's start with the hold that got Rob lumped up." Coach Dan walks to the center of the mat, Dave smiles from the corner, and Rob's face beats red. Coach lies on his back. "Amir, put me in a choke."

Amir bounces up, lays his body across Dan's, and locks his arm around Coach's neck.

"Now, Rob, correct me if I'm wrong, but is this the position you had on Dave?"

"That's it." Rob's voice is low.

"Good. So what did Rob leave open?"

"The gap by his head," a kid from across the room answers.

"Right, which allowed Dave to leverage his elbow and . . ." Coach Dan brings his arm up and lands his elbow an inch from Amir's face. I wince. "What Rob needed to do was close the gap with his hips. Amir?" Coach returns his arm, and Amir shifts his hips toward the mat, pressing deeper into Dan. "Now?" Coach tries to bring up his arm but can't. "You see?" The group nods and then Coach taps Amir twice on the back. They separate. "All right. Pair up and work on that. Close the gap."

Around the room guys are choking and pressing and talking and switching. Coach is on the mat, watching and giving pointers and patting guys on the back. He smiles and I watch his hand, thick and meaty, come down repeatedly on heads and shoulders and backs, as he nods and gives advice. I want that. How fucked up? I turn to Rob. "All right. Let me get my squeeze on."

"Switch partners!" Coach Dan hovers over us. "Rob, get with Dave. He needs the competition."

Rob gets up and moves across the room without argument. I stand and look for someone else. Fuck, the only one not paired up is the Blob. Fucking figures. I walk over. "Hey, I'm Tony. New guy."

"Bill." He extends a hand. We slap. "You wanna roll?"

I don't, but really, what the fuck am I gonna say? "Sure."

"I'll get on bottom." The Blob lies on his back and spreads his legs. I can't look. We slap hands and get to it.

The Blob locks his ankles behind me and tries to drive up his hips. I grab his wrists and push down on the jiggly mound. He strains and sweat pops across his forehead. I bring up a knee and press it into his thigh. His ankles separate, and I spring out of the mount. I go for another arm bar, but for a fat fuck, he's lightning. He pulls away and leaves me lying on my side. He rolls and goes for my head. I remember someone saying, "Tuck it away before you lose it." I do and the Blob's got nothing to grab.

I roll and get to my knees. Guys are paired up around the room, rolling with their new partners and through them I see Dave and Rob. Both are red-faced and breathing heavy.

Holy Fuck, the Blob's on top. If Rob was a truck, this dude's a fucking fleet of semis. I try to lock my ankles, but he's too big. He pushes down while I try to get up. No use. But he slips in his own sweat and slides back onto my legs. It's like a motherfucking zoo attack, and the hippo's got me. I wiggle, but can't find a way out. I press into the ground with my hands, like a reverse push-up and feel a leg slip loose. I look over his shoulder and then whip my leg around the Blob's neck.

His weight shifts, and I push up and squeeze. He shifts off my other leg and to the mat, grabbing at the one around his neck. I use the leverage and pull him toward the floor. Once he's there, I lean back and sit on his head. His meaty hand comes up and taps me twice. I release and he gasps for air.

Across the room, Dave's working a choke on Rob, but Rob keeps sliding his hand up through. Most of the room is watching, no longer rolling. I turn, slap hands with the Blob. He doesn't say anything, just nods and wheezes.

Dave pulls Rob's arm at the elbow, removing it from the space, and squeezes his hips and draws down on Rob. Here it comes. Rob squirms but can't get free. He taps the mat twice.

The room applauds, but it's not like last night. Not like when Rob beat Dave. Coach Dan says, "Nice work," but even his voice seems softer, less enthusiastic. Both guys are spent though, and I doubt they hear much of anything.

Class ends and we head for our gear. I take my pants into the bathroom and my legs are covered in sweat. Putting them back on feels like sliding into a used condom. I'm tired and sore, but again feel good about it. I dig this shit. I walk out and, again, Rob's talking to Coach. He turns to me as I approach.

"Coach's got a beater of a truck that he'd like to get running for the winter."

"That way I can plow the parking lot here and pick up some driveways."

"All right." I don't understand why I should give a shit about this, but I can be polite.

"So I told Coach that if we could use it for the Vo-Tec project, we'll get it back in shape."

I have no idea why he wants to do this, but I'm sure Rob's got a reason. I smile. "Sounds good, but where are we going to work?"

Rob takes a step toward me, and his face pulls serious. "Greyson will let us bring it to the shop." His eyes pop wide, telling me to fucking agree, like we've done this shit before. Coach is eyeballing us, and his smile is gone.

"Right, right. The hell was I thinking?"

Coach's smile returns. "Great. I can barely drive my piece of shit hatchback through the snow as is."

"We'll talk to Greyson tomorrow and then let you know at practice." Rob's all business, and I remember the protégé comment. This is starting to make a hell of a lot more sense.

"Works for me. You want to go check out the beast?" We nod and follow Coach out back. The air bites at my damp skin. "Here she is." Coach spreads his hands before a busted Ford 250. It's hard to see its condition in the dim light, but Coach's smile is obvious.

"Sweet ride, Coach." Rob runs a hand along the hood.

"Had her forever." He turns to us. "Do whatever you need. All right?"

"Absolutely." Rob shakes hands with Coach Dan and then Coach shakes mine.

"See you tomorrow, boys." He turns and heads back into the gym. We take off up the street.

Rob throws on his hood. I don't bother with mine; it's so fucking thin. "You need to pick up some gear."

I nod. "You think Big O or Coach Dan will spring for that?"

Rob stops walking and looks at me, all disgusted.

"It was a joke. Come on."

He walks.

"Hey, I understand what you're doing. It's cool. I was just playing."

"Sure?"

"Hundred percent. Shit, if this works out, I'll have to figure out how to pay Big O back. Can't fix his ride, though. Drives a damn Escalade."

We laugh and pound fists.

"Coach is a good guy, and I appreciate what he's doing. You know?"

I do. I want the same, someone to give me a way out. "If you like him so much, why don't you say anything about Dave and what he's up to?"

Rob stares ahead. "I've thought about it. Really I have. But it would just be my word against his. I don't have proof or shit." He looks at me. "And what would Dave do then? You know how crazy he is. Outside the gym there's no one to hold him back."

Shit, Rob's as fucked as I am.

We're quiet for the rest of the walk, but when we roll into the park we say the same fucking thing, "The hogs are back." And there are more. Six altogether out in front of Charity's. We head straight to Amy's, and Rob knocks.

She pops her head out the door like some animal coming out of its hole, but sighs when she sees us. "Thought you might be Char."

"Still ain't home?" Rob steps down the stairs.

"The fuck'd I say that for if she is?"

Neither of us answers. Amy comes out with a cigarette pressed between her lips, lights it, and holds the smoke for a long time. "I've been watching these guys. They rolled up with some nasty-ass bitches, all scabby on the face and shit. Must be fucking 'em for a score."

"Maybe it's better that Charity's not with them." Rob watches Amy.

She nods and we all look at the trailer. Every light is on, but the blinds are drawn. Laughter pops. Someone yells, and one thought screams through my head. "I gotta go." I take off before Amy or Rob has a chance to say anything.

My trailer's dark, but the door's unlocked. I step inside

and hear voices in my mother's room. I'm uneasy but walk down the hall and tap the door. The bed squeaks, feet shuffle, and my mom's face appears. "'Sup?" She looks at the floor.

"You all right?" I reach toward her, but she pulls the door.

"Shut that fucking thing and come back!"

Every muscle tenses at the sound of Cameron's voice. "Mom, what's going on?"

She bobs from side to side and doesn't answer. I could just walk away, head down the hall, and forget about this. But I can't. That move has stopped working. I push the door back, and she stumbles then falls onto the bed. I move into the room and Cameron stands. He's wearing a pair of boxers, and every muscle is exposed, stripped of fat and roped along his frame. His neck is thick and strained, and his face is jumping off his body. "Get the fuck out!"

I step back but look at my mom. It's like her brain's been ripped out of her head. She's sitting where she fell, her chin resting on her chest. "The fuck's she on?"

"Get out!"

I crouch and look at her, but she doesn't see me. Out of the corner of my eye, I see the nightstand. There's a glass pipe. I turn and see residue in the bottom. Motherfucker. "What did she smoke?"

Cameron's eyes bore into me. "This ain't none of your business, so don't go messing little boy."

My body flames, and I look at her. Right now anything could happen and she wouldn't know it. He could kill me, and she'd wake up and wonder how. Damn it, I said I wasn't going to stand up to him again, that I have to forget that stupid fucking fantasy, but right now, I don't have a choice.

It takes all the energy I have left to speak. "Get the *fuck* out of my house!"

He laughs. "Who's gonna make me?"

I know I can't. I know I shouldn't. I know there's no chance. But maybe? Just maybe? I pin back my shoulders, and he pops into a boxing stance.

"All right, bitch. I heard you've been learnin' how to fight. Come on, let's see what you got."

I don't know what the fuck to do. All the fights I've been in have been with guys who street fight like me—sloppily. We haven't learned about sparring at the gym, and I can't try and get in the clinch with this wiry ball of muscle.

He jabs and catches my cheek. It stings, and I step back.

"Ha, ha fucker. You don't know shit."

The anger or the embarrassment or the shame sinks my body into position to match his. I look over the top of my fist and throw, but it's a wild punch, my nerves far too fucking jumpy. Cam steps out of the way. I'm carried forward by the momentum, and my legs wobble so bad I can't gain my balance.

He cracks me off the back of the head, right at the base. My vision goes blurry, but I find a corner and use it to turn and regain my position. Cameron bobs in front of me, smiling. "What do you think, you gonna even land one?" He's not even breathing heavy. "Doubt it." He drops his hands and laughs harder. Fuck, he's right, I can't take him. Not like this. I lunge.

He catches me with a solid upper cut to the jaw on my way into him. Everything jars, but I continue forward and into him. We topple, and I land on top. But my face feels busted, and I can't think of what to do. Cameron doesn't give me the chance, just starts throwing hooks at my ears and neck. I put up my hands for cover, and he pops me in the throat. I jump off and clutch my neck. I can't breathe.

I suck the air as hard as I can but get only a mouthful. My face feels shattered and my throat like I've got a fist jammed inside it. I wheeze while Cameron gets to his feet. Fuck, what's he going to do now? I'm done. I can't fight. I can't even breathe. I turn to my mother for help, but she's nodded off on the bed.

"A fucking bitch. Just like your mom." He stands over me and I cower. Cam leans, and over my wheezing, I hear the throat grating sound of him churning a hawker. Please, no.

He spits and it lands in my hair. I cannot describe how dirty I feel. I see him adjust his feet, and I know what's coming next. I close my eyes and take the kick square in the ribs. It doubles me over. He steps away, laughing, and takes two jumpy steps like he's going to do it again, but stops his foot midair. "Try that again, and next time I'll take your head clean off."

I watch him squat down next to my mother and whisper in her ear. She doesn't move, barely seems to breathe. But he smiles and kisses her, and I tuck into myself.

"Look at me, boy."

I move my head and feel his spit slide across my scalp. I'm on the verge of tears but know that if I don't do what he says, this will get worse. I look at him.

He's wearing his jeans and holding on to his shirt. "I ain't going nowhere." He slides the shirt on and then points at me. "You remember how that feels before you go fucking around again. Got me?"

I nod because I have to.

He jerks his head quickly, looks down at my mother and then turns out of the room. A moment later the door slams, and outside, I hear him draw another hawker. It smacks the window.

I use my sleeve to wipe away the spit on my head and feel more anger than I've ever felt before. But I also feel more like a pussy than ever before. I can't even slip into my fantasy about killing him because I know, without a doubt, that it's just that, fucking make-believe.

I sit up and look around the room. It's littered with laundry and garbage. My mother is passed out on top of the piece of shit she calls a mattress. A fucking meth pipe sits on the dresser. And here I am, in the corner, like some dog. There is no point in playing pretend: my life is worthless.

8

Everything hurts. I roll out of bed and pull on the nicest gear I own, because maybe it will distract from how I look. When I showered last night, I only glanced at myself in the mirror, but that was enough. I've never looked this bad.

My muscles scream, and my heartbeat bounces inside my face, which is so swollen it doesn't feel like it's a part of me. There's a clamp around my throat, and I'm not sure I can speak. Shit, just breathing hurts. I don't think the rib's broken, just cracked.

I shiver in the cold, and my bed calls to me as I tuck the comforter in, but there's no way in hell I'm staying home. Staying here means I'll have to nurse my mom back from the pile of shit she fell into. Taking care of myself is enough.

I pause at her door to make sure she's still breathing and then hit up the kitchen. There's milk, but not much else. I fill a glass and drink. The cold feels good, but I have to grab my throat when I swallow. The pain is just too intense. For once it might be a good thing that there's no food here. Eating would feel like swallowing sand.

I finish the milk, take a piss, and brush my teeth. I don't look in the mirror. There's no point.

"Jesus Christ, Tone, the mask is a little early. Halloween's in two weeks." Amy walks over and examines me. She exhales near my face but waves the cloud away. "I heard it. The fight."

I look at my feet and will them to move, but my body is uninterested.

"He's one bad-ass motherfucker. Your mom all right?"

I shake my head. I wish I could explain, but from Amy's look I don't need to.

"Strung out?"

I shrug. "Yeah." The word rips along my throat, and I grab my neck.

Amy's eyes pop wide. "Damn, what the fuck did he do to you, Tone?" Amy's voice is soft and caring, something I've rarely heard, especially from her. My insides well up, and I'm glad I can't answer. Crying would only make me look worse.

Amy shakes her head while taking a drag. "Them fuck-ing bikers. Never bring any good, and now they're pulling in this shit."

Rob appears in the distance, walking slow. His right leg drags behind, slightly, but he rolls up, smiling. "Mornin'." Then he looks at me. "The fuck happened?"

"Cameron." Amy points at me with her cigarette. "Tone can't speak because of him."

Rob stares, open-mouthed and confused. I point at the hogs. When he turns back he seems to understand, but still looks unsure. We may all live in this park and share a lot of the same shitty, fucking situations, but none of this crew has it like I do. I'm like the symbol of everything people think when *White Trash* comes to mind. And they're right. And I know it. I take a deep breath, and it still fucking stings. Always will.

Greyson's got the laptops out, and three new junk cars at our disposal. "You've got to share the cars, but there's plenty of laptops. Remember, by the end of class you need to identify all parts of your system on one of these cars and then give me the pitch for your presentation."

Kids nod and flip open packets for the project. Rob turns to me. "I'll get a computer. You go check the one in the middle."

It's a beat-up Chevy SUV that's been stripped of all that made it pretty. Perfect for us. I pull on a pair of gloves, and a couple of other kids slide beneath, checking out the exhaust. I look in at the engine and find the easy parts: oil cooler and filter, the fan and radiator. I step over one of the kids lying beneath and tap the water pump and oil pump with my pen. The exhaust kids slide out, and I slip onto one of the creepers. It's painful to get down, but once I'm flat I feel fine.

The oil pan's simple to find, and right next to it is the transmission filter. I tap these as well, but instead of sliding out, just lie still for a moment. I like being beneath a car, in spite of how filthy the thing is. It's like it's so close to collapsing on me, but I know it won't. Something about the danger and the safety.

"Yo, you find everything?" Rob's voice filters through the metal.

I slide out. "Yeah." My voice is busted, barely audible, but hurts less to get out.

He nods and gives me a hand up. "You think Greyson will be down with our plan?"

I look over at Greyson. He's talking to a pair, checking off their packets. I flip mine over and write on the back: *Whose truck do we say it is?*

"We'll just tell 'im the truth. He knows we're too broke to

have our own. And we tell him about Coach; it may explain how fucked up you are."

He's right. Greyson's been eyeing me since we tumbled off the bus. No doubt he's seen his share of jacked-up kids coming through here, but he isn't like the rest of the teachers who just look away. He's used to staring down the middle of a pile of shit and asking kids to come look. He's not afraid of the ugly, but I don't know about the truth.

Greyson joins us. "Boys, how we doing?"

"Not bad, not bad." Rob nods and looks around. "Tone's got all the parts covered and we've got the presentation worked out."

Greyson smiles. "Let's hear it."

I point to the Chevy and walk over. I'm about to start labeling the parts, but Greyson's looking at me like I've got shit falling out of my pants. "What?" My voice sounds like a torn muffler.

Greyson's eyes dart between my injuries. "I thought I could wait until you finished, but I can't. What happened?"

I catch Rob shaking his head as I bow my own. "Nuthin'."

"Don't lie to me. That's not nuthin'."

My head flushes. The last thing I need is for Greyson to go poking into this and talking to Big O and getting CPS all involved. Who knows how that would fuck shit up? No, let's just stick to cars and Rob's plan.

"Practice got a little intense last night." Rob's voice is strong. I look at him out of the corner of my eye.

"Practice? What practice? You two playing ball?"

"MMA. We fight mixed martial arts," Rob says.

I stare at Greyson. His forehead wrinkles. "You mean like those guys on TV? The ones in the cage?"

"Yes." Rob sounds proud.

Greyson chuckles and shakes his head. "I didn't even know kids could get into that crap. You know what they call it. The *sport*? Human cockfighting." He clicks his tongue. "Cockfighting? You know what that is, right?"

We both nod, but Rob's twitchy and his face is red. I can feel his anger. He ain't saying shit, though. I don't give a fuck what Greyson says, so long as he forgets his question. He looks me over.

"And that's how you got these?"

"Yeah." My voice is dry.

Greyson shakes his head. "Your life. All right, show me the parts."

I nod and take my place again. Rob just stares at the space in front of him. I list each and Greyson says "uh-huh." It hurts every time, but if Rob can do his part, then so can I.

I climb under and show him the pan and filter. He looks under while lying on his side. "Good. That's all of it." He stands and I slide back out. Rob's with it again, looking calm. "Okay, the presentation."

Rob clears his throat. "We'd like to bring in a truck for that."

"Really?" Greyson crosses his arms over his chest. "Explain."

Rob does, how we'll use the truck to show how the coolants and lubricants are added to the vehicle, how they run through and what they affect, and finally how to change them out.

Greyson puts a finger to his lips. "So why is the vehicle necessary? You could do that on a PowerPoint."

Rob swallows. "Sure, but this is real. We can't fake knowing what we're talking about. We mess up, it's obvious."

Greyson is still for a moment. He looks at Rob and then at me. "Where are you getting the truck?"

"It's mine."

The fuck? Why'd he say that?

"Really?" Greyson frowns.

"Yeah."

Greyson puts his hands on his hips and smiles. "It's a big risk, but all right. If you're willing to take the chance, it's fine by me."

"So I can bring it in?"

"Yeah. As soon as you can. Just drop it off around back." He turns away, but whips around. "And think about that nonsense fighting, will you? I can't see any good coming from it."

"How the fuck are we going to get Coach's truck to the garage?" My throat is shredded as I speak, but I gotta ask. I've been thinking about it since class.

Rob kicks a rock, and it strikes a trailer. "We'll get it runnin' over the weekend. We can figure it out."

I look down and imagine this: us with no tools and no fucking clue. "I don't know. Why didn't you just tell Greyson that it's Coach Dan's? He might have helped us work something out."

"You heard what he said. *Human cockfighting.* No way he woulda let us help a guy who coaches that."

He's right, but it doesn't change the fact that we're fucked.

"We'll talk to Coach tonight. Figure something out. You're still coming, right?"

"Yeah." I rub my face, forgetting about the bruises and wince. Fuck, I'll go anywhere just so long as I don't have to be home. I have no clue how I'll deal with my mom when I see her. Or Cam. I thought fighting back was the answer.

Clearly it wasn't. I've got to try something else, but until I figure out what the fuck that is, I'll keep my promises. The ones I've made to Big O and Rob. If I back out, I'm even more of a pussy than I already am.

"All right, see you later."

Rob takes off and I stand in front of my trailer. Last night comes back in quick scenes: my mother, the pipe, Cameron yelling, the first punch, the spitting. I've been here before, lumped up and having to return home, but this time feels worse. Maybe it's because Cameron is by far the craziest one yet. Not the most brutal, my father still holds that title. Regardless, I'm sick of it. I've had my ass kicked more times than I can remember. Can this MMA shit really help me now, or is it too late? I've got some natural skill, so Coach thinks, but I need more. I wish I knew just what. But even if I did, what would I do?

I climb the steps and head straight to my room, only glancing into my mother's as I go. Food containers from her work are strewn across the floor and dresser. Her blankets are heaped at the end of the bed, and the bottom sheet doesn't cover half of the stained mattress. I can't remember if it looked like that last night or not, but at least she's no longer in it.

I untie my shoes, place them under the bed, and lie down. My face and throat throb, my side is a dull ache. I doubt Coach will let me practice, but I'm going. Even if I have to just sit there. I close my eyes and start to drift off.

Pop! I sit up. Gunshot? *Pop! Pop!* "Come on!" someone screams from outside. I go to my window. Up at Charity's place, her dad is holding the handle of his hog and looking at the bike like it just pissed on him. Two other guys lumber out of the trailer and join him. They all squat down and look.

Chaz tries to start it again and nothing happens. Fuck, meth-head bikers angry at a hog that won't run. I roll off my bed and don't know why I'm doing this, but head out the door.

All three look up as I approach, but Chaz gives me a long once-over. "The fuck happened to you?"

"A fight. It's nothing." I shift my weight from foot to foot, feeling like I may need to bolt at any second. Why the fuck am I doing this?

"Damn. Looks like you got the shit of it." Charity's dad laughs, and the others follow his lead. Their eyes are red-rimmed, and their mouths are caked-white in dried spit. Chaz is wearing the same clothes I saw him in the other night. They're beyond fucked.

"Yeah. Guess you can't win 'em all."

Charity's dad smiles at this. "No. No, you fucking can't." The air around us stills, and I know I'd better do something now. I can't just stand here looking like an asshole.

"Need some help with your bike?"

Chaz screws up his face like I just farted.

"I take Vo-Tec, Auto. I know some shit."

He opens his mouth like he's gonna laugh. "No shit? Over behind the bus garage?"

"Yeah, with Greyson."

A smile breaks out beneath his grizzled goatee. "Took the same classes back in my day. Fucking Mr. Prucell. Mean son of a bitch, but knew his shit." He looks back at his bike and then at me. "Fuck, an extra pair of eyes can't hurt. Have a look."

I swallow. My throat is still raw, burning from all the talking, and my heart's beating inside it. We all squat, and I ignore the pain. Charity's dad straddles the bike and tries to pop it, again. The bikers eye me, but I stay focused on the bike. It sputters and does not turn over. Chaz gets off. He wobbles on his feet, and the other two seem to have trouble staying still. "The fuck you think?"

I don't know much about bikes, and jack shit about hogs, but I know a fair amount about fucked-up people. They don't think straight. Don't remember to do shit, like buy food. Or pick their kids up at school. Or wake up for work. Or fill the tank. "Got a gas can?"

Charity's dad spits on the ground. "You fucking kidding me? You think I'm outta gas?" He laughs and the other two stand. This was a bad idea. "Run along, Vo-Tec."

I don't need to be told twice. I turn and take two steps and my heart's pounding up in my temples now. My face is flush and hurts, but I stop. I turn back. I move to the tank and unscrew the cap before any of them registers what I'm doing. "Hey, motherfucker!" Chaz's hand's on my wrist, but I've got the cap off. The other two close in, and we all look down into the empty tank.

"No shit?" Charity's dad shakes his head. "I'll be." He turns to one of the bikers. "Ed, go get me the can." He walks to the back of the trailer and returns with the gas, then snakes the neck in and pours the two gallons. Chaz juts his chin for me to screw the cap on. I do and he restraddles the bike. He starts it, but it hesitates. He throttles the gas, and the Hog rumbles to life, throwing that deep, *rat-a-tat* growl. My heart beats in tempo, and I force myself not to smile.

"Fucking gas! No shit?" Charity's dad turns to me, and he kills the engine. "Well, well. Thank you, Vo-Tec." He clasps my shoulder. "We've been busy, and fuck," he throws a hand toward the trailer, "you know, partying, man."

I want to ask about Charity, because this is the perfect time, but I can't bring myself to speak. It's not because of the pain in my throat, but something else altogether. There's something up. Something bigger than I can understand. Charity's dad squeezes my bicep.

"I 'ppreciate the help. You need us to take out the fucker who clipped you?" He laughs, a deep gravelly sound and looks to his friends. All three have the same set to their eyes, letting me know it's no joke.

I remember what Rob said about Chaz always being on the lookout for new bodies. I glance at the other two and wonder where he picked them up. This park or another? "No. Thanks. It's not like that. This is from class." I'm not telling these beasts that Cameron got me. Considering Dave's ties, I don't know what he means to them.

"Class? What class? Gym? You beating the fuck out of each other in gym?"

I don't like how he's taking such an interest in me. It's like with Big O. With interest, comes conditions once they've helped. Whether I've asked for it or not. "No. Fighting class. Outside of school. In town."

Charity's dad drops his hand, looks me over again. "Down there with Dave Jensen?"

Everything inside clenches, and the sensation is like getting kicked in the ribs again, but I keep my shit together. I can't believe he's talking to me about Dave. Then again, they're all fucked up. "Uh, yeah." The three look at each other and something unspoken passes between them. My legs go slack, and I'm not sure if I need to run now I'll be able to.

Chaz pats my back. "Well, any friend of Dave's is one of ours." All three nod, and I try to speak, to say, what, I don't know: *I'm not Dave's friend, but I know he deals for you. Where the fuck is Charity? What are you dealing and is my mom on it?* But nothing comes. I stare at the bike I just helped start and wish I knew how all these pieces fit together. Chaz pulls me close. "You ever need anything. Cash or whatever. You find me. Or let Dave know." He looks me in the eye. "I know how things are. I've known your mom forever. And I know Cameron. You need something, let me know. That's what we're here for."

He lets me go, and I feel sick, like he's just reached down the front of my pants. I want out of this place, not to become a fixture. And I don't like all that he knows because that shit is dangerous. People always hold shit over you. Use you when they can. Kind of like how Big O is with me and Rob. Fuck, is there anyone who will help me without wanting something in return?

Chaz smiles and pats my back. "I'll be seeing you, Vo-Tec."

I say, "All right," and move on, and know the answer to my question.

The guys lie dead on the floor, but look up at the chime. "Damn, Tone, what the fuck?" Amir stops stretching. So does Phil. I shake my head. I have no idea how to answer these guys. They don't know me, and no one needs any info about my shit at home.

"What happened?" Phil sits on his heels.

I turn away and kick off my shoes, head to the corner and do not speak. I see them look at Rob, and he cuts his hand across his throat. They nod, look at me, and then return to stretching. I feel a mix of respect and disappointment. These guys could help, I'm sure. Not exactly how, but come on, they're tough as nails. But I can't drag them into the bullshit of my life. Not with them still being cool with me once I have.

Dave walks in while I'm trying to stretch. It hurts too bad to get much out of it, so I watch him. He just kicks off his shit like nothing's different. But why would it be for him? I look away before he notices me. Phil and Amir are speaking low and looking toward Dave as well. Coach Dan crosses over the mat.

"Today's a good day, gentlemen. Beautiful weather. Good day to be alive." He looks around the room, and I dart my head back to my knees. "Whoa, Tony. Hey, look up here." I exhale and do as I'm told. "Woof. That's nasty."

Guys look over and everyone gets a good look. Dave smiles and I tense.

"What happened?"

I keep my eyes on Dave and he laughs. He knows. I bet Cam told him. I turn to Coach Dan. "Nuthin'." My voice barely scratches out.

Coach's face loses its playfulness. He closes his eyes and sighs. Everyone goes silent. "I do not tolerate being lied to in my gym, so I am going to ask you again, and this time you will tell me the truth." He opens his eyes and fixes them on me.

I shift my weight so my rib doesn't feel like it's stabbing me. This guy has no fucking idea what he's asking.

"Tony, what happened?"

I look him in the eye when I answer. "Nothing."

He clenches his jaw and swallows. "I do not allow liars in my gym."

I'm not smooth about it, but I stand and Coach stops speaking. I'm not going to make him repeat himself, and I sure as shit don't want to hear it. I am not a liar and will not be forced into that position: lie and stay, or be honest and reveal way too much. There are certain things I simply will not do. Like ever ask Chaz for help. Or talk about my piece of shit life. I've never asked anyone in here about theirs. Wouldn't even think to. That just isn't right.

I look around the room. All eyes are on me, all confused, except for Rob's and Dave's. Coach Dan's face is a mix of frustration and concern. I don't like that he called me out, but I do get his point. He's got principles, and they are good ones. Shit, he took a chance on me based on Big O's word. I respect that more than he could understand. And somehow I hope he'll understand and respect what I'm about to do, because I don't want to do this, and I know it's going to fuck up that offer and all that Rob's worked for, but I don't have another option.

I turn, grab my sneakers, and walk out the door in my bare feet. No one says a word as I go, and I don't wait for anyone to come after me. Rob knows better. I cross the cold asphalt and then slide on my shoes.

I walk for I don't know how long, but long enough so that I know I won't run into Rob when I get back. He waited, no doubt. He probably talked to Coach Dan after, maybe smoothed things over and then waited by my trailer. Or maybe not. He could be fucking pissed enough to finally cut me loose. Big O will keep helping him without me, though. Fuck, maybe I did him a favor?

My trailer's dark. Maybe Mom's working late. But who knows? She could be passed out on the kitchen floor. I just hope Cameron isn't in there.

"What took you so long?" Dave's voice cuts through my heart and scares the shit out of me. He's seated in the shadows on the couch. I turn to run, but arms grab me. The rest of the bodyguard emerges from the dark.

"Easy, now." He speaks close to my ear. "You don't want me to have to break anything."

I ease into his hold. Dave flips on a light, and I'm moved

into the recliner. The thug then stands at the arm, hovering over me. My mouth's dry, but I manage to speak. "What the fuck?"

Dave smiles. "I'll cut to the chase. This has nothing to do with the gym, if that's what you're thinking. I don't give a fuck about your big scene with Coach Dan." He looks around the trailer and raises an eyebrow. "And it's not as if I've enjoyed waiting here for you. I'm here to help, just like I helped Cameron and just like I helped Rob."

Hold up. What? What the fuck is going on? Cameron *and* Rob?

"And now it's your turn."

I square to Dave. There is no doubt in my mind that Chaz sent him, but I don't know if it's safe to say so. "What are you talking about?"

He leans forward, resting his elbows on his knees. "It's real simple. I have money, you don't. Neither did those two, and when they needed it, I hooked them up. As payment for a service."

My head continues to spin. I just got tossed from the gym, and I'm sure shit's fucked up between Rob and me because of it. Who knows what the fuck's going to happen with Big O? Dave's figured this out somehow and is fucking with me. It's that simple. He's lying. Rob wouldn't take anything from him. Cam might, even though he's his uncle. But that's beside the point.

"Let me help you figure this shit out. You hooked up Chaz today. He appreciates the favor and wants to repay. He doesn't like to be in anyone's debt."

I grow cold, as if I'm back outside. Dave knows too much and is way too calm for this to be bullshit.

"He's had his eye on you ever since we picked up Rob. He knows the two of you are tight. And now that you're fighting . . ." He pauses. "Or were. Whatever. Chaz figures you're good to go. You follow?"

I nod, because, unfortunately, I do.

"So they don't want Marcus here to hurt you." Dave looks up at the thug. "But he will if you fuck this up."

I lick my lips. "What do I have to do?"

"Easy, deliver a package. You'll be paid, of course. The guys believe in making good on their deals. And, honestly, you could use the cash."

Fuck! How can this be happening? How can Dave have Cam and Rob be under his thumb? And why the fuck am I getting pulled in? I breathe slowly to calm myself. "So why am I talking to you and not Chaz?"

Dave nods. "He tried earlier, but you snubbed him. Not good." He laughs, and it's evil. "Besides, this is part of my job. I'm the go-between. They're obvious targets and don't want the attention. I fit anywhere."

Shit, he's got an answer for everything.

"Listen, I don't have all night to convince you, so here it is. You deliver a package tomorrow night, you get one grand." He looks at me for a moment, his eyes lighting. "You refuse, and things'll get a lot worse round here."

Marcus shuffles next to me, and my insides go tight. Does he mean for me, or for my mom, or both? Fuck. How much worse can it get? I don't want to find out.

Dave stands. "I'll be back tomorrow, round eight. Be ready." He pauses. "Not like you'll be at the gym." Dave laughs and Marcus crosses the room and joins him. Dave looks me over. "Don't be stupid, Tone. This ain't the ring. There ain't no tapping out of this one."

They leave, and I sit in the semidark, completely drained and thoroughly lost.

9

It's cold when I wake up, past the nip of fall, feeling more like winter. I pile on layers of clothes because walking to school is going to take at least an hour. There's no way I can see Rob. Not after last night, the gym and the shit with Dave. I have to think. I tried last night, but couldn't figure anything out. What am I going to say to Big O? Coach Dan called him. I know it. Regardless if I figure that out or not, I still need to figure out what to say to Rob. How do I ask him if he's been dealing? If he's been doing the one thing we said we'd never do? And, fuck, what the hell am I going to do about tonight? I'm full of questions without answers. Story of my fucking worthless life.

I head out and brace against the wind. It pricks my skin like a cold shower, and I'm wide awake now. The sun's not yet up, so it could be last night. And wouldn't that be fantastic? I could just skip going to practice and wouldn't be in this mess. No, I would. One way or another, my life would have made me submit.

The walk wasn't as bad as I thought. Moving that much seems to have helped my rib. My face is still busted to fuck, but I didn't expect that to change. Big O was prowling the halls when I slipped in. I made sure to go the opposite direction and kept my eye out. Did the same with Rob, who was definitely looking for me. It was like he'd lost a pet. I'm surprised he wasn't calling my name and whistling. At least he cared, though. Shit may not be that bad when I talk to him. Then again, he may just drop me in the middle of the hall when we do meet up. For now I'm good, rolling through the morning, done with history and math. Cleaning duty now. Maybe Big O will be waiting?

The wall-eyed janitors aren't in front of the TV, aren't around anywhere that I can see, but the big fuck is. "Good. I was hoping you wouldn't bail on me." He steps out of the office.

"I haven't missed once."

"Yeah, but it's homecoming. Planning on more fun like last year?"

The fuck is this dick talking about? He doesn't know me.

"Didn't know I knew, huh? Getting high. Getting in that fight." He laughs. "If you call *that* fighting."

I feel like turning around, walking out and checking to see that I'm in the right fucking place, because this feels like I'm in Big O's office. "What are you talking about?"

He rolls his eyes. "Please, don't play stupid. I see and hear everything around here. Just letting you know where you stand."

"All right."

"And Big O and I go way back."

I try to play it cool, but my eyes pop.

"Yeah. I know that's what you call 'im. So did we. Back in the day."

This is just weird. Period. Maybe I'm sleeping in Sagehorn's and the bell's gonna ring and I'll wake up.

"So he gives me the dirt on the riff-raff he sends me. Like you." Franks puts his hands on his hips and looks like the Jolly Green Giant.

I don't understand why he's telling me this or why it matters. So him and Big O used to be friends, or are friends, or whatever. What the fuck does that have to do with me? "All right. What's your point?"

Franks crosses his arms over his chest and looks at me with his hard-ass stare. Yeah, I can see how the Big O and him could get along. "My. Point. Is that the best indicator of future behavior is past performance." He lets that hang in the air, like he's some teacher or shit, waiting for me to have some fucking "lightbulb" moment. Haven't had one of those in years. I shrug.

"You don't get it do you? You're not like the rest. You've got that edge, but, no, something's different. Even though you're trying to be a bad-ass with your MMA crap, you don't have the heart to be completely lost. Or you're too scared to be."

"You don't know me, and I don't know what the hell you're trying to do here, so just give me a damn broom or I am ditching. I don't need to take this from you."

Franks pops off the wall. "Hmm. Maybe I'm wrong." He grabs the sweeper and hands it over to me. I take it and rush out before he has a chance to say anything else.

I sweep the hall, thinking about what Franks said. That motherfucker. *Trying to be bad-ass.* He's got no fucking clue. *Or you're too scared to be.* Like he has any idea what I've had to face. Of course I'm scared. If I wasn't I'd be stupid. And as much as it's done jack shit for me, I know I'm not stupid. The fucking opposite.

I slam the sweeper against the wall, leave a pile and walk past lockers all decorated for the athletes: *Go Jake #65. Slay the Cougars, Jeremy!* I feel like ripping them off, but don't. Franks would know. I just sense it. That fuck's got me weirded out. How's he know all that shit? Big O really tell him? They really got it on camera? Thought that was typical bullshit. And who the fuck told him I'm a fighter? I'm not. I can't be. Not after what I did. Does Franks know about that?

I finish and return to the office. But no one's around, so I put the sweeper back and bolt. I hit the hall and make my way toward the main entrance, toward the buses for Vo-Tec. Now I've got nowhere to hide.

They're all there, bunched into a pack like they've got an inside joke. Amy looks like she's gained at least ten pounds. She's eating her nerves calm because Charity still isn't back. Must be nice to get away. I roll up just short of them.

Amy and Rob look over but I don't give them a chance to speak. The bus pulls up and I hop on, sit up front and look out the window. Rob stops. "This how it is? You ain't talking?"

I refuse to turn. Not talking? No, more like needing a fucking conference room for the two of us to figure this out.

It sounds like he goes to say more, but doesn't, just shuffles to the back.

That hurts more than the collection of my wounds.

"All right, gentlemen, today you should be one-third of the way through the project." Kids groan and take out packets and slap them on the wooden tables. I lost mine. "I'm glad to see that you're catching on. I don't even have to ask." I turn from Greyson, and Rob's staring at the table. I have no idea what he's thinking, but I'll bet he's got no clue that I'm on to him. If what Dave said is true.

Greyson continues on about the project and shit. I look through the windows cut into the garage doors. There's just a couple of clunkers and Greyson's SUV and a . . . what the fuck? I sit up straight and look harder. Can't be. But it's the same make and model, and there's the window sticker for the gym. I turn. Rob's watching me.

"All right." Greyson claps. "Get cracking." Kids get up and get laptops or check out the clunkers. Rob picks up his packet and sets it down in front of me.

"You saw?"

"Yeah. How?"

"Shit, you actually talkin' again?"

I look away.

"Oh, did I hurt your feelings? So sorry." He picks up his packet and stands. "You *are* a fucking bitch."

My heart pounds. He's right, but he doesn't get to say that shit to me. Not now. "The fuck you say?"

"You fucking heard me."

I've seen this face so many times before he fights, his sneer. He rolls up on a kid, gets his shoulders pinned, and his fucking lip creeps up his face. It's weird being on the other side. Weird, but it also pisses me off. I'm a pussy, but not with Rob. "The fuck's that supposed to mean?"

"Really? You're the smart one. Don't need me to tell you." He juts his chin toward the garage. "We had a fucking deal and you bailed."

I look over at Greyson, who's across the room looking at some kid's laptop. "Coach Dan had no right to fucking call me out."

"His gym. He can do what the fuck he wants."

Fuck, what I'd like to say. Even more, what I'd like to do—drop an elbow into his face, but he'd just fucking deflect it, then pin me. "So you just agree with whatever he says? And *I'm* the bitch?"

"Fuck you, Tone!" His face beats red, and he loses the sneer. "Least I take care of my shit. You had a deal to stay. But because someone wanted to know shit about you, it was too much. Coach Dan would've helped you. Don't you get that?" He steps to me, and I can feel the anger pouring off him. "Did you take care of Cameron? Get him out of your life? Is that why you don't need the help? Or is he still beating your mom?" He pauses. "And you?"

I shove him as hard as I fucking can. His words fall away, and all I can hear is the thudding in my head. That and Dave's words from last night. Rob trips on a stool and goes down. Greyson flashes in front of me, on his way to Rob.

"Tony? What's going on?"

His words seep through, but I can't say anything.

"It's cool. We were just messing." Rob laughs and stands. "Tone forgot his packet, and I was dissin' him. My bad."

The thudding softens, but I'm still amped, still ready to break my hand against Rob's fucking face if I have to. Greyson shrugs. "Well, at least you've got the truck here. Work on that. I'll get your packet on Monday." He eyeballs me and then smiles. "Relax, Tony." He walks past and pats my shoulder. I jump but feel my head clear.

"I know, Rob. I know about you and Dave."

He stares at me but says nothing.

"So it's true? You're dealing?"

He lowers his head and steps closer to me. "One, it ain't that simple. Two, we can't have this conversation here. Let's go out to the truck."

I have to swallow my anger first, but I say, "All right."

The truck's a piece of shit through and through. That

much is obvious in the light, as are the rust spots and chipped panel. The engine and transmission are solid, though. "How'd you get it here?" The question just pops out, and I'm pissed at myself for not staying focused.

Rob shakes his head. "The bikers."

"What?"

"It's not what you think. Last night, I stayed after, talked to Coach Dan—he wants to talk to you about shit, too. Anyway, I stayed to look at the truck, and that's when the Front rolled up."

This makes no sense. "Why were they there? Nothing but the gym is open this time of year." Then it hits me. "Or are you bullshitting me and they were there for you?"

Rob closes his eyes and breathes one deep breath. It's like he's calming himself before giving a presentation. "I dealt for them *once*. That's it. One time. I'm not like Dave."

I believe him. I just do. But still. "Why?"

He turns away. "Why else? I needed the cash. It's not like I wanted to, but some shit's fucked up, and I don't have the kind of scratch I need to cover it."

"What the fuck's up?"

"Don't worry about it. I got it under control." Rob looks me over. "How'd you find out?"

"Dave."

"Huh." Rob looks down at the engine. "Last night, they asked if I'd seen Dave."

"He was at my place, waiting."

"He bring Marcus?"

"Yeah."

Rob nods and some of my anger fades. Shit, if they put him in the same position as me . . . but, no, he said he needed cash. Did he go to them?

"Anyway, I told them I didn't know where Dave was and they started asking about the truck and we got talking." He pauses and laughs. "They asked if I knew you. Called you Vo-Tec."

I shrug just because I want to hear what else happened.

"I told 'em I did, and they said they owed you a favor. What the fuck'd you do?"

I shake my head. "Nuthin', just helped with an empty gas tank."

"What?"

"Isn't worth it. Go on."

"Well, they thought it was, cuz Char's dad called somebody, and in like ten minutes the tow truck was there."

I stare at the truck, this beat-up piece of shit that we're somehow supposed to get up and running. How the fuck are we going to do that? How the fuck am I even going to make through tonight? But, shit, if Chaz had the truck towed here, maybe I don't owe him anymore? No, they've got me regardless.

"There's a deal going down tonight. Bet that's why they were there. Dave was recruiting me."

"Fuck, tonight? You in?"

"Like I have a choice?"

Rob tries to look at me but turns to the floor. "You don't." He sighs and shakes his head. "How much?"

"Huh?"

"How much they paying you?"

"Dave said a grand."

Rob whistles and his eyes bug. "Fuck, Tone."

"I know. That's a lot of cash."

"Not what I meant. I only got five hundred."

My stomach drops, and I grip the hood of the truck to keep steady. "The fuck does that mean?"

"Wish I knew."

Behind us the door opens, and Greyson calls out, "You boys all right in here?"

Rob says, "Yeah," but I don't know how.

"Tone, you coming out?" Amy's smoke curls around her chins. I want to ask just how much she's been eating, but know she'll put the butt out in my eye if I do.

"Where?"

"The game? *Homecoming?*"

Amy doesn't give a fuck about football, just likes the drugs and the fights. Both of which I need to avoid. I know Big O will nab me up at some point, and I can't have one more issue for him to hold against me. That is if I survive the deal. Holy fuck. I can't believe I'm doing this. "That's all right. Thanks."

"What? You should go." Rob looks at me and then motions behind Amy's back for me to play along.

"*You're* going?" I ask. "You hate this shit." This isn't completely true. Rob loves all violent sports, just hates the dicks who play them.

"Nuthin' else to do."

I kick a stone down the lane and wish my only concern was whether or not to go to the game.

"Come on, Tone. Let's get ripped and start a brawl like last year." Amy takes a drag and laughs at me. The smoke puffs out her nose.

"I didn't start shit. Remember? I just fell on that kid, tripped because I was too high."

They laugh. "That was some good bud." Amy goes dreamy at the memory.

"You see? That's why you need to come back to class."

Fuck, he's relentless. I already told him I'd think about talking to Coach. But I do owe him. The only reason I survived the fight last year was because of Rob. He rolled me under the bleachers before it hit the fan. Broke some fuck's nose right in front of me. Bet the security tonight will be tight, and I can't afford one more fuck-up. That and I'll need to leave at halftime to be home for Dave. So if I don't go, I'll just be home, waiting. And no doubt Cameron will be tanked, reliving his glory days on the field. Shit. "All right, all right, I'll go."

They cheer and Amy shakes her ass. "Better be careful with that thing." Rob laughs, but there's something more than a joke in his look. Amy laughs along and whips her hair, slows her rhythm. Shit, she's gained weight, but she knows how to work it. Fuck, I'm getting wood.

"See you at six?"

Rob keeps his eyes on Amy. "Yeah, I'll get us a ride."

"We goin' through the fence?" The football field's lights shine in the distance, and Rob scans inside so he can answer my question.

"Looks like they got pigs at each corner, but there's a crew blocking the hole, so we should be able to squeeze."

"I ain't squeezing through shit." Amy stops walking.

I keep the joke to myself.

"It's that or we pay." Rob looks at her, then me.

"I'm all about free. Not like I have any cash."

"None?" Amy says the word like a curse.

I think, *Not for long*, but walk on, along the side of the

field that bumps up against the woods. The stands are full, and there are packs of kids standing in clumps along them. The pigs will be too busy to notice us. Perfect. I wait for Rob and Amy.

"Looks good," Rob says.

"Some shit's going down tonight, I can feel it." Amy steps over a root popping through the ground. Rob follows her, arms out like he's ready to catch her if she falls.

We make it to the fence and spy the slit, the one the Vo-Tec kids made with a set of bolt cutters. If you don't know where it is, you can't even tell it's there. A cop is standing a solid fifty feet away, and a group of seniors is between the fence and him. I squat down, push the chain-link, and slide through. No one even looks up. Rob and Amy do the same, with Rob holding the gate like a door.

"Ladies and gentlemen, the Albalene Cougars!" The announcer's voice rips through the air, and everyone looks up. Amy jolts to the side and puts a hand beneath her stomach.

"Fuck that scared me. I almost pissed my pants."

The opposing team runs onto the field, and our fans' booing drowns out their side's cheers. The team runs along the sideline and then branches off at the yard lines, forming columns for their warm-ups. We move toward the bleachers.

A hardcore-metal guitar riff pierces the air, and our side gets to its feet and cheers. The stomping reverberates, and in the distance, our team is walking from the locker room and moving along the outside of the fence toward the entrance.

Our school loses its shit, pounding the bleachers and each other. The team breaks from the gate and punches through a paper sign that a group of cheerleaders hold. The heavy, hardcore song with a throbbing drumbeat follows their run. They stop on the fifty-yard line, just a few feet away from the opposing team. Pinpricks form on my arms, and I rub them away.

"Let's go see who's around." Amy pulls Rob's arm and I follow. He walks tall, shoulders pinned back, hoodie on display. Some kids from the other school are walking through, douche bags obvious in their school's yellow and blue. I watch the pigs eye them and then see Big O, standing at the edge of the stands. I duck to avoid his look.

We settle in with some other park kids and pound fists. Amy slinks off with a couple girls, giggling and whispering into each other's ears. Someone's got a flask, and it's making the rounds. It's Jack and feels good going down. I haven't had Jack in forever. It warms me, and I take another pull before passing it to Rob. He takes it and just hands it off to the kid next to him. I go to ask what's up, but the kickoff rolls and there's no point in bothering. The noise is like a wall.

It dies and the cheerleaders cheer and someone hands me the flask again. I'm feeling good. Loose. I take another drink.

"What's up fuckers?" The voice is unmistakable. My insides draw down, and I swivel to look at him. Dave pops into the center of our crew, pounds fists with Rob, and ignores the hard stares from the rest. He finds me and moves in closer. "There's the little pussy."

Why the fuck is he here? Can't I get two hours of relief before I have to tangle with him? The Jack mixes with my anger and I don't feel like holding back. "Fuck yourself, Dave."

Dave cocks his head, looks at Rob and shakes it. "If he weren't your boy, Rob . . ."

"What? What would you do?" My heart's pounding, but I sound calm. I know how to keep my shit together.

Dave levels his stare on me. "I'd make you my bitch, cuz you're used to that."

My joints stiffen, and kids around us turn. They've heard, but I'm sure they've got my back. It will always be us versus them. The haves and the have-nots. It's not that we want this shit, but it's people like Dave that don't let us out. I stare him down and can't help but think how much he's like Cameron. I don't know how the fuck I didn't see it before. It's like looking into a beefier version, but the eyes are the same: empty. I swallow. "That ain't what your mom said. Fact, just the opposite."

The park kids laugh and wait for more. Dave's face ignites, and on the field a crushing hit draws cheers from the stands.

"We'll leave moms out of this, since you really don't have one. Burnouts aren't people."

I forget where I am, who is watching and what will happen. I lunge and get a hand around Dave's throat. He wobbles. All I can see is his face, turning red, and his eyes, not so empty now.

"Tone, no!" Rob rips my hand off Jensen. "Not here." He twists my wrist and draws my arm up behind my back. Like when we used to play Uncle.

Dave straightens and his eyes dance, but his face stays red, his jaw set. I could have fucking taken him, I know it. I whip my arm out of Rob's grip and turn on him. "The fuck?"

Rob stares me down, just like in Vo-Tec. He's trying to tell me something, I know it, but I'm too pissed or too buzzed to get it.

"The Front," he whispers.

Fuck. My head spins. Rob's right. What the fuck am I thinking? I turn away from Rob and back to Dave.

Dave's eyes are dancing. "You get permission or does your daddy want you to play nice?" He steps closer to me. "Oh that's right, you don't have a dad, either."

My entire head is engulfed in flames and my arm

twitches, but I hold it still, swallow and speak. "Don't worry, next time I meet up with your dad, I mean, Charity's dad, I'll be sure to let him know you've been doing your job."

Dave's face melts to hatred. He looks around to see who's listening. Some kids nod slowly while others cup hands to spell it out. Dave works his tongue along his bottom lip. "I don't know what the fuck you're talking about. Douche." He steps closer and whispers. "You watch yourself, Antioch. You have no idea what you're fucking with."

The slap is fast. Even though only his fingertips catch me, they clip the corner of my eye and make me cry out. One of the pigs turns as I grab my face. When I can see clearly again he's heading our way and Dave's gone.

"What's going on over here?" The cop bellies his way through the crew to me. The crowd roars again and feet stomp the bleachers.

"Nothing. I just had something in my eye."

The cop cracks out a flashlight and shines it in my face. He sniffs. "You been drinking?"

"No." I turn and try to blink away the spots in my eyes.

"Liar." He leans closer, sniffs again. "You've got two choices. Breathalyzer. Or leave."

Fuck me. I sure as shit won't take a breathalyzer. Who knows what Big O would do? "I'm out." I take two steps, and Rob grabs my arm.

"Yo, be careful."

I nod and move on.

"I'm watching you," the cop says, and then I hear him speak to the rest of the group. "So who else is joining him?"

I jam my hands in my pockets and pull my head into my shoulders, trying to become as small as possible. I can't go back through the fence, not with the pig watching. I have to pass Big O and all the screaming kids. They light up as we pick an interception. The announcer's voice booms, "Warrior Ball!" Everyone's smiling and the cheerleaders are bouncing and the air is cool. It's perfect. And here I am, busted, pissed off, and tossed out.

Big O turns as I pass, and I pick up the pace and get the hell out.

10

The walk home, like this morning, should take me another hour, but that's fine. Maybe someone will run me down before I get there. Headlights burn up ahead, and I step out of the road. The car doesn't move, though. The headlights blink off and then back on. "Shit." I know this car.

Dave's Mustang rolls to a stop next to me. Marcus is in the passenger seat. "Get in," he says.

I hesitate, and for a second consider running. But it's a pussy move that will get me nowhere. Not that this ride may take me much further. But I climb in the back.

We drive for a few miles and no one speaks. I breathe slow, trying to calm my nerves and convince myself that I'm doing the right thing, that it's what I have do to survive. That I don't really have a choice. That I'm not like them. I hope I'm right.

"Glad you made this easy, Tone. That scene back there was fun, too. Nice way of making it seem like we're not on the same team."

We're not, and I wasn't playing, but telling him that is useless. "Thanks."

"You see, Marcus, a smart one. Like Rob."

Marcus grunts and I imagine Rob in my exact position. I wonder how he kept from shitting himself?

"Listen. Here's the plan. We're making two stops. One, to pick up the stash. Two, to sell it. Marcus and me will make the first. You're on your own for the second."

My heart leaps and twists, and I choke it back down. "*I'm* making the deal?"

"Exactly." Dave's smile is illuminated by the red dashboard lights.

Last night he said I was just delivering a package. I know there's no point in arguing, though. He'll just have Marcus break me, and then I won't get paid at all. Have to just take it. "But I've never sold anything."

"Doesn't matter. It ain't that fucking hard to walk through a door with a box and then wait to get paid. It's like delivering a pizza." Dave pulls off the road and down a street I've never been on. "First stop." We're at the edge of town, near the old warehouses. There are still a few homes scattered here and there, mostly vacant, all busted. We pull into the driveway of one that is clearly uninhabited, unless broken windows is their thing. Dave turns to Marcus. "You know where, right?"

"Uh huh." Marcus walks toward the back of the house, and Dave keeps his eyes trained on where he disappears. He either doesn't trust him or the scene, because he's gripping the wheel like he's trying to choke it. His other hand's on the door handle.

Marcus emerges with a shoe box–sized package wrapped in black plastic. He smiles before getting back inside.

"Box cutter's in the glove," Dave says as soon as Marcus is settled. Marcus grabs the knife and carefully removes the plastic. It's a plain cardboard box sealed in packing tape.

"Want to check?" Marcus asks.

"No. Leave it. They won't want it if it's been opened. Think it's been fucked with."

Marcus retracts the blade. "But what if it ain't all there or is shit?"

"That's *their* fucking problem."

Marcus laughs that same unnatural squeal, and I go numb, as if already dead. I see the picture now. I'm worthless, expendable. I'd laugh if I could. It's all so ironic. Me thinking I'd somehow end up with a better life, only to be sitting in the back of Jensen's ride, headed toward the exact opposite.

We drive into the warehouse district, a landscape of sagging buildings, cracked pavement, and decay. Only a few streetlights still work, and their weak orange glow does little to ease my fear. We're going to drive into one of these shit holes, and I'm going to have to go into the dark and somehow come out alive.

Dave slows down and starts checking the signs on the fences that surround the old parking lots. He nods when he sees the one he wants and turns to Marcus. "Go roll back the door."

Marcus nods, bends over in the seat, and grabs something from beneath. He tucks it inside his coat and then is out the door. Dave watches him every step of the way.

I could bolt right now. It's so dark, and there are so many places to hide. My chances are good. But somewhere there are dealers. Maybe watching? Maybe the kind who would kill me on sight? If not, Dave will find me eventually. Or he'll get my mother. I settle back into the seat and watch Marcus open the chain-link enough for Dave's car to pass through.

Once the car's inside, Marcus swings in, and Dave's lights illuminate two vehicles in the distance. "That's them," Dave says, and he parks, positioned to fly straight back out.

"Here's how it will go." Dave turns in his seat, and

Marcus keeps an eye over his back. "You take the box, walk up to the door and knock. They'll ask who you are, but they don't want your name." Dave's worked up now, like I've seen him at the gym. If he's nervous, I should have already shit myself. "You say that you're with Agnostic Front. If they ask who from AF sent you, you say Chaz. If they ask for more, you fucking leave."

Agnostic Front. Chaz. These facts makes all of this now so much more real than before. There's no room for me to fuck this up. My face is jumping, I know it, because Dave cocks an eyebrow and speaks real slow.

"Just chill. Cuz you can't afford to freak out now. It's too late." He runs a hand over his face. "Most likely, they'll be happy to see you, will check the stash, and then pay." He settles his eyes on me. "You just take the cash. Don't count it if they ask you to. Just tell them that you trust them. You have to use those words: *we trust you*. If it's short, we'll take care of it later." He nods and slides back into his seat. "That's about it. You return with the cash, and I'll pay you tonight."

Every part of me is vibrating in fear, swimming in my adrenaline. I feel like I could fight or cry. But I'm walking away tonight with more money than I've ever seen. *If* I'm allowed to walk away. Fuck. I can't pussy out now. "All right. Let's do this."

Dave taps the clock on his dash. It's just after 9:00. "Perfect."

Marcus hands over the box and smiles, looking like a Rottweiler. The box is dense but not heavy, and the contents shift inside. I don't look at Dave for last-minute advice or support. I force my limbs to move, to open the door and to stand outside the car.

The shutting door echoes across the lot, and I cringe, but nothing follows, no movement, no shouts. Doesn't seem as if anyone is watching. I tuck the box like a football and head across the pavement, keeping my eyes on the large metal door.

I don't allow myself any time to hesitate. I knock and a hollow sound booms, followed by a shuffle of feet beyond. The door slides open a crack, and a soft light emerges, along with the edge of a face. "Who are you?"

My mouth moves but the words catch. "T . . . T . . ." I shake my head. "I mean . . ." I remember Dave's words. "Agnostic Front. I'm with Agnostic Front."

The eye widens, and the lip curls. "You sure?"

I nod, and the movement is exhausting. Now that I've got the words out, I feel weak and incapable of any more. If they're going to kill me, they might as well do it now. The eye hesitates, watches me, but then lingers on the box. The door slides open enough for me to walk through. I step inside, and the door is bolted behind me.

The owner of the eye is six-three, thin, and wiry. He lifts the box from my arm and crosses the room to a card table with a lantern and portable heater. Seated at it is a large fuck, like Marcus, but white, who's just set down his glass of vodka, the bottle at his elbow. He doesn't speak, just stares at me.

I don't move, just let my eyes adjust and try to take in the rest of the room. It's impossible. There's nothing but shadows, and the random speck of moonlight through missing sections of the roof.

"He's with the Front, so let's find out, eh?" The guy from the door places the package on the table and takes a knife from his pocket. The other turns to him, leaving me be. I'm torn between watching him open the box and finding an escape route. Even if they are happy with the contents, who knows what the fuck they'll do? There's light pouring in from the far corner. Can't be more than thirty yards. I could make it in seconds, but I can't see the ground. I could trip and fall, and then I'm fucking toast. But I've come this far. My chest tightens as the knife slices through the packing tape.

"Ah," the tall one says to the other. He reaches in and grabs a sealed plastic bag, then cuts a small slit with a flick of the wrist. The lean one dips in his finger and then runs it across his tongue. My heart pounds faster than I have ever felt it move, but his face transforms into a smile, and I can't help but do the same. The big man tastes as well and appears as pleased. My heart skips a beat, and my body relaxes a notch.

"Come, have a drink. We will take care of you now." The tall one waves me over. His accent sounds like it's from one of those cold European countries. The big man pours himself a vodka and then fills two other glasses. They grab theirs and look at me so I grab the third. "To success," the tall one says, and the big one mutters something in another language. They tilt their heads back and take the shot. I stare at the liquid and know I have no choice. I'll piss them off if I don't, and so far so good. The vodka burns down into my stomach, but I nod and pretend to enjoy. They set their glasses down, and the tall one stoops, reaches beneath the black of the table, and emerges with a brown shopping bag that he sets next to the lantern. "Fifteen, as agreed."

Even with the weak light, I can see inside the bag, and indeed, rubber banded stacks of cash lie inside. I can smell them, and can't help but smile. They laugh. "You see, he smiles. He must be one of them, they always smile once they see the money." He pours another drink. "Yes. Good business with the Agnostics."

We drink and then I pick up the bag.

"Count it first, please."

I shake my head. "We trust you." The words come out a hell of a lot smoother than I expected.

Both men go still and then the big one stands. My heart slams around, and I lose some of the grip on the bag. Fuck, was that what I was supposed to say? The vodka and the relief of them being happy made me too loose.

"Yes, okay." The wiry one nods and moves to the door. "Yes, I understand."

I nod to the big one and do the same to the other as I pass through, back into the cold. Holy fuck. I did it. I hug the fifteen thousand dollars in my arms and then run like the fucking cops are behind me.

Halfway to the car the taillights flash and the engine comes to life. For a second I think Dave's going to take off, but no, I have the money. He needs me. I grab the handle and am safe. For now.

Dave drives and takes a tight turn out of the lot. "You got the money, right?"

I'm breathless. "Yeah."

"Good. Now pull back the middle of the seat."

Marcus turns to watch me. I fumble around the top. He snorts.

I find a tab and pull. The seat back flops forward, and I'm looking into the trunk.

"Now, pull up the trunk bed and stick the cash in there," Dave says.

I do and it fits tight and secure. I reset everything and sit back.

"Not bad, trailer trash."

Normally, I'd tell Dave to fuck off, but right now I don't give a shit. I succeeded and that feels good.

"Yeah, muthafucka," Marcus says.

"Tell me, how close you'd come to shitting yourself?"

"I may have. I don't know."

Dave laughs and speeds up. "Two Hungarian guys, right? Talk. Like. Dis?" His impersonation is spot on, and I wonder how long he's been dealing.

"Yeah, one real tall and the other a grizzly looking fuck."

"Sounds right. No problems though?"

I'm still alive, so in my book it went fucking perfect. "They did act weird when I told them I didn't want to count the money."

"Did you say what I told you to?"

"Exact words."

"What they do?"

"Just went stiff and then real polite. I'd count the money if I were you."

Dave laughs, again. "No, it ain't like that. The cash's all there. It's something else, a respect thing." He waves a hand. "You did good, Tone. Don't worry, you'll get your cut."

I know I will, and that's fucked up. Maybe it's the vodka, or maybe it's just the thrill of the moment, but I trust Dave. He's been honest. He sure as shit isn't telling me everything, but I don't doubt him. Everything went as he said it would. He's the real deal, tight with the Front. Now so am I. And so is Rob. And Cam, too. We're all on the same side now, with *them*. Fuck, have I just made that decision? Am I really okay with this?

Dave turns on some music, and I just drift with the bass. I'm too exhausted to think. The lights outside the park appear in the distance and I feel like I could crash through my bed. We pull up to my trailer.

"Get out, Tone." Dave's voice is low and even, but I can't tell if it's because he's tired or serious. Marcus opens his own door, and I know that if I don't move, he'll do it for me.

I jump out and Marcus walks around the driver's door. Dave steps out, goes to the back and climbs in. Marcus nods at the passenger door he's left open. I get what he means and climb in. Marcus settles behind the wheel and watches me watching Dave count the money.

"It's all here." Dave pats the fifteen stacks he's made. He then picks up one, fans it and hands it to me. "Fucking positive the most money you've ever held."

I keep my mouth shut and take the cash. Of course he's right, and telling him to fuck off won't get me anywhere. I stick the wad into the front of my waistband while Dave puts the rest back into the bag and settles it into the trunk. "Tone, I'll let the guys know how good you did. Trust me."

Fuck, that word again. I'm embarrassed to hear it. I don't want to trust or respect any of these guys, or to receive any from them. But I was told I'd make a grand and I did. There's something to that. I just don't know what. "All right," I say and climb out.

Marcus whips the car around and brakes in front of Char's trailer. Bet they're going to hand off the score. Wonder how much Dave gets to keep? I exhale, touch the money, and turn toward my house.

I head inside, and a sweet smell fills the air. I flip the switch in the kitchen and nothing happens. The fuck? I step into the living room and trip over the chair. It's on its side and my heart moves up into my throat. "Mom?"

No answer.

"Mom, it's me." I stand and move forward, only to get tripped up by the stem of the lamp, also lying on the floor. Something's not right. I've been here before. It's like a fucking snow globe version of white trash: *Domestic Abuse*,

Trailer. I move to the junk drawer in the kitchen and rummage through. I find a lighter and flick and flick until the flame dances a soft orange glow.

The house has exploded. Shit lies everywhere: cushions, the TV, garbage, knickknacks. Cameron's work, I bet. But where is he? A moan comes from my mom's bedroom and I stop dead. I light the doorway, but it's mostly shadow. This is like some horror movie, and I'm the kid about to get whacked. I know what I have to do. Just don't know if I can.

I move slowly into her room and step over the debris. Another moan sounds, and I drop the lighter. I sift around the carpet and filth until I find it. I try to restart it, but the metal singes my skin. I pocket it and blindly make my way toward the sound. The sweet aroma I smelled has grown. "Mom?"

I wait and inhale and the aroma has lost its fruity scent. It's metallic. I know that smell. I pull the still hot lighter from my pocket. It burns my thumb but doesn't light. Another moan, this time right next to me. I click against the burn, again and again, until the flame hisses to life.

There, beneath the shadow, lies my mother, half on, half off the bed, her shirt soaked through with blood. I move toward her, but then pull up short of the bed and spew. My stomach spasms and empties. I hack until I know I'm done, but I don't feel any better. Fuck, she might be dead.

I've thought of this ever since I was little, when she'd be passed out or smacked around. In my vision I was always stoic, shutting her eyes like they do in movies. I wouldn't cry but pack my bags and wait for the police. They'd come and someone would take me away.

Now, I don't feel any of that bullshit. This is my mom, and I'm fucking scared, but I have to look. I have to find out. And if she's . . . Fuck I don't know what I'm going to do.

I move the light over her.

I can't make out her face. Everything's cast in shadow, but it's more than that. What I can see is wet, swollen, and dripping. There's an opening that could be her mouth, but it doesn't sit in the center of her jaw. She moans again, and I steady myself by biting my tongue. I touch her shoulder. Hot blood sticks to me. "Mom? What happened?"

She doesn't respond. I'm not surprised, and for a moment wonder why the fuck I even asked. But a bubble of blood forms over her nostril and I know. I'm a scared and stupid pussy whose mom just got fucked up by her boyfriend. I don't care how much the lighter burns. I keep the flame going and lean close to her. "You'll be okay," I say as close to her as I can without the tickle of gagging pulling at my throat. I slide my hand across the bed and find hers and squeeze.

She breathes. That's all.

"I'll be right back." I stumble over the shit but make it to the door. I hit the steps just as Rob's walking past.

"Yo, you're bleeding."

My hand is still coated, and I've smeared it across my shirt and pants. "Mom's."

Amy pulls up beside Rob, and her eyes pop wider.

"I need a phone."

Amy nods and tosses me her cell.

"Your mom?" Rob's voice is barely audible through the pounding in my head.

I flip open the cover, nod, and punch 9-1-1.

"Nine eleven?" Rob steps closer.

"Yeah." I spit the word. Isn't it fucking obvious?

He puts up his hands. "All right. But . . ." He looks over his shoulder, comes back. "You should ask for two."

The phone connects, I shrug.

"Char's back and she needs help."

"Nine-one-one, what is your emergency?"

My mouth freezes. I know the answer. I know to just tell the dispatcher that I need help and to give her the address. I don't even need to say any more and the cops and ambulances will be here. But for some reason I can't speak. When she asked me, "What is your emergency?" I thought: *I'm trapped.* There's nothing she can do to help with that.

11

We roll off the bus and instead of going directly to my trailer, I head to the mailboxes, this giant, metal birdhouse-looking thing out by the manager's office. It's been two weeks and her jaw's healing, all wired shut, but Mom's thinner than ever. Her ribs are mostly solid and most of the swelling is reduced. It's just inside, the internal bleeding as the doc said, that's taking forever to dry up.

I fish out my key and slide it into the lock. Every day the envelopes multiply, fucking bill after bill. I stuff them into my back pocket without looking to see who they're from. Like it fucking matters. There's no money to pay a single one. I already used my cash from the deal to cover the ambulance and some of the ER shit. Rob watches. "When she getting out?"

"Don't know. Maybe next week. Maybe longer."

He clears his throat though, and I know what's coming. He's been good, hooking me up with some food and grocery stuff like soap and toilet paper. But I know him, and it's only a matter of time before he starts lecturing me about what I gotta do next. That's his fucking thing. I respect it, but fuck, I'm limited.

"So tonight, I think it'd do you good to come back. Coach Dan does too."

I close the mailbox and walk on, almost laughing to myself. "You told him about *this shit*?"

"Some of it." Rob curls his hoodie closer to his head.

What'd he leave out? The fact that she didn't press charges? Or that Cam's walking around bragging about how he keeps his woman in line? Or that the whole fucking park got to watch the show while I talked to the cops and tried not to lose my shit? Did he mention Charity? Did he even go *there*?

"Tone, you all right?" Rob's voice brings me around.

"What? The fuck you talking about?"

"Yo, you were just breathing heavy and shit." He steps in front of me. "Seriously, you need to come back and burn that shit off."

"What shit?" I sidestep.

"That anger."

I spin. "What, I don't got a right to be angry?"

"Not saying that." He throws his hands up. "You need to use it, that's all."

This is exactly what I thought would happen. He'd turn all dad-like on me. "How the fuck you know what I need? You dragged me to that fucking game. I would have been here."

Rob screws up his face and fills his chest. "So it's *my* fucking fault? *I'm* responsible for what happened to your mom? That's fucking whacked, Tone. That's fucked and you know it." He pauses, then says, "Like you being here woulda changed anything. Cam woulda put you in the hospital with your mom."

He's right. No doubt about it, but I don't fucking care. I'm just sick of this shit and don't need him telling me how it is. Like I don't fucking already know.

But I lunge at him anyway and we hit the stones, my

breath catching on impact. I stay with the fight, though, and reach for Rob's head. But it's like the fucker's greased, sliding under every grasp, and in a second he's off the ground and on me. His bicep clinches around my neck. "Let it go, Tone. I ain't your problem." I flail and pull at his arm but know it's useless. I go from mad to on the brink of tears and tap twice. He lets go.

The blood filters back from my head, and the sensation tingles along my neck. I rub my eyes to keep the tears in and we sit. Rob looks off into the distance. It's just so hard, all of it.

"It's just fucked, Rob. Without her working, we got no money. Worse than before. Nothing to pay the regular bills. And now . . ." I pull the envelopes from my pocket. "How the fuck we gonna pay for all this medical shit?"

Rob shakes his head and doesn't say anything.

"We were fucking broke before, but now we're just fucked." I read the return address: *Saint Coleman's Medical Center.*

"Too much shit, man. Your mom. Charity." Rob's voice is low. "Un-fucking real that her dad did that. Just let his supplier . . ."

Rob doesn't finish and I picture Char from that night, like a zombie. Twenty pounds lighter and all from brain loss, just nothing upstairs. The track marks explained. She's damn lucky that she drifted outside the trailer when Rob and Amy were coming by. She might still be gone.

"I don't know." Even as I say it, I know I'm lying. If my dad had had the opportunity, he would have pawned me off. Few of his friends that came by were extra nice, with candy for sitting on their laps and shit. I can't think about this now. I push myself up. So does Rob.

"Tonight then? For real? Cuz you can't say you don't need it."

I nod. "Yeah, but Coach Dan's still down, even though I walked out and didn't do shit to fix his truck?"

"Why would he think that?"

"Huh?"

Rob just looks at me in that way he has, like he is old enough to be my dad. Some better version of him. It takes me a second but I get what he means. I turn away because the tears are back, and I don't know what the fuck to say.

"Your list of I-owe-fucking-yous just keeps growing." He laughs and slaps my back.

"The fucking truth. All right, swing by at six."

"Done."

I didn't need to lie to CPS this time. Since I'm seventeen, they don't give a fuck if someone's home or not, and by the time they get to the paperwork I'll be eighteen. They did help with getting the power back on. I only had to spend one night without heat or light, but it isn't like that hasn't happened before. Cam cut the wire. Somebody on a job site must have told him how to do it and not get electrocuted. Wish he'd missed a detail or two. But when CPS saw that, they got someone on it without looking at our bills.

I set the mail on the counter with the rest, only to watch it all spill into the sink. The air still reeks as well, even after two weeks. I closed her door after the police were done and then cleaned once I had hot water, but in spite of all my scrubbing, working three towels to a frothy pink, the stench lingers. Just like the image of her. All of it etched into my head like I've been fucking branded.

I hit the fridge and pull out some bologna and cheese I

snagged from the hospital. I crook the bottle of fruit punch into my elbow, the one I stole from the corner store, take all to the couch, and eat my dinner.

The bell chimes and guys look up. "There he is!" Phil's on his feet in a second, popping up from a stretch. Amir follows.

"Big Tone. Tony the . . ."

Phil holds up a hand. "Don't, man. Don't finish that fucking sentence."

Amir blushes and laughs, pounds fists with me. "Sorry, it's just so perfect."

I go to answer, tell Amir it's all right, but Phil puts me in a headlock. "Good to see ya. Where the fuck you been? Laying some pipe? Huh?"

I'd like to laugh but can hardly breathe. I know Phil's playing and all, but Jesus fucking Christ he's strong.

"What's going on out there?" Dan's voice is as crisp as always, and Phil releases my head. I tense and wait for our encounter.

But Coach Dan extends his arms wide. "Tony! The second half of my personal pit crew." He walks over and raps my back, his knuckles like a hammer. "Glad you're back."

I wasn't expecting this. Rob said Coach understood, but that didn't imply he was going to be nice to me. I'm not sure what to say and look for Rob, but he's off talking to Phil and Amir. "Thanks, Coach," I manage and look away, but Coach Dan grabs my shoulders and squares me to him.

"Rob's kept me in the loop. I'm sorry about before. That wasn't fair. Had I known . . ."

I nod but can't look at him.

"I'm also sorry about your mother."

I don't answer. Can't. My throat seized the first time he said sorry.

He leans to my ear. "Big O and I have been talking, too. We're all on the same page. Don't worry, son, we'll make sure this doesn't happen again. That warrior in you is coming out."

I could melt into a fucking puddle right here and not give one fucking shit about what anyone says. Coach Dan has no idea how much I need his words to be true. And if he can do what he says, I'll owe him even more than I owe Rob. I swallow and manage to say, "Thank you."

"My pleasure. Now, go stretch."

I join Phil, Amir, and Rob and they seem to understand that I need some time to let this settle in. They don't ask me shit, just stretch, and soon I match their positions.

Coach Dan's clap brings me around. "Tonight we're going to cover some stand-up fighting. A few of you have matches in a week, and while I know you are solid grapplers, you all need work on striking."

I completely forgot that Rob's fighting his first match in a week. I'm a terrible fucking friend.

"Go get your gloves and then everybody but our three fighters, against the wall."

Rob turns to me. "I got two pairs, hold up." He goes to his bag, comes back, and tosses me his old pair. They're worn down at the knuckles and reek of sweat, but I don't give a shit.

"Thanks."

Rob laughs. "Wait on that. Try washing the smell off first and then see if you still want to thank me."

I slide the gloves on and then join everyone else along the wall. Coach Dan trots to a back room and then emerges with various pads. He holds a bunch, kicks some more in front of him, and sets them down just off from the center of the mat. "Before we hit the shields, let's review proper stance." He points at us. "Guys on the wall, spread out and mirror these three." We do and I look up and see the Blob. He nods at me, and I return the same. Still no Dave, but I'm keeping my eye on the door.

"All right. One piece at a time." Coach Dan stands behind the three fighters. "Heads." All tuck their chins down, close to their necks. I follow. "Protect the chin, don't make it a target."

"Eyes." All three stare at whoever's in front of them, and for Amir, that's me. His eyes burn so cold I have to look away.

"Arms." They tuck their elbows to their sides but keep their shoulders loose, ready to drop a bomb, while their hands hover around their eyes, protecting. All have their right side slightly forward. I position myself the same and feel tucked in, coiled. I know this one.

"Body." Each bends at the waist, only a bit, but it shrinks their open space, their strike zone. Makes sense.

"Feet." They all shift the left foot forward and bounce on the balls of both feet. I look to the left and right, watching us all get ready, and it feels as if we're about to brawl.

"Excellent. Relax." Coach steps out from behind and smiles. "Perfect form. And we must remember that form matters. Not only when we're fresh, but when we're beat. Especially then. When it's two minutes into the second round and you want to drop the shoulders or rest on your heels, that's when you need to tighten up." He pauses and looks at us. "Because if you don't, that's when you lose."

Heads nod and Coach crosses to the shields, scatters the pile. "We should have enough for you to pair up. I'll give you combos."

Rob trots over and picks up a shield, then comes back to me. "This is the fun part."

"Nothing fancy, just four punches, four combos." Coach claps. "Amir." Amir slides his arm into the pad, and Coach Dan pops into stance. He looks different, younger, somebody I wouldn't want to fuck with. "Jab." He tosses a few into the shield. "Alternate hands and remember your feet. Don't stand still." He bounces in and stabs, quickly bounces back, looking like a boxer. "Now, double jab." He does the same but sticks two lightning-fast strikes into the shield. Amir rocks back.

"Now, cross. Remember to settle the weight on the opposite foot and rotate from the hips." Dan dances and then plants his left foot, draws up his right shoulder, keeping his left hand near his face and blasts the shield from a right angle. He follows through by bringing his right hip across. Amir has to reset.

"Last, the hook." Dan again dances. "Remember to drive the hips to full extension. You want to go through, not just meet the jaw." Dan turns to Amir, drops his hips, and brings his hands to his face. When he pops, it's like a fucking jack-in-the-box. His left leg stays bent and he powers off the right, extending his fist into the mat, through and high up in the air. Amir falls on his ass.

No one laughs; instead it's a thunder of applause.

"Nice, Coach D."

"You going Golden Gloves on us?"

Coach helps up Amir and then smiles. "That one felt good. Damn." He rubs his knuckles. "All right. I'll call out the punches and then the combos. Don't think, just react."

Rob slides the shield in place, and I adjust my gloves, pushing them down, making sure they're tight.

"Stance."

I drop into it and Rob nods.

"Jab right."

I do but forget my feet. Rob points at them.

"Jab left."

I remember this time, and the hit stings.

"Right. Left. Right. Left." Over and over. My arms are already tight, I'm sweating and breathing heavy. "Stop. Shake 'em out." I look around. Guys are wiggling their arms and rolling their shoulders. I do the same, and it seems to help.

"Stance!"

"Keep low, Tone. Looking good." Rob's watching me like he's examining a car.

"Double jab, right. Double left. Double right." And on and on. The crosses are tough, but Rob tells me to follow through with my elbow, and that makes all the difference. I even knock him back on a few. The hook is easy for me, cuz most guys I've fought have been bigger. I'm always trying to take off a head at the chin.

"Rest and switch up."

Rob drops the shield and rolls his shoulders. "Fun, right?"

"Hell yeah." I notice the lift to my voice. It feels good.

"Wait until we work on knees and kicks. You land one of those right during a fight, fucking devastating."

I pick up the shield. "You nervous? You know, about the fight?"

"Yeah, but I'm ready, too. Not like I haven't thrown down before."

"True."

"It is different, but I'm more excited than anything." He pauses. "You know what does make me nervous?"

I shrug.

"We gotta have that fucking truck working by Friday. Two fucking days, man. That's it."

Shit, I didn't realize it was that soon. School and Vo-Tec have just been a blur. But, fuck, I owe Rob. "We'll get it tomorrow. You'll see."

Rob goes to say something, but Coach yells, "Stance!"

He hits the bag hard on each call, and I grip the mat with my toes so that he doesn't knock me on my ass each time. Every punch is crisp, every angle correct, at least from what I can tell. Even Coach Dan hovers for a bit, looking for flaws, much in the way Rob watched me. Coach only smiles, though, and yells for the next combo.

I watch Rob, really examine him, and it's more than just position. He's not really here with us. It's like he's in his head, or maybe out of it, and just letting his body do the work. He looks dumb, like some fucking cow or shit. Not a pissed-off bull, all stomping and grunting. No, he's just loose, and kind of stupid with his mouth hanging open and his eyes glazed.

But his image screams strength. I can hear it. And I want it.

I hit the button for the elevator and wait. I feel bad showing up soaked in sweat, but I didn't bring anything to change into, or even have a bag so I could. She won't care, though. Visiting hours are almost over, and she'll be hopped up on her meds already.

I head to the nurses' station, where Camilla, the head nurse, has been every single night. I wonder if she ever gets up from her chair. It looks like it's crammed up her ass.

"Just made it, Tony." She smiles.

"Yeah? Is she all right?"

"Rough evening. The jaw's healing well, but she says it's throbbing. We're giving her as much pain meds as we can." She looks up and down the hall. "I think she's just sick of being penned up here."

I bite my tongue so I don't laugh. This place is a fuck lot better than our trailer. There's heat, food, and security. *She* doesn't feel pent up. No, she's got it good. "Can I still go see her?"

"Of course, sweetheart. Go right in. Probably be the best part of her day." Camilla smiles and her eyes disappear into the wrinkles. I walk down the hall and take a deep breath before entering the room.

When I was a kid, she used to be bruised and swollen and lying in bed a lot. I didn't know any better, thought it was normal, what fathers did. Then I went to school and the other kids talked about doing crafts and shit with their parents. Playing board games and watching TV. All I knew was arguing, beer cans, and staying in my room where it was safe, for the most part. She looks like she did then, when my dad really went over her. Her nose is wide and flat and extends out beneath her eyes. Her lips are swollen like some celebrity's, but instead of looking sexy they're cracked and oozing. Her jaw balloons out on the left side and makes my own hurt just looking at it. But her eyes are open, not slits like they've been. "Tony?" At least that's what I think she says.

"Hey, Mom." I move to the side of the bed and sit in a chair.

She moves the bed upright but winces at the effort. There's no fucking way she'll be out of here in a week. Fuck, not even two. She stops, breathes deep through that deformed nose and then says, "I'm all right." It sounds like someone's sitting on her head.

I look at my feet. "Nurse said you're in pain. Jaw's bothering you."

"Don't worry."

I don't know what to say. Not worrying is an impossibility.

"You okay?" She reaches for me.

Her hand is bruised from the IVs that still run from it. I don't want to touch it. Last time I did, it felt lifeless. I've never felt that question before. Whether she was alive. But I grab her hand and squeeze it lightly and remember that she's asked a question.

"Sorry. I'm fine, just tired. Practice wore me out."

She smiles, an odd faraway grin. "Back to football, huh?"

"No, Mom, that was years ago. I'm . . ." I don't know how to explain it, and it's probably not worth it. She won't remember.

"That's good. Make sure you eat. Need energy."

I feel like squeezing real fucking hard and asking her just how the fuck I'm supposed to do that without her home and without any money. But I nod. Cameron did this to her. She didn't do it to herself. "All right."

"Good. Be home soon. It'll be like it used to be. Just fine."

The fuck? She must be high as a fucking kite. Like it used to be? When? When was the *good* time? I don't remember that period. Fuck, I'd better go before I say something I shouldn't. "Just take your time." I stand and pat the back of her hand.

She nods, closes her eyes, mumbles something, and I wait for more, but she's out. I watch her for a moment, just look at her busted face one more time. I can't remember if my father did worse. Sure if he didn't then he came close. I don't want this. I want a normal fucking life, or whatever stupid fantasy I have for what that is. Sounds like she does, too. I can't wait as long as she has. I've got to figure something out. My brain was intelligent once. Maybe I can get it jump-started?

The cafeteria's mostly empty: a couple of docs sit at a table talking in some foreign language and an old dude sits by himself, staring down into his soup. The cashier looks like she's about to nod off and take a nosedive into the register.

I head over to the refrigerator and grab a carton of milk, the only thing I'm gonna pay for. Then I get a tray, make a sandwich, grab a fistful of cookies, and take it all to Sleeping Beauty. She startles when I slap the tray down, but pretends nothing's wrong, doesn't even look up at me, just at the tray and starts pounding numbers.

"Eight fifty." The cashier has the wet and sticky voice of a lifelong smoker.

I pat my pockets, back to front, then just let my hands dangle and say, "Hmm." She looks up, face closed in on itself.

"I forgot my wallet."

Her expression stays flat.

I root around my pocket, find the change I need for the milk. "A-ha, guess I'll be dieting tonight." I slap on a chuckle and hand over the change.

She stares at her hand and then at the tray.

"I'll put the rest back. Sorry."

"The sandwich?"

"Oh. Yeah. Well . . ." I look at it and then back to the counter where I made it. "How about I wrap it up and put it with the other pre-made?"

She remains still for a moment and then nods. "All right."

They've all said the same thing, must save them work or filling out a form or shit. I don't know how I came up with the plan, but it's been working, so I don't fuck with it. I bring the tray back to the service area, where they keep the spoons and forks and salt and shit. They've got a giant roll of plastic wrap as well. So while the hag voids my order and then re-rings the milk, I wrap the sandwich and cookies into one big blob, drop it into my underwear and pretend to return everything. My pants are so baggy that no one has noticed.

I return for my milk. "All set?"

She nods and hands over the carton.

"Sorry about that. You have a nice evening." I walk away, and she doesn't respond. My dinner shifts along my crotch but does not fall out. I pass the docs, who keep talking. The old man takes a sip of his soup and then goes back to staring at the bowl. I pass through the doors, and there are no alarms or security guards. Go me. I'm eating tonight.

12

Miss Myers smiles at us from the blackboard, where she's written an outline on one side and "Thesis" on the other. I can't read the thesis because her fucking head is in the way. But it doesn't matter. I've just got to get through this class and then it's time for me to shine for Rob.

"I want you to follow the outline here. It will make my life easier." Myers smiles and steps in front of the outline, revealing the thesis. I read it before she does, aloud, "Man's true self is revealed when the boundaries of society have been stripped away." Her face is set to serious when she turns to us. "Think about this and which characters and their actions speak to its sentiment."

I don't have a fucking clue. The last part I remember about this stupid-ass book we've been reading is about this Jack kid and his fucking mask, but I do remember somebody in here talking about a pig getting crushed by a rock. Or maybe it was that fat fuck, Piggy?

I read the thesis again, just to focus. Man's true self? Hmm. I can write about that. Maybe not the way she wants it, but if she really is interested in what a man can do when he has no fear of getting caught, well, now I've got something to write.

The pencil moves itself and works over three pages and to the bell. I'm not even sure of what's there, but when Myers sees the volume, her face brightens. "Tony, I didn't think you read the story."

I hand over the essay. "Me neither."

I turn out the door, directly into Big O. There's no going around him, so I look up and say, "Hey."

"Don't 'hey' me, Antioch. My office. We need to talk."

I knew it would come to this. Coach Dan said he'd been in touch with the big man, but that doesn't mean shit. Big O does as he pleases. I've seen that much. My gym membership is about to be revoked. Shit, maybe I can make another deal for the Front and then be all set. No. Shit, no. That's not even funny.

There's a large folder sitting in the middle of his desk, and I read the label before sitting down: *Antioch, Tony*. My record. Shit.

Big O swings in from behind me after closing his door. "As you can see, I've pulled your record." He hesitates a second at the corner of his desk, hand extended to the file, but not touching it. "To be honest, I was surprised by what I found."

He sits and I relax in my own chair because he wants to give some speech on my life and how I should spend the rest of the school year. I'm pretty sure I've heard this one before. I wonder if he has anything interesting to add, or will it be about how I am wasting my talents? There's no waste when there's no opportunity.

"Don't you want to know what was so surprising?"

I shrug. "Not really."

Big O frowns and the skin on his bald head tucks around his eyes. "I don't get you, Antioch, not one bit." He flips open the cover, and there are pictures of me from when I was younger paper clipped inside. They're the school pics that my mom never bought. Pages of notes and typed forms fill the rest. Big O finds a tab amidst all the pages and thumbs it, turning to a page of charts and graphs. He places a meaty finger next to one. "This is what I didn't understand. When you were ten, your IQ was 120." He turns the page toward me, and I see a set of numbers and percent signs, but they mean nothing, now. I understand what they indicate, but that's old news.

"So?"

He pulls the page back. "So? *So?* Don't you understand what that means?"

Of course I do. I'm smart. I've known that since Kindergarten, when I could read all the signs around the classroom and the other kids couldn't tell A from Z. Who gives a fuck? Give me that same test now, and I'd probably come up retarded. I sink in my chair. "It's a pretty good score."

"Pretty good?" Big O says it all flat, like there's no air in his lungs. Then he laughs, just like Franks. "I guess compared to your score in eighth grade. You remember that?"

How could I forget? Mrs. Danielson practically creamed herself when she found out. Hugged me and smiled her big-ass bleached teeth, telling me I'd be in the gifted and talented program at the high school. Then my mom wouldn't sign the papers, or forgot, or passed out and puked on them. Who knows? All that came of those tests is nothing. But I remember the score. "One thirty, right?" I look up.

Big O stares at me, trying to keep eye contact. But I break. "Your name came up quite a bit before you got here. They talked about how smart you are, and what a shame it was. I figured it was just some fluke, because you were enrolled in the Vo-Tec program." He pauses. "You didn't give me any reason to doubt my instincts."

I look at the file, probably filled with referrals for all the trouble I've been in, and reports about all the shit at home. Big O's right, I am a fuck-up, and maybe at one time I was smart and had a chance, but what does that matter now? "So what's your point?"

Big O goes to say something, his mouth open to the side, but then he clamps it and shakes his head. "This is why I've been working with Coach Dan, who, by the way, has told me things have been rocky, but seem good now. Is that right?"

I nod. That about sums it up.

Big O grins. "Good. Keep it that way. Now, what's your plan for next year?"

I laugh. "I don't have a plan for tomorrow."

"That's what I figured." He inches forward in his chair. "What if I could get you a scholarship? Could get you into college, a regular college?"

I stare at the floor, even though I understand that at this point I should be staring into his face all shocked. But he's either delusional or just fucking around. What he just said is like telling me that Santa's real. "How you going to do that?"

"I've got ways, connections, so to speak. And with your IQ, *not* your grades, I could sell your potential. You're staying out of trouble, helping Rob. All good things."

I hear his words and picture what he's saying. It's like a faded memory resurfacing. All the shit they said before about my bright future. Fuck, I remember how that felt. A bunch of adults who had their shit together, weren't falling down drunk or getting hit by their boyfriends. They looked at me like something special, not the white trash I was, am. That may be the best I have ever felt about myself. But none of that shit ever happened. Nothing they said ever worked out, so I just forgot about it, pushed those emotions down and moved on.

That's what you do in life. Take shit and keep going.

That's why I dealt for the Front. Not that I wanted to, I had to. And fuck, if Big O knew about that, there's no way we'd be having this conversation. It's not right for me to even entertain the dream again. Rekindling those embers is impossible.

"Why do you care?" I look at him now.

Big O sits back, his eyes wincing. It takes him a moment to find the words. "I've got my reasons, Tony." He looks toward the door, but more beyond it. "You remind me of someone in particular, someone else I helped in the past." He looks at me again. "I've tried to help others, since, but they weren't made of the same stuff. You're different. I know it and you know it."

"What about Rob? You're helping him, right? You saying we're the same?"

Big O grins. "It's different with Rob, but similar. He'll get his chance with Coach Dan. I don't think he understood when we brought this to him. Coach Dan will mentor him so that he can become a trainer. Dan wants to open another gym. This could be an excellent opportunity for him. But it's finite. Like him. You have more potential."

Potential? Fuck, the last time I heard that word about me regarding school I felt as good as I did the other night with Coach Dan. He sees something in me. And I guess so does Big O. But none of that potential from last time ever amounted to shit. What's the difference now? I don't think it matters if I have all this possibility. What I need is a way to use it. I don't know if this is the answer. "I don't know."

Big O holds up a hand. "Not now. Just think. There are conditions to these things, and I'll need to know by January." He sighs and sits back. "But for now, just think. Please, Tony."

We clap for the pair who just finished showing us how brakes and rotors work, even though it was the most boring presentation yet. My brain is asleep. These lame-ass PowerPoints are like a fucking narcotic, and Greyson's making us go last because our presentation is different. Rob's leg has been thrumming faster with each one, though, and is about to dislocate from his hip at this point. I turn to him. I want to talk to him about what Big O said, but now is not the time. "Fucking chill."

He stops his leg. "We're up after these two." His eyes dance, and there's no point in talking. He's as amped as Amy was this morning, talking about having to take care of so much now that Char's living with her. The girl's a vegetable. Won't speak. Barely sleeps. Her mom's nowhere to be found. Took off the same night Char returned. Probably put two and two together and bailed. Can't say I blame her, except she should have taken Char with her. She's living with Amy because there was nowhere else for her to go. A bike rumbles in the distance and she cowers. I don't know what the fuck they did, but I think they ruined her. And Amy says, "I've got my own shit to worry about." Whatever that means.

"Tim, Steve, ready?" Greyson closes out the previous presentation on his laptop, and the projector displays the background—his Hemi engine. Tim shakes his head, and Steve looks at the floor. Greyson frowns. "Seems as if we have only one more presentation." He pauses. "Rob, Tony, will you please?"

Rob springs up like we're at the gym. I follow. He goes to the truck while Greyson opens the bay and I get the oil and antifreeze. The truck starts right up, and I hear Rob shout,

"Fuck yeah!" before rolling in. Greyson shuts the door, and Rob pops the hood. I join him, and we get started.

"We've got the lubrication and cooling unit. In case you haven't figured that out by now." Rob smiles and the grease monkeys do as well, more awake than they've been all afternoon. "So Tone and I are goin' to show you the ins and outs of checking levels, proper maintenance, and troubleshooting problems with each."

I look over at Greyson, and his face is lit up brighter than one of the shop bulbs. This is the shit for him; it's obvious, and I feel good seeing that. He's been good to us. Because of him I know my way around enough to make it. Rob's a natural. Took to this shit like he did fighting. So I'm glad we spent the three hours we did last night after I got back from the hospital getting the beast to work, even though I'm exhausted and feel like a douche just standing here with these fucking bottles. But whatever, I'm along for the ride. And being on this ride with Rob is a good thing.

I move to my spot for our first demo.

"I think Greyson would have sucked your cock if you'd asked him." I laugh and Rob keeps smiling, the same one he's had since he started that presentation.

"You might as well, because I sure as shit ain't doing it." Amy breathes heavily, like she's been running.

I look at her to see where she's headed with the joke, but she's serious and seems pissed off.

"Whatever. Rob did a kick-ass job, and he'll do the same when he fights. Girls'll be crawling all over him. Won't need your crusty ass." I slap Rob's back. His smile has faded.

Amy stops walking and so does Rob. She looks at me, her eyes drawn to little beads, and I almost start apologizing, but she cuts me off. "Just what I fucking need, my baby's daddy going off and getting his face busted and then fucking some other ho."

The fuck? What'd she just say? Rob's gone white, and Amy's staring at him like she's just waiting for him to open his mouth and say the wrong fucking thing. I get my voice to work instead.

"You're pregnant?"

Amy snaps her head but doesn't look at me. "The fuck you think this weight's about? I ain't getting fat for no reason except this boy here forgot to wrap it up."

I put my hands up because I don't have a clue how to respond. Rob stares at the ground, looking at it like he's never seen rocks before. I don't blame him one bit. If he really is the daddy, he's fucked. Amy's not the kind to let him slip away, and Rob's the kind of guy who will take care of his responsibility. So I have to ask, "You sure he's the father?"

"Fuck you, Tone! I only been with Rob. I mean, for the past six months. I'll take a paternity test . . ." She bursts into tears, her words falling apart. Rob looks up and swallows, his face still haunted. He reaches for her, but she slaps his hand away and screams "No!" before running awkwardly to her trailer.

We both watch her, and my brain dances, trying to put this shit together. "I'm sorry. I didn't mean it to come out like that, but you sure?"

"That she's pregnant?" Rob's voice is a dry whisper.

"No, that you're the one."

He shrugs.

This is beyond fucked. "How long you two been hittin' it?"

"Off and on since the summer. No big deal. Ya know?"

I do and I don't. Amy's always been there, an option, but one I never actually wanted. I shake my head. Rob's still watching her trailer. I look over at mine just so I can think of something else for a second, but that doesn't really help things. "All right, man. Go talk to her. Tell her I'm sorry. Okay?"

"Yeah. Yeah I will." Rob's voice has no energy.

All the happiness in him is gone and I feel sorry. He really did an outstanding job today, and I haven't had the chance to let him know what Big O said, but it's like none of that matters now. He may get to work as a trainer, but he'll also be raising a baby. Not exactly what he wanted, I'm sure. But that's what happens to dreams around here. They stay just that, or turn into nightmares that haunt, because they either never came true or did in ways no one wishes they had.

"See you tonight?"

He waves as an answer and is already moving toward her trailer. I walk toward my own and am glad for once, in a long fucking while, to be in my own shoes.

13

The bell chimes and Coach Dan pops out from the back, looking as if he's been watching the door. "How'd it go? You get her started?"

Rob's spaced out, didn't say a fucking word on the walk here. He's trying to speak now, but nothing's coming out.

"What was it? What was broken?"

"Rob, wasn't it the ignition coil?" I nudge him with my elbow.

"Yeah. Yeah it was. Easy to fix once we figured it out."

Coach Dan's smile rips his face in two. "So you did it? Fantastic! I knew you could." He pulls us both into a bear hug and slaps our backs. "When can I pick her up?"

I look over at Rob, and he's still struggling to get his head out of his ass. "Whenever. We're all set. I think Greyson put the keys under the visor. But check the tank if they're not there."

"Thanks, boys." Coach walks to the center of the room.

"You all right?" I ask Rob.

He stares ahead. "The fuck you think?"

"Listen up. We're sparring tonight, so get your mouth guards." The room grumbles in response.

"Maybe this will help?"

Rob gives a little smile. "Yeah, I wouldn't mind throwing down a bit." His eyes brighten and he looks over at me.

"Fuck, let's go stretch."

We join Phil and Amir, and Amir says, "Nice to know some mechanics."

"Hell, yeah. Might get you some regular work. Just tell the rest of the guys in here." Phil rolls onto his back, throws his legs over his face, but keeps talking. "You seen some of the bombs these fools drive? Shit, there's a gold mine out there."

"Not a bad idea." Rob's voice sounds like he's coming around.

I work my hamstrings and consider the idea. I'm desperate for cash, but I can barely find some of the parts on my own. I'd need Rob, but he doesn't need me. Found out the problem with Coach's truck without any input from me. Fuck, I really do owe him. Better find a way to pay back before there's another debt I can't get out of. His world is falling apart pretty quickly, though. May not be too hard to do. Fuck that's an awful thought.

Coach claps and we all sit up. "As if I needed to remind you, we've got three of our guys on a card this week."

A cheer rises up.

"They'll represent, and I expect that any of you who can make it to be there." He looks each of us in the eye. "We're a family. Period. We support each other busting our asses in here, and outside this ring."

I look down because guys are nodding like Coach is some kind of preacher or shit. Like his words are their words. They believe this, but I don't know how to react. What do I know about *family*? They shit on you.

"I've got one more thing, a bit of a surprise. Rob, come on up."

Rob joins Coach, but looks like someone who doesn't want to pose for a picture.

"You all know that Rob's been here for over a year training his ass off."

The room applauds, and a smile creeps over Rob's face.

Coach stifles the clapping. "Well, I just got conformation that Rob is my official mentee for personal training certification."

The room applauds again, and Rob's smile disappears as shock overtakes his face.

"Therefore, starting tonight, Rob will be working as my assistant, learning the ropes and preparing for his exam." Coach Dan squeezes Rob's shoulder. "No offense, but I couldn't think of a better candidate."

Again, we clap and shout Rob's name, and again, I watch Rob deflect the praise. Coach's right, he deserves this. He's a good kid. I don't know how many people I can say that about, myself included.

"Tonight, we work hard and then lay off these three for the rest of the week. So let's take care of business."

There's a low murmur, and I watch Rob. His face moves to happy to uneasy, eyes wide, mouth drawn tight, almost like he's going to puke. I go to speak to him but stop, because I see Dave in the corner. I don't know how I missed him before, but he's there, hunched up like a fucking gargoyle.

"Gloves, mouth guards, cups. Make sure you got 'em and line up."

The room moves as one, and Rob goes to his bag. Fuck, I meant to snag a mouth guard, but with checking on my mom and shit there's been no time. I don't want to bother Rob, so I go to Coach Dan.

"What's up, Tony? You gonna slip me the bill for my truck now?" He laughs and I play along.

"No, I don't think you could afford our services, since we're so good, but if you have a mouth guard we could call it even."

"Shit, that's all. I've got a whole box. These idiots forget all the time." He leans close to me. "Grab one, but then tell me one thing." His voice has lost its playfulness. "What's the deal with Rob? Seems like something's eating him."

He's got that fucking right, but it isn't my place to say, even with how nice he's being. He better not press me with any *This is my gym* bullshit. "Think it's the fight. He's nervous."

Coach watches me for a second. "Thought so." He nods and looks like he's trying to convince himself. "All right, we'll get his confidence up. Mouth guards are in the bottom right drawer in my desk. You'll have to mold it later."

Rob tosses me his old gloves when I join back up with the class. I try to get used to the wad of black plastic in my mouth, but it feels like I'm suffocating. Rob, Amir, and Mike stand out in the middle. The rest have formed three lines. I enter Rob's.

"Here's the progression. Each line will run through three times. No switching. First, stand-up sparring only. Five punches max. Second, go straight to the clinch. Take 'em down if you can. You'll stop on my whistle. Third, start from the ground and go for submission. Again, on my whistle, or a tap out." Coach steps back to the far wall. Rob is slouched before him, weight on his heels. Dave's bouncing like a jackhammer.

"Fighters set!" Coach barks and all three pop into stance. "Go!"

Punches fly, but most are dodged or deflected. Many are way overthrown. The next group does the same. "Come on, make some contact! Let's go, Dave!"

Dave and the third group set out.

The other two rage against Rob and Mike with flurries, but they just block and it's over. Dave's patient. He jabs left and gets Amir looking. He then plants his foot and lands a solid hook in Amir's side. The air blasts from Amir and he sags. Dave switches feet seamlessly and pops Amir a quick kick to his other side. Fuck, Coach never said anything about feet. He's clenching his jaw now, biting his whistle, and watching Dave, but not saying a word.

Amir rights himself, but is slow to react to Dave's next punch and it clips his ear. Fuck, Dave's four for four. No one else has even landed one.

"Come on, Amir," Rob says. Dave cocks his head but doesn't look. Amir sets himself and deflects Dave's last jab. Coach blows the whistle.

"Nice job, Dave. Come on everyone, give 'em some."

The guy in front of me goes toe-to-toe with Rob, but he couldn't punch his way out of a playground brawl, and looks almost glad to return to the end of the line. I step up.

Take away the gloves and this is just another day for Rob and me. We've been slap boxing and doing takedowns since like the first fucking grade. I fake with my shoulder, get him to lurch, and then pop him with a quick jab to the eye. He steps back and smiles. Coach Dan yells, "All right."

Rob charges me, but I sidestep and catch him in the kidney as he passes. He turns and isn't smiling anymore. We weave and I jab a couple of times. "Last throws, right here," Coach says and Rob flexes his entire body.

I stay loose and look for somewhere to strike. A combo from last class surfaces and I move in. Rob backs up, but can't resist changing direction when I go to a knee. I clip his chin with my right as I drive up, standing. He struggles back and hits the wall.

"Sweet Jesus, Tone." Coach Dan blows his whistle. "Nice goddamn work."

I look at Rob one last time before I return to the line. He's off the wall, shaking his head to clear it, and seems to be laughing. Guys in line clap my back, and even Dave nods as I settle in.

"Now for the clinch."

Same rotation and similar results. There's a lot of pulling and head tucking and leg whipping, but no one goes down. Coach blows his whistle, and the second group sets out. Rob, Amir, and Mike get in the clinch at the same time, and like a set of dominoes, each opponent goes down. "There we go!"

Rob's got his fire back, and he gets the next kid on his hip, but can't get him down. I turn and Dave and Amir are fighting for leverage, each with a hand around the other's head, pawing at the free arm with the other. Then Dave tucks his body, drawing Amir down, shifts his weight to his outside foot and strikes the other behind Amir's leg. They wobble as Amir fights for balance, but end up in a heap, Dave on top. The whistle blows.

I step out after the guy in front of me who basically lets Rob throw him to the ground. He makes me look like a raging hard-on compared to his pussy ass. Rob and I lock up, push and pull and I try to get a feel for where he's headed. Coach is yelling something but I can't make it out. And I really don't care. Rob tries getting me into a choke hold, but I slide out by bringing my arm up and through. Then momentum shifts. Rob's beneath me and I'm weightless, and in a second staring at the ceiling. Coach's whistle blows.

Rob helps me up. "Nice job, Tone."

I try to speak but the mouth guard's in the way.

The guys keep rolling, and I care only about watching Dave. He's the only one in here who's fucking shit up. It's strange, but I feel my body shift as he shifts, mimicking his moves, trying to learn them. He's a motherfucking asshole, but damn good at this shit, and right now is fucking up Amir in a thousand different ways. And I know he and Rob have been doing this for about the same amount of time, but it feels like Dave's been at it longer.

Dave straddles Amir and pins his arms to his chest. Amir bucks, lifting Dave up by raising his hips. Dave teeters and Amir gets a hand free. He ropes it around Dave's neck and spins out from beneath him. Dave keeps a hand leveraged and tries working the other through Amir's hold. Amir works his legs around Dave's extended arm and even I can see where this is headed. Dave waited too long and now he's trying to pull away. He pitches to his side, Amir's legs around him like a snake. Amir releases Dave's head and sits upright, crushing Dave's arm.

Dave reaches to tap, but then refuses. His arm's out and we're all watching for it, but it's just lying flat. Coach's biting his whistle and shaking his head, but, like before, Dave still isn't tapping. Coach mutters something, his words forcing the whistle to chirp. Amir looks up and Coach juts his chin at Dave's arm and then shakes his head. Amir nods and Coach gives the whistle a full blast.

Dave stumbles out, just like he did when Rob got him. "Coach, I didn't tap."

Coach Dan clenches his jaw. "And you should have. You always do this Dave. You're not Silva, okay?"

Dave's face crushes into itself. "No, I'm not. I'll be better than him. If I ever . . ." He looks around the room, his lip curled.

"If you ever what?" Coach steps closer to him. "Go on, finish what you were saying."

Dave looks at him and then away. "Nuthin'." He turns to get back in line.

"Don't *nuthin'* me, son. You answer my question."

Dave's body tenses, his traps and rear delts forming knots of anger. He spins on his heel. "I ain't your son! And *you* don't make *me* do shit!"

"Excuse me?" Coach Dan's voice is low but fierce. It's a decibel I am all too familiar with.

"You heard me."

The room is silent, and I imagine we're all thinking the same thing: *Take him the fuck out.* Coach Dan could do it, I'm sure. And Dave's eighteen, so why not?

"I did and *you* heard *me*. Now answer the question."

Dave shrugs, looks around the room. "Fine. I'll fucking answer."

He pauses and looks at us again. In that glance I'm reminded of the football game. I'd like to bust his fucking jaw because everything about him reminds me of Cameron. He's a shifty liar who's got trouble always at his side.

"If I ever find a real trainer, not some washed up Marine who ain't done shit with his life, then maybe I'll have a shot."

Coach Dan breathes deep, his chest rising. His nostrils flare, and the muscles in his jaw pop. "That's how you feel?"

Dave doesn't answer, only licks his bottom lip.

"Then get out of my gym."

"Yeah, yeah, whatever." Dave waves a dismissive hand. "Coach Dan has his rules that we must follow. Even though they're fucking pointless. Don't matter one bit in the *real world*." He laughs. "'Get out'? I'd love to see you fucking make me." He turns from Coach to us. "Any one of you."

Coach Dan opens his mouth but Rob steps forward. "Let's go."

"Yeah, that's what I'm talking 'bout, muthafucka." Dave slides into his fighting stance and the rest of us back up. I'm boiling, though. Fuck, if Rob doesn't do this, I will.

"Rob, don't." Coach reaches out. "He's not worth it. Think of your fight this week."

Rob's face ripples in doubt, and Dave steps toward Coach. "Fuck you! Let him man up if he wants to. Ain't that the point of all this?"

Coach lunges but catches himself after two steps. Dave doesn't even flinch. Coach's face is red, as if the whistle is choking him, and his words are tight. "You're just a punk, Dave. Nothing but a thug. You have no idea what this sport is about. I knew that the day you walked in. Why I never . . ." Coach turns to Rob. "You don't have to do this, but if you want to, I won't stop you."

Rob nods. "It's the right thing."

Coach stares at Rob for a moment and then returns to Dave. "This is it. You're out of here after this."

"Only if I lose." Dave swings his arms and jumps up and down.

"No. You are not welcome back. You understand me? I'll call the cops."

"And be a bitch? No you won't." Dave rolls his neck but doesn't take his eyes off Coach. "This is your code, Samurai. Live by it."

Coach's cheek twitches beneath his eye, but he doesn't speak.

"It's all right. I got this." Rob takes off his shirt, exposing his skinny torso, all ribs and tortoise-shell abs.

Coach looks at him and then to Dave, taking in his line-backer girth. There's doubt in his eyes, but respect, too. I know that look well. All my life people have been doubting me, but on some level saying, *I understand.* They don't, but the guys in here do. No one gives me shit. Fuck, I don't care

if Coach Dan isn't the best coach; he's done some shit right.
Still is. He's taking care of Rob, and that's more than enough
in my book. My head surges with this, and I'm more amped
than I've been in a long time. Feels like if Rob beats this
douche then some part of this world will be right.

"Circle around the mat."

We fall into a circle around the room, making a roughly
shaped ring. Dave and Rob move to the middle, and it all
feels like slow motion. Coach Dan steps to them and touches
their gloves. He looks at each one more time, but they are
staring each other down. Guys whisper for Rob, and next to
me Amir mutters, "Crush this fucker." Coach blows his whistle, and all hell breaks loose.

Dave charges like a bull and throws a wide punch,
misses, and follows with an uppercut. Rob blocks it and tries
to use the position for leverage, but Dave slides away. He
kicks and Rob catches Dave's foot at his chest and twists.
Dave topples to the mat, hands out for balance, though, and
he spins from Rob's grasp.

The room's loud, guys all yelling for Rob. It's like a fight at
school, but there isn't a teacher around, just a coach who's
watching as intensely as us, and wants the same fucking result.

Rob advances on Dave, who is still on all fours, and cracks
a shot off the back of his head. Dave hits the mat, arms splayed
at his sides. A cheer rises up. Rob hops on his back and throws
jabs. He shouldn't be. He should be trying to choke him out
now. I know this, and I see the same look of concern on Coach
Dan, who's moving his arms as if to guide Rob, but Rob's plain
old fighting. Right now, this isn't about sport.

Dave takes the hits and doesn't react. Rob reels back to
blast the son of a bitch and Dave spins, grabs Rob's wrist,
and in one fluid motion, pops onto his free hand and pulls

Rob beneath him. He slams a knee into Rob's back and Rob cries out, but his voice is muffled by Dave's arm, which coils around his neck.

Rob slithers, tries to get his arm through Dave's, but can't. Dave slides his body along Rob's back, crunches into himself and ratchets up the triangle hold. Rob flails and tries to connect, but Dave is safely tucked behind his neck, out of harm's way. Coach steps in and blows his whistle. Least Rob won't have to tap.

Dave holds on, though, and looks up. His face is evil, lips curled, face nestled so close to Rob, it's as if he's going to devour him. I've seen this image before, too many times.

Coach blows the whistle again, harder. Around us guys are screaming, but it's unintelligible, just guttural sounds. Rob continues to flail, but then goes limp.

"Release him!" Coach screams, and Dave just smiles. Again, that image, and something breaks, just loosens inside of me. And I am no longer here, on this mat. I'm little and he's standing over her, snarling in her ear. I'm older and it's someone else in a drunken stupor looking to see if I want to fight for my mommy. I'm older still and it's a mask of evil, high on smack and ready to take me out if I say one word. And I am silent. And I am a pussy. But no, not here.

I see myself move, take two steps, and feel the energy I've been coiling up to release. I plant my foot and squeeze my leg into a solid weapon, my foot a ball. I tell myself to drop my hips, engage my torso, contract as hard as possible, and then like a spring, release. And I watch myself do just this, my foot slamming into the side of Dave's face. Something within gives and his body sails off Rob, settling to the ground in a heap. I stand next to Rob and my senses return.

Dave lies on his side like a dog, and Rob rolls over on his

back, sucking air like he's just surfaced from water. He looks at me and I crouch to him. "You're all right." He nods even though it wasn't a question and looks past me. I look over my shoulder and Coach is shocked, eyes wide, eyebrows arched. His lips move but nothing comes. He looks to Rob and Dave and then back to me. He straightens. "Tony?"

I stand, prepared to take whatever I have coming, because it's dawning on me that what I did isn't fair play. I did not engage under Coach's rules. "Yes, Coach?" My voice is surprisingly strong.

"Guess I was right about you."

I tilt my head like a confused dog.

"Warrior, Tony. Pure." Coach goes to say more, but is cut off by the room, which erupts in cheers and crushes me like I've scored a touchdown.

Rob's got a zombielike look to him, feet shuffling, eyes glazed. I'm fucking amped from knocking Dave out, but can't really celebrate with Rob, not considering the reason. He would have been chocked out. He knows it. And after Coach escorted Dave out of the gym, which he went along with without argument, without even asking how he got knocked out, Coach grabbed Rob and said, "You need his fire, son."

He hasn't said shit since then. Hasn't even thanked me, but I understand. Fuck, I owed him, anyway.

The park lights glow from just down the street, and a hog rumbles in the distance. We both stop walking. Another rumbles to life, and the noise grows like a swarm. The first one peels out, its back tire fishtailing. The driver doesn't spill though, just revs it and bullets away. A procession follows, and all my good feelings go with them.

"Fuck, I gotta go see Amy." Rob runs a hand over his face.

"Why?"

"Really? You forgot?"

The realization punches me harder than any of the hits I've taken all night. "Shit, I'm sorry. I just . . ." I can't finish.

He bites his lip and nods, keeps looking at the ground.

"You know when she's due?"

"Said some time in May. We get to hear the heartbeat next week."

Fuck, as soon as he hears that, it's over. He'll be an awesome dad, but what else? Damn I feel for him. But who knows, maybe he'll get this shit right? "Man, I didn't even know you two were hittin' it."

"We just started. You know, something to do." He shifts his weight. "Better 'n beatin' off."

"I hear ya. But now, with the mentor program. You got a real opportunity."

Rob sighs. "I know. I can work as a trainer by the summer if I complete the course. Coach said he'd even give me a job if it works out."

He can't fuck this up. I won't let him. I reach out and clasp hands and then hug him. "That is fucking awesome!"

"I know." He smiles. "I start the program in January. Fucking A."

We walk on and I'm glad I didn't get the chance to tell him about my conversation with the big man. I don't want to take away from him, and besides, my deal—if it's even something pursuable—is a giant *What if.* . . . At least Rob's got something tangible in front of him. Some way out of this fucking trailer park.

He sighs, again, though, and has that far-off look like he

did back at the gym. He's lost and shouldn't be thinking about this now, not with what just happened and his fight and all that's in front of him.

"Fuck, forget about that for now. Your fight is all that matters." I turn and start walking.

"Yeah, right."

"Don't sweat that shit with Dave. It'll never happen in the ring."

He doesn't answer, and I think it's because we both know I'm full of shit. Honestly, who the fuck am I to talk? What the fuck do I know after being there for a fraction of the time he has? We enter the park, and the air is still laced with the dust from the bikes. I look toward my trailer, and Rob looks over at Amy's.

"Char's all up her ass about this baby, too."

"You know what her deal is?"

"No. She ain't talkin' 'bout what happened." He pauses and shakes his head. "She's still got fucking bruises. On her thighs. Around her arms. And the way she looks at me now, it's just different. Char never had fuck-me eyes before. She does now. And won't shut up about the baby and how fucking great it will be. It's like her world. I can't even talk to Amy about an abortion." He looks away. "That's why I agreed to deal, to pay for that. Amy was going to at first, but then Char came home and found out, and that plan's gone now."

I look at the trailer and imagine the scene inside. I'm sure if I did the same for all of the pieces of shit here, every one would be filled with some tragedy. This place is a collection of despair. Poor Rob. I clap his back. "Shit, man, good luck."

I leave him and step inside my trailer and feel the change immediately. Something's off. Something in the air isn't the same. I don't move, just stand and sniff and listen. There's an odor I can't pinpoint and a soft smacking sound. My heart races and I'm glad I'm still loose from the gym and that my brain's ready to fight. I grab a piece of shit steak knife from a drawer and step into the family room.

My heart pounds in my ears, but I strain past it to listen for the noise I just heard. Nothing in the room is out of place, but the noise snaps again. I stop. It's coming from the back. Maybe it's just a mouse or a raccoon? Fuck, I hope it isn't an opossum. That happened once. But, shit, none of them sound like this, like a cabinet opening and closing.

I step down the hall and the noise grows, clearly coming from the back of the house. I pass our bedrooms and the bathroom, holding my breath and keeping the knife tight to my side. I stop. There's light from outside. But there's no window here, just the back door, which we never use, because there aren't any steps beneath it.

A breeze kicks up and the door pops open and then quickly it snaps shut. It's been cracked along the hinges. A chill runs up my spine. I turn to my room and flick the light. All is as I left it. The same in the bathroom. I hesitate before my mother's room and have to swallow before I throw on the light.

Her bed is immaculate, as I left it, untouched. But every drawer has been emptied. Her dresser, her nightstand, the TV cabinet in the corner, all hang open as if they've puked up their belongings. What the fuck was he looking for? I know it was Cam. That smell must have been his. Something rotten. He's been gone long enough for me to not recognize it. But he's back now. So are those bikers. Fuck, it doesn't seem like anything's missing. But it's not as if I did a fucking inventory of her room. I cleaned and then got out. But what if he left before he had the time to find what he wanted?

I bolt from her room and to the furnace nook behind the

bathroom. It's just a closet filled with the boiler and hot water tank, but she keeps a screwdriver and a hammer and shit in here. The shit her boyfriends have left behind. A roll of duct tape rests in the corner. I grab it and head back down the hall.

If there's something here he wants, he'll be back. This duct tape isn't going to save my ass, but it's all I got.

I rip off a length of tape and stick it over the hinges. I rip section after section until the door is sealed shut. There's no more light, and when the breeze blows, it doesn't flap. That noise would have kept me up all night. That is if I could actually sleep. No, I'll be up, because I want to hear him coming. As if that will make a difference.

14

'm exhausted, couldn't sleep and have no fucking interest in school, but I'm here because it's safe. How fucked up is that? I stayed up all night waiting for Cam. Or Dave. Neither showed. Maybe Cam found what he needed, but my guess is whatever it is wasn't here at all. I'd put money on the fact that he'll be back and that Dave will get even with me. Here or at home. It's just a matter of time.

Rob's fight's tomorrow, and Fridays are when Cam usually gets tore up, so I've got to get my head straight.

The wall-eyed janitors are watching TV, looking stoned. Neither even flinches when I bang around with a sweeper and dustpan. Franks isn't here, probably stalking kids in the hall, so I take off to the English wing. I'll sweep there and over in Bio. If he wanted more, then he should have been here to tell me.

The English hall's as boring as Lance's class, a whole lot of teachers talking and kids melting in their seats. I peek in Myers's room, and she's sitting at her desk reading a stack of papers, red pen in one hand. It'd be fantastic if she read my essay while I'm out here. I'd love to see her freak out. I sweep by and nothing happens. I pass by again and she's just reading and writing notes.

The Bio hall still reeks, but at least there's more action.

Some lab's using the burners. I pass by and a kid takes the tubing from the glass piece and lights it, waves it at his partner. They laugh until the teacher turns around, and the partner slams into the glass piece, which smacks the ground and turns into shards. The first kid turns off the gas and is looking all innocent at the ground by the time the teacher approaches.

I step into the room. The teacher's about to speak, probably to give them hell, but stops when he sees the sweeper. "Did someone call for you?" His head's wrinkled in confusion, and I feel a little bad for him. All these years around douche bags like us and these pickling chemicals, bet his brain's shot to shit.

"Just passing by." I point at the mess. "You want me to get that?" I don't know why I felt the urge to help, but I look up from the pile and the lab partners stare at me like I'm Jesus.

"Yes. Yes, thank you."

"No problem." I twitch my wrists and set the head flat, then twist and slide the bristles around the pile and scoot the mess into the hall. I push it forward and hear the teacher behind me, "Now, what were you two doing?"

"Look at the grease monkey turned janitor." Dave moves away from the classroom he's left. "You trying out all the cocksucking jobs until you find the right taste?"

I grip the handle to steady myself. He steps and I can see that from the edge of his chin to the middle of his forehead is an oval bruise, dark purple and swollen. Some of my fear dissolves. "Yeah. Something like that."

"Always knew you were a cocksucker." He steps closer and I watch his body, see how he's angling me, just like on the mat. I move the sweeper, cutting off his line of attack. No doubt he wants to settle the score. He stares down at the handle and nods. "Yeah, I'll pass it around, just like that little cunt, Amy."

My mouth drops, and Dave smiles like he'd punched me in the nuts.

"Too bad your bitch-boy Rob doesn't know how to pull out. She don't mind getting sprayed." He laughs again, and I don't bother to ask how he would know. That's what he wants. I messed with him, and now he's trying to get in my head. Fuck him.

Dave steps to my left, against the lockers, and I turn with him. "That's right, don't give me an in." He lowers his body. "Seems like that trailer-trash head of yours has some brains in it after all."

The glass crunches beneath my feet as I swivel and step, keeping my guard up. "Seems like you don't mind using us trash when it means you get a cut."

Dave drops his hands and stares at me like he's trying to see inside. "From what I hear you could use another cut of your own. Those hospital bills ain't cheap."

I clench my jaw. That hurt. I could get a job and try to help pay, but it wouldn't make a dent. Dealing though, that pays. And Dave fucking knows it. And that's because Cam was in my house, rooting around for bills. Here I am, in another corner.

"Yeah. And I've got your piece of shit uncle to thank for that."

"So go thank him. See what he says. Maybe you can get someone to pin him and then kick him in the head."

I turn my back on Dave. If I look at him one more second I might go for round two. But I don't know if the outcome would be the same as last night.

"You tell Rob we might need him. And you, too. Busy season's coming."

I turn back. "Fuck you, Dave. We don't need you." My

words sound weak, and Dave smiles at them.

"Yes, you do. But it's not like you have a choice. The Front says jump, you're fucking jumping. If not . . . well, let's not go there." He spits on the floor. "Missed a spot." Dave laughs and walks away.

I lean against the wall and breathe. I can't get wrapped up in this shit, not with what Big O's put on the table. And there's no way Rob's getting near it. He's too close to something good. I've got to keep him straight, keep him away and focused on the gym. I need to be there, too. Fuck Dave and Cam and the Front. We'll survive. Somehow. I take one last deep breath and then walk back to the office. I do not clean up Dave's spit.

"Nice work getting on top of that beaker." Franks is loading a pallet of paper onto a hand cart. "I'll make sure to pass that along to Big O. He likes hearing good things about his charges."

"All right. Thanks." I set the sweeper aside and empty the dustbin. Hold up, how the fuck did he . . . "How'd you know?"

"Mr. Nelson called to thank me." He puts down a box and leans on the cart. "What, you think I'm psychic?"

I put the dustpan away. "Maybe," I say and then mumble, "more like a stalker."

He lets go of the cart. "What's that?"

"I said, no, just a janitor."

Franks steps out from behind the cart, and my heart jumps at the size of him. He looks bigger without hundreds of pounds of paper hiding him. "Listen, because I'm only going to say this once."

I give him my attention because his voice is raspy, just above a growl. Reminds me of too many men from my past.

"Yeah, I'm a janitor, but *you're* headed toward a garage,

not college. So you may want to rethink who you're calling out. And there's one thing I've done that you haven't." He leaves the statement hanging there so I have to ask. This fuck must have wanted to be a teacher; his lines are like a fucking script.

"What's that? Grow up?" I jut my chin. "You're simply amazing."

He laughs, a quick burst of hot air along my neck. I wasn't expecting that. "Grow up? No. Some people never do that. I'm not concerned with growing up, not how you think."

My head's buzzing with thought, because I'm actually trying to figure his cryptic ass out. "So what are you saying?"

His face tightens, and the lines around his eyes grow deep. "Proving yourself. Being a man."

Now *I* laugh. "You have no idea what I've done. What I'm doing. 'Prove yourself.' I do that every single fucking day."

"Jensen would have kicked your ass just now."

I stop, completely. My words, my thoughts, gone.

"That's right. All your talk got you through that. Not necessarily a bad thing, but"—he jams a finger into my chest and I refuse to flinch—"he'll be back and what will you do then?"

"You saw that bruise then, right?"

His eyes dart but he nods.

"Who the fuck gave him that?"

"Some punk who kicked him when he was down." He pauses. "*That's* what I heard."

I open my mouth to speak but the bell rings. Franks waits to see if I've got anything else. But before the bell dies away, I'm out the door.

Big O eyes me as I walk down the hall, heading for the Vo-Tec bus. He doesn't say anything, just lifts his chin and raises an eyebrow. Him and the big fuck must be more than old friends. No fucking way that broom-pusher knows what he does without a daily update. Although, Big O is all about nonviolent resolutions. At least that's what he always says. So it's hard to believe that this *man up* shit is coming from his mouth. Is Franks just saying what he thinks or what Big O wishes he could say? Either way, Franks is right. Dave's coming for me. One way or another, I'll find out.

The bus pulls up and I get on.

My fucking fridge is empty, seriously not one goddamn thing. I polished off the ketchup yesterday and had the last can of soda for breakfast. I have to go see my mom tonight and steal some shit. Enough to tide me over. But it's not as if once she's home we'll be going on a shopping spree. What the fuck am I going to do then?

I head to my room, grab my gear, and step outside to wait for Rob. I can't stand to be in this place for another fucking minute. Cigarette smoke hangs in the air, and I immediately turn toward Amy's. She isn't out; Charity is, sitting on the stoop, a full ashtray next to her. She stares at me and the twenty pounds she's lost is obvious along her jaw line. Just hard bone now. Her hand shakes when she brings it to her lips, but she looks at me, real steady. Rob's right about her eyes.

I kick a stone and walk over. "Hey, Char."

"Hey, Tone." Her voice is as hollow as the rest of her.

I look around, desperate for a topic. "So, uh, you whipping up anything good for Thanksgiving?" Char used to rock food prep, which is probably why she was so fat. She looks at me through a cloud of blue smoke. "Huh?"

I wave the smoke away from me. Damn she's out of it.

"You know, next week. Pumpkin pie or some shit?" I don't know why the fuck I'm talking about food, because now my stomach's gurgling.

Char looks between her feet. "That's next week?" She doesn't look back up.

"Yeah."

She keeps staring, and I hear gravel crunch behind me. Rob rolls up. "Hey, Char."

She maintains her position but takes a long-ass drag from her cigarette.

"What's the deal?" He looks at me like I'm up to something.

"Nuthin'. I asked her about Thanksgiving."

"Oh." He looks back at her and shakes his head. "Char, we're taking off now. Go inside soon. All right?"

She pulls a wobbly hand to her mouth and the ember burns from beneath a stack of ash. She doesn't nod or speak or in any way seem as if she's heard Rob. We turn and head for the gym.

"That's how she is now?"

"Yeah. Except for when Amy starts talking, baby this and baby that. She perks up, but then goes back to that."

"She say anything about what the fuck happened?"

"No, but it doesn't really matter, does it?"

I stop walking, look at Rob. "What do you mean?"

He shrugs. "Not like we can change it, you know, do anything about it. Just gotta deal with the here and now."

I want to say something to him about how he should be using his same advice with Amy, but I can't. It may be because I still don't want to fuck his head up before the fight. Or maybe it's because he's making a lot of sense, and maybe I should just listen.

Coach Dan's face is clouded when we enter. "Boys, how's everything?" His words are clipped, and he moves like he's hopped up on too many energy drinks.

We say, "Fine," at the same time.

"Good, good. You seen Dave?"

Rob and I look at each other and shrug. I told him about running into Dave today, even though I didn't think I should. But he put my mind at ease saying that it was just Dave talking shit, like always.

"All right. Light class tonight, but go get warm." He moves to the front door and stares out while we join up with Phil and Amir.

"Yeah, he's fucking tweaked." Phil curls toward the ceiling while lying on his stomach. "Found a dead deer in front of the door when he came in this morning."

"Car hit it or something?" Rob straddles the ground.

"No, man." Phil turns his head. "Somebody fucking slit its throat and left it there."

"You didn't see the blood?" Amir rolls his shoulders.

We shake our heads and Rob says, "It's dark, or I wasn't paying attention, I guess. Is that why he's asking about Dave?"

Amir stops rolling, looks at us. "He thinks Dave killed that deer."

Phil laughs out loud. "Probably the only way that psycho can get tail."

"True." The two pound fists, and my head swims.

I don't know if I should say anything. I mean, I don't know if these guys want to know what I do. Then again,

Coach looks scared as fuck and that puts me on edge. If a man like that is frightened, then my ass better start looking for help.

"Dave didn't, but someone he knows could have."

Rob shoots me a look, and I can't tell if he wants me to shut up or that he hasn't thought of this yet.

Phil rolls onto his back. "Who does Dave know like that?"

I settle into the stretch and open my mouth to speak, but Rob does for me. "No one. Tone don't know what the fuck he's talking about."

I read his eyes loud and clear this time and swallow the answer I had for Phil.

I'm sweaty and tired and uninterested in being here, but I've got no choice, I need to eat. The hospital doors slide open and I walk in.

All we did in class was drill kicks with the shields. Rob and I paired off, drew knees, aimed at shins and sides, and took out legs while Coach talked up maintaining balance, striking hard and fast and pulling the leg back so we don't get caught. But mostly he just glanced at the door.

I hop on the elevator and punch the button for the third floor.

At the end of class Coach Dan just told the guys fighting to rest up, and for us to come and show support. That's it. No fucking inspirational quote, nothing dramatic. Fucking bull-shit. The guy's scared out of his head. I don't blame him. If that deer isn't some freak coincidence, then he's got some bad-ass motherfuckers on him, and that means Dave is real tight with them. But Rob said it was all right, not to worry.

He's in his fucking Zen space, and I'm not fucking with that. We pounded fists and went our separate ways. I didn't say shit about the bikers, or Dave or Amy.

I step out of the elevator and head to the nurses' station. Camilla smiles. "Well, long time, no see."

"How's she doing?" I don't want her getting interested in me. Mom is her only concern.

"Very well. I think the plan is to have her discharged by the weekend."

I smile even though I don't want to. "That's great. Can I see her?"

"Go right in."

I head down the hall and find my mom sitting upright, relaxed, watching TV. The bruising around her eyes is gone and though her face is still swollen, she's got a healthy glow. It hits me, like a crack upside the head: she's clean, inside and out. I haven't seen her like this in years.

"Tony?" She brightens.

"Hey, Mom." I walk to her bed, but don't reach out, even though part of me, right now, feels like we should. But I'm fucking gross anyway. "Camilla says they might release you this weekend."

She lowers the volume on the TV. "I know. Can't wait." She smiles, but I can see the lie tucked inside her cheek. Home is dark and cold. This place is a warm spring afternoon.

I shift my weight and don't know what to say. There's so much, but I'm so fucking hungry. "Do you want something from the cafeteria? I haven't eaten all day."

"No, no, I'm fine. Go, fill up." She's got her hand on the remote before I'm out of the room.

Another old bag works the register, and I play my scheme, loading up with as much shit as I can manage without looking ridiculous. I pay for my milk after pretending to return my tray of items and apologize, again.

"It's all right, son." The geezer with a face like a raisin pats my hand. "Least you were nice about it." I resist pulling my hand away and she continues. "Had a fella just a few minutes ago, before you came in, wanted me to give him some food for free." She crinkles her face and the lines hide her eyes. "Between you and me, I think he was drunk." Her face reddens. "I told him that nothing in this world's for free. Well, he didn't like that. Slammed his money down and didn't wait for the change." She releases my hand and props hers in the air. "Imagine that, looking for a handout and then forgetting your change. Some people!"

"Hopefully he won't be back."

She smiles. "But you make sure that *you* do."

I promise I will and head toward my mother's room, eager to plow into the food tucked in my underwear and happy to have enough to get me through a few days. I turn the corner toward the elevator and something that old bat said wriggles inside my head. The way she described the drunk.

I head up the stairs to my mother's room, and when I walk in, standing beside her bed, is Cameron.

"Tony." Mom's voice is steady, a command. She keeps her eyes on me, and I do the same with Cameron.

I haven't seen Cameron in a while, and with everything that's gone down from the break-in at the trailer to the dead deer, I know he's been up to no good. And now he needs something. It had better not be Mom.

I step back into the hall and walk to Camilla. "What do you need, hon?" she says. I drop my trousers and start to unload my haul. "Tony? What? Where?" She sputters as I set cookies, sandwiches, and fruit on the counter.

"They didn't have any bags in the cafeteria." I look up and her face clears, slightly. "So could you just hold these for a minute?"

"Well, um, all right. But where are you going?"

There's no point in explaining. By the time I do and she gets security, Cameron will have slipped out, and I'm not missing this chance, not with witnesses around. I don't care how scared I am, some shit is more important.

"What were you looking for?" I stand a few feet inside the threshold, allowing enough space to maneuver.

Mom gives me a hard look. "Tony, what's going on?"

"The question's not for you." My heart's hammering in my chest, and my legs feel wobbly.

Cameron runs a hand along his cheek and leans against the bed. "The fuck you talkin' 'bout?"

I step forward and my heart tickles my throat, but I swallow and steady my stance. "Really? You're going to pretend that you weren't the one who broke in?"

"Someone broke in? Again? When? Why didn't you tell me?" Mom sounds genuinely concerned, but I'm confused. The first break-in? The fuck is she talking about? But that doesn't matter at the moment. His answer does.

Cameron moves away from the bed. "Told you. Don't know what the fuck you're saying." He loops his thumbs over his belt. "Now, if you don't mind, your mom and me were catching up." He smiles. "Seems there's a lot she don't remember."

Her face has darkened. "It's true, Tony. I can't seem to get it back. Cam's been trying to help. He told me how I got here, the break-in and all. Well, the first one, now, I guess." She puts a hand to her chest and her eyes mist. "But I've got nothing, for at least the past month. Just blank."

I'm certain that if I'd eaten anything, it'd be covering the floor now. If she can't remember, and he's feeding her lies, has he already created some fucking story? Then we're back to square fucking one. No. No, I can't fucking do this again.

I clench my jaw and fists, close my eyes and growl. When I look, Cameron has retreated the step he's taken, and my mother is wide-eyed.

"*He* fucking put you in here, Mom! There was no break-in. He fucking broke your face, cut the power, and left you for dead."

Cameron's eyes narrow, but he doesn't speak. Mom looks at him out of the corner of her eye.

"You've been using again, too. But I bet you fucking forgot that."

She startles and rises up. "What? What are you saying?"

"This asshole's been getting meth from Charity's dad." My rage is consuming and I'm losing focus.

"Better watch how much you say there, son." Cameron's unhitched his thumbs, and his arms dangle at his sides.

I'm so fucking angry, or I just don't care, or some part of me wants that fucking fantasy to come true right now that I lash out. "Or what? You going to put me in the hospital, too?" I laugh. "We're already here."

He crosses from the bed to me. I adjust my weight to the balls of my feet and lower my hips as he moves.

"I'll shut your fuckin' mouth for good." He pops into a fighter's stance. I eye his body for weakness, but there's not much of a window. He moved so effortlessly, without having to think; it's obvious this is second nature. Thank God he's drunk.

"Tony! Cameron! Stop it!" Her words are muffled noise in the background, like the hollers from the guys at the gym. I'm there now, on turf I know, and Cameron's just someone to tangle with.

He swings and I step to the side, but he slides right back into position. I step and jab and clip his chin. The impact startles me more than it hurts him. I fucking punched Cameron, felt his whiskers against my knuckle. No turning back now. He catches me with a shot to the ribs, then recoils just as quickly and is out of reach. I jab anyway and he weaves. Fuck, I can't throw like this, not on his level.

I fake a right, just pop the shoulder, and get him to lean back. Then I settle my weight onto my left leg and slam my right foot into his shin. He screams and grabs beneath his knee. I move in and get my arm around his neck. He releases his leg and squirms, trying to shift me off, but I grab his right arm and wrench it back. "You little fuck." He pants and I position my body for the takedown.

We hit the ground with a crack, and I crunch my body as compactly as I can while he flails. I almost lose him twice, but I can smell the beer on his breath and can feel the strength of his body go slack. Fuck, it's not even close to how I imagined it, but I don't care. I've got him now, and I'm not letting go.

But hands are on me, and I'm ripped away, forced upright and into a choke hold. My face is level with the holster and the guard says something that I don't understand but rumbles through his chest. Another one crosses the room and checks on Cameron, who is wheezing on the floor. Fuck, all I needed was another minute. I could have held on for that long. The guard stands up, looks at me, and then to my mother. I watch her now, too, and see the call button in her lap.

"Mom?"

The guard tightens his hold, but more importantly, she turns away, refusing to make eye contact.

"Mom, tell me you didn't."

She stays as she is but Cameron rises. "You got nobody now." He laughs his redneck shrill note, and I go limp in the guard's arms, too overwhelmed to fight.

15

t's Friday and that means only one thing to me: Rob's fight. Fuck everything else. She pushed that button. That's all it took. I thought maybe we'd come out of this all right, she'd wake up and realize what the fuck Cam is. No chance of that now. No, she made her decision loud and clear. Wouldn't even explain to the security guards what was what. I had to, told them we were just messing around. Cameron's smart enough to have agreed.

So what do I do now?

I wish I were fighting, because I'm feeling it, the flow, that hum throughout my body. I was so close last night, could have choked him the fuck out, shown him that I'm not a pussy. But I am. My mom made me one last night. Maybe that's the way she's always wanted me. Not like my father.

Fuck, maybe that's the point? If I take on Cameron, is that really the same? If I learn to defend myself, aren't I just being smart? Intelligent like I'm supposed to be? Not an animal like him. Like Cameron. Like all the rest. Life sure isn't like any standardized test where the results spit out just where you stand. It's messy and full of problems where there really aren't solutions. Does that mean I should give up or keep trying to figure shit out?

Myers hovers by her desk with a stack of papers at the

corner. "Shit," someone says, "she's returning our essays." Myers likes to talk to each of us about our writing. She calls us up, and we have to sit in this uncomfortable chair while she reads the comments she's written in the margin. Real fucking useful.

Myers moves to the front at the bell. "Today we will conference on your essays for *Lord of the Flies*." She purses her lips. "Some of them were outstanding. And some, not so much." Myers lifts her eyebrows and looks over the class. I know where I fall on that spectrum. And I know what she's going to say to me. It's all right; after this I got Vo-Tec and then Rob's fight. I can handle whatever bitch session she throws.

"While I conference you'll be reading a short story that we'll discuss next class, so take notes and be prepared." She smiles but no one joins her. "Grab a textbook from the back. I've written the title and page number on the board."

I read her chalk handwriting, join the rest, grab a book, and head back to my desk. I open to the page and try to read but the words slide out of focus. Last night keeps popping into my head. How could she? I can't think of an answer.

"Tony."

Fuck, I don't want to listen to this. I'll just keep my mouth shut, and it won't last as long. I tuck my chin to my chest and take the seat, but have to glance at her face. It's serious, eyes dancing over the page of my sloppy handwriting and her flurry of red-ink notes.

"Well, first off, I should say thank you for being so . . . honest." She looks at the paper, not at me, and holds the corner just off the desk, like she wants to flip it over. "But, second, you should understand that you didn't address the essay with any reference to *Lord of the Flies*. This is all personal response."

I shrug and want to say "No shit?" but keep it to myself. I think she sees my shrug because she pauses for a second, but then continues.

"However, based on the information you provided, I don't have a choice but to speak with administration and guidance."

I look up and her eyes are enormous, scouring every inch of my face. I've seen this look too many times over the years. Some teacher gets concerned, like in kindergarten, when I had bruises all up my back, or like when I talked about not eating when I was in third grade. Always the same shit about *speaking with administration*. Like that's ever done shit. Big O knows, anyway. I've told him enough so he understands. It's like that with all the Vo-Tec kids. So she can go tell him whatever the fuck she wants. I'm pissed at myself, though, for opening up. The fuck was I thinking writing what I did?

Her face changes though, her eyes widening, almost like she's happy or some shit. "Unless . . . Did this, did what you wrote really happen?"

I can't remember all of what I put in there, but I know it was mostly about my dad, before he left and how he hurt us. Stupid shit like twisting my mom's arm behind her back or pulling her hair. Making me sweep up broken glass from his beer bottle with my bare hands, and the hours he'd make me stand, facing the corner of the room, yelling so much his words became like white noise. To the point that one time I fell asleep. Only once, though, because what he did after was a permanent reminder to never do that again.

But if I say yes right now, even with what Big O knows, guidance will haul me into the office as soon as I take a step out of this room. And nothing will come from that. I'm too old now. That shit's all in the past anyway. And if I have to deal with that, I might get so caught up that I'll miss the fight. Fuck that. Like Rob said, the here and the now. I know what the answer needs to be. "Well, uh, some is, you know, like fiction."

She draws her lips into a line, eyes still dancing.

"I made the story fit the thesis. You know, man's true self without boundaries."

Her face softens. "Oh, okay, I see." She leans in. "Well, which parts? What's real and what's fiction?"

I lean back. "All of it, really. You know I didn't read the book, so I had to write something you might like. You know?"

She nods and looks back at the essay. "Well, yes, and for fiction this is gripping." She looks back at me, and her eyes latch on, probing for any shred of a lie. "You're sure it's fiction, because like I said—"

I put up a hand. "It's fake. I'm sorry. I won't do it again." I stand up before she can say anything else, and I head back to my seat, ending the conversation before I'm caught, but I feel compelled to look back up at Myers. She's shaking her head and moving my paper to the bottom of the pile. I don't even know what my grade is, but it doesn't matter. She's burying the story. Just like I've done. It's better that way.

Greyson's playing some documentary and not paying attention to us. Half the kids are sleeping, and the rest are zoned out or talking. "So, you ready?" I keep my voice low. Rob stares at the TV.

"Yeah, I'm good." His voice is as energetic as the slugs snoozing on the table.

"That's it?"

He turns away from the TV. "All right, Coach. Settle down."

I feel stupid, but not enough to let him off the hook. "Seriously, it's all you've been talking about since I don't know how the fuck long. And now?"

Rob sighs. "I hear you. It's just I got a lot of shit on my mind with Amy and the baby and everything."

"Why the fuck you worried about that?"

"You know how much a baby costs?"

I shake my head again and keep my mouth shut.

"I do. I got all sorts a numbers worked out, and it's a fuck lot more than the nothing I've got." Rob pounds his fist against the table and his eyes pierce me.

I know where he's going with this, and I don't like it one bit. He dealt so he could afford an abortion. That didn't happen. Now he's looking at the big picture, and there's only one surefire way around here to make a lot of cash. There's no way I can let him make *that* decision.

"Rob, don't. Don't go there. Don't even think what you're thinking."

"How you know what I'm thinking? You so smart you just got it all figured out?"

I shake my head. "Not like that. It's just obvious. You're in a tight spot, and finding the easiest route out only makes sense." I pause and look at him. "That is unless that route only leads you to something worse. You know what I mean?"

He holds my look for a moment and then glances away, sighs. "Fuck, Tone, I hear you. But damn it, the fuck am I supposed to do?"

"Stick with Coach. You've got time. You'll earn. You've got the skill."

He looks at me and nods.

"Meantime, put that shit behind you. Tonight is all you need to think about. *The here and the now*, motherfucker. Got it?"

Rob smiles and I feel good. "Since when you get all philosophizing?"

I laugh. "It's always easier to figure other people's shit out. Just have to give the advice, not take it."

"Guess that's true. Just don't expect me to tell you what the fuck to do. I got no idea there."

I don't answer because there's nothing to say. I doubt there's anyone who could give me the advice I need.

"Fuck!" I spit and my heart quickens. Rob sees the bikes, too.

"These guys must be making a killing."

We walk past slow, even though I want to race to my trailer to see if Cam's been by. Five hogs rest on kickstands, and all is quiet in the trailer. I pick up the pace and envision the rest of my house as ripped up as my mother's room was.

"Tonight?" Rob's standing in the lane, not keeping up with me. He juts his chin toward Amy's.

"Yeah. Swing by."

I take off at a run. The door's still locked, but I enter and hold my breath and listen. There's no flopping from the back door, no sound except for the wind outside and my heart in my ears. I exhale and go room to room. Nothing's been touched. No one's been here. I plop down in the recliner and breathe and feel my heart slow. Tonight's the fight. Tomorrow she comes home. The bikers are in town. I'd better save my strength.

I finish the last of the hospital sandwiches and then grab my old Carhartt and slide it over my hoodie. The walk to the civic center is a half hour, easy, and it's cold enough to snow. Rob rolls up and we head out.

"You set?" he asks me.

I laugh. "That's my question."

He nods and keeps walking, his steps light, and his body at ease. He seems energized, his eyes darting and fingers tapping. It's good.

"Give me your bag."

"What?"

I stick out my hand. "Just do it, save your grip."

He hands it over and I shoulder it. Rob stays quiet, mumbling to himself a couple of times, but I don't ask for clarification. Whatever he's saying is for him alone. Whatever gets him through. That's just how it is sometimes. One step, one word, and then another.

I grab the door handle at the center and steal a look at him before opening it. His eyes are fixed and hard, his jaw's set, and he's breathing from his nose. Fuck yeah. Let's do this.

The ticket window blocks us. Fuck, we have to pay.

"Ten bucks each." The woman behind the counter doesn't even look up.

I turn toward Rob but then back, because I don't know what to say to him. There's a small sign taped to the window: *Fighters, lockers in the basement.* "He's on the card."

The woman looks at us now, just glancing at me, but her eyes linger on Rob. She returns to me. "And you?"

"I'm his trainer." I lift Rob's bag off my shoulder.

She looks at it and then back to Rob, who hasn't said shit. I so want to turn around and see what bad-ass motherfucking glare he's throwing this bitch, but I won't risk it, she's on the verge. I can tell. Sure enough, she sighs. "Go on in."

We pass through, and I feel like I've just won a round. I turn back to Rob to pound fists, but he just points straight ahead.

Amir, Phil, Mike, Coach, and a handful of the guys from the gym crowd around the seats at the corner of the ring. Even the Blob's here. "All right, you made it." Coach steps forward and claps Rob's shoulder twice, really fucking hard. But Rob doesn't wince. His face is stone, and I completely understand why the counter woman didn't give me any shit. Rob looks like he could eat someone's heart. "Fighters, to the locker room."

Rob turns and I hand him his bag. I feel like saying "Good luck" but know how pussy that would sound, so I keep it to myself and watch Amir, Mike, and Rob follow Coach down a set of stairs, into the basement.

"There's the prodigy." Phil steps forward and clasps hands with me. "He ready?" He cocks his head toward where the group just disappeared.

"Yeah. I think."

Phil laughs. "Sounds about right. Amir had the shits all day. He's good now, though. Let's go grab those seats."

We all move to the far end, where the corner's labeled for our gym, and sit on the cold folding chairs. Diagonal from us is the other gym, a crew from thirty miles away. They leer while the crowd filters in and begins to fill the space.

"What's the card?" Phil asks our crew.

The Blob answers. "Mike's first, then Amir, then Rob, then the other gyms."

"All right." Phil throws jabs into the air and looks over at the other gym. "I'm on next time. Can't fucking wait." He looks at me. "When you eighteen?"

"June."

"Shit, we need to forge you some documents, get that

karate kick on the mat sooner." He laughs and nudges me with his elbow and I laugh along, in spite of how my stomach's churning.

It's fucked up, because Rob and I have fought more times than I can remember. We've been throwing down since kids at school realized what Pleasant Meadows was all about. But I haven't ever been as nervous over a fight as I am now. It's worse than the time we fought a bunch of freshman when we were in seventh grade. And then I almost shit myself. Should have. It might have helped. But maybe it's because I'm not in there with him? Or maybe it's something else altogether? Whatever it is I don't like it, and I can't wait for the fucking show to start.

Two girls in boy shorts and bikini tops step out of the announcer's booth and make their way toward the ring. Phil nudges me. "See what I mean? Get you on the card and you'll be up close and personal with them titties." He claps my shoulder and laughs in my ear. "Not that you'd know what the fuck to do, but you'll learn."

I smile and take in the girls. They are hot as hell, dirty hot. I look past them and to the back of the center, and see Dave buying a ticket. My breath catches but seeing him makes complete fucking sense. It's as if my nerves have been signaling to me that something else is up besides the fight, but I've been too fucking stupid to get it. Well, here it is.

Dave steps inside and then stands at the back wall, his shoulders pinned. Marcus stands next to him. Dave sees us and stares.

"Ladies and gentlemen, tonight's first lineup is about to begin. Please take your seats and get ready for Friday Night Fights!" The crowd cheers and Phil pops out his phone. "Gonna get this shit for YouTube."

I'm lightheaded and disoriented. I close my eyes and breathe and focus on getting straight.

"Our first fight of the night is one of three between crosstown rivals East Coast Boxing and MMA and City Grapplers." The crew screams and tries to drown out the guys from the other gym, but I'm silent because Dave's here. I remember what he last said, about the "busy season." Shit's going to go bad for someone. Probably me.

Off to the side, Coach Dan and Mike emerge.

"For East Coast we have Mike Drumore and for City, Jesse McTigue." Mike looks possessed, eyes wide and jumpy. He keeps his focused on McTigue and adjusts his mouth guard nonstop.

"All right, Mike!"

"Fuck 'im up, son!"

"Show that bitch how East Coast rolls!"

Our crew pumps up Mike, while Coach Dan speaks close to Mike's ear, but I don't think Mike's listening. The card girl walks around with her sign.

I look up to check, even though I know what I'll see, and sure enough, Dave's still planted with his bodyguard. I look down to the entrance from the lockers, hoping to see Rob, but there's just an empty doorway.

McTigue comes to the center of the ring, and the ref says some shit I can't hear because the crowd's starting to buzz now. Both fighters nod and then touch hands and separate. The ref raises his hand and when he brings it back down, the fight is on.

Mike slips a few jabs, as does McTigue, but none amount to anything. McTigue kicks and Mike catches it, but McTigue's either fast or Mike is slow, because he pulls out of Mike's grasp. Mike staggers and McTigue closes the distance between them, gets Mike around the neck and takes him to the mat.

"Come on, Mike!"

"Ground game now, muthafucka!"

Mike locks his ankles around McTigue's waist and keeps his hands up, deflecting each shot. Then he manages to get a hand around McTigue's wrist, and with that gets out and around McTigue's neck. Our corner loses its shit and I inch forward in my seat, but the round is over. The fighters separate and move to their corners.

"He's yours, Mike."

"Get that son of a bitch!"

Dave's still at the back, motionless.

The bell rings and round two begins. McTigue gets in a few kicks while Mike only lands one solid throw. It cuts McTigue's eye, though, and he rushes Mike with a flurry, fists and knees flying. Mike takes the attack and somehow gets McTigue in a clinch.

"That's right, Mike! Feel 'im out."

Mike snaps a leg into him, and McTigue loses his balance and is on the ground. They scramble but McTigue bends and twists like his bones aren't solid. The bell rings.

"Fucking wrestlers. They're like rolling with spaghetti." Phil holds up his phone and snaps a picture.

The card girl goes round, and it doesn't look like Dave is watching her, only us.

The third round begins, and Mike drops a spin kick into McTigue's side. He winces and puts a hand to his ribs and steps back. Mike sets himself and then charges. McTigue draws up his knee just as Mike is closing in and they strike at the same moment. He reels back and McTigue advances, whips his leg, and catches Mike behind the knee. Mike crumples to the mat, and McTigue cracks a jab into his face. Mike's blood sprays over the canvas as the bell for the match rings.

The opposing corner goes fucking nuts, jumping up and down and high-fiving. We're all quiet until Mike emerges after the ref declares McTigue the winner.

"'S all right, Mike."

"Keep your head up."

"Get his punk ass next time."

Coach claps Mike's shoulders, says a few words, and then Mike disappears, back to the locker room, while the staff cleans up his blood, preparing for the next fight.

Phil leans back and sighs. "Fuck. Least Amir's next. He should take this fucker out in the first round."

"Why's that?" I ask and check on Dave, who hasn't changed position.

"Can't remember who told me, but the dude he's fighting is barely trained. He's just some cocky street fighter. Think I even tangled with him once."

I've seen Phil's work at the gym, and I can't imagine how scary he'd look fucking up some shit in an alley. "So he's a pussy?"

Phil's face straightens. "Nah, man. Ain't like that. The punk's for real. Can fight with those hands, but this ain't no street. Say you fight a dude, how often you grapple once you hit the ground?"

"Never."

"Exactly. Here," he points to the ring, "you go to the ground and that's where the fight *begins*. And no picking up bricks and shit. Just flat out man-to-man combat. And based on how well you've trained, may the best man win. Get it?"

I do, completely. A fair fucking fight. What I wouldn't give for that.

"Here with our second fight, from East Coast, Amir Ricci and City Grapplers' Tom Fragale." Fragale is a big fucking dude. I don't know how he and Amir are in the same weight class. He's flabby around the middle where Amir's every muscle casts a shadow. Amir rushes over to us. "I'm gonna fuck this fat fuck up!" He pounds fists with us and then enters the ring, bouncing on his toes and holding up his arms to the crowd. I look up and Dave plants a foot against the wall.

The ring girl goes round and it's on. Fragale moves in a slow arc while Amir glides around the ring, tall and taunting. He pops Fragale in the face twice before the fighter has a chance to put his hands up. Fragale charges forward, like a football player, low and leading with the head, and Amir just sidesteps and cracks him with a punch to the back of his head. Fragale stumbles but doesn't go down. Amir waits for him to advance, and he does, but with his fists just under his nipples. Even I know that's fucking suicide. Amir throws a combo, catching him with each blow, and the guy goes to a knee. Amir strikes twice. Fragale blocks one, and when he does, Amir slides beneath the arm and coils around him like a snake. He pulls him to the mat, and within seconds Fragale's tapping out.

Now our corner loses its shit, while Amir waves to the crowd. He's declared the winner and then joins us. We huddle around and congratulate him. He's barely sweating and all smiles. "Coach, I need a real fighter next time."

Coach claps his back and smiles. "If I can't find someone better, I'll step in the ring myself."

Phil scrolls through the footage he's just captured. "I'm telling you, Tone, get on the next card. This shit's too fun to just watch."

I agree. I expected tonight to feel like this, and I'm glad Rob dragged me in. I could hop in that ring right now I'm so pumped. Give me some chump like Fragale and even I'd fuck 'im up. But most likely I'd get someone like McTigue, and it'd be like tangling with Cameron. Fuck, I wonder if he'll show up tomorrow with Mom coming home and all? I may have my own ring inside the trailer. But that shit don't matter now. Here comes Rob.

"And the last fight of our first series is Rob O'Connell from East Coast and Todd Stetson from City Grapplers."

Rob rolls out, looking total bad-ass, shoulders pinned, swagger cocked. He nods his head like he's got a song trapped inside and then pounds fists with us before entering the ring. I look past Rob for Dave. Shit, he isn't at the back. I look around and can't find him or Marcus. Fuck, I hope he left, but that doesn't make any sense.

"Who you looking for?"

I don't want to tell Phil because it's not his problem, but I have to. "Dave's here."

"Muthafucka, where?" He spins around, looking.

I keep scanning. "Don't know. He moved."

"Sure it was him?"

"No doubt."

Phil sits back. "Tell me when you spot him, cuz that bitch is up to no good, and if he thinks he's gonna fuck some shit up, he's got another thing coming. My fucking fist."

The ring girl circles, and I still can't find Dave. The bell sounds and I give up.

Rob dances to the middle, and even though they're both 145 pounds, Stetson has him by an inch in height. Rob kicks first, glancing Stetson's knee, but he doesn't seem affected. He moves in with his long-ass reach, catches Rob with a shot to the head and then one to the kidney. Fuck, Rob's got to take him down.

"Clinch, Rob!"

"Wrap his ass up!"

"Ref, them monkey arms can't be legal."

Stetson swings again, but Rob dodges it and steps in, delivers a nasty shot to Stetson's side and then hooks his bicep. Rob plants his feet and tries to get him on his hip, but Stetson's free arm is like a hammer, dropping on Rob from every angle.

Rob gives up and slides out of the clinch. Stetson pursues and lands a right, but Rob uses McTigue's move and crushes Stetson with a knee. Stetson swings again, but it's wild, and Rob pivots off his leg and kicks Stetson in the waist. Rob's too slow in drawing his leg back, and Stetson grabs a hold and down they go.

Rob jerks but can't get his leg back, and Stetson's got his legs around it now. Rob bends the knee and sits on his opponent. He throws down punch after punch, but Stetson won't let go, he just keeps working the angle. The bell rings, and the round is over.

I don't know when I stood, but I'm not the only one. Our entire corner is up, not speaking, just shaking our heads. This is one tight fucking matchup.

The ring girl goes round and the fight resumes. Rob keeps his distance while Stetson tosses jabs. Rob moves in a slow arc, like Fragale, but his eyes dance. He's got a plan.

"What's up, Tone? Watching your boyfriend get his ass kicked?" Dave's voice worms in my ear, and I stop breathing. I hesitate to look, but there he is, crouched on the seat next to me, his big-ass friend looming, looking at me like I'm the next event.

"The fuck you want?" I speak but turn back to Rob. He's still steering Stetson toward a corner.

"Just watching my boys, same as you." He laughs. "But

I've got some business as well."

The word makes my heart pound harder than it already is. *Business* means too much shit for me. I nudge Phil. "Look who turned up."

Phil looks at me and then over at Dave. His face clenches. Marcus leans forward, and Phil's eyes cut in on him. "You with him?" He points at Dave.

Marcus nods. "Sure am."

Phil nods, repeatedly. "All right. So's you know, you here to bring shit, I'm your man. Touch my boy Tony here, or any of these guys, and you're fucked."

"That so?" Marcus smiles.

"Heard it, right?"

"Mmhmm."

Dave laughs and I try to ignore him. Rob's still bobbing and weaving, looking more like a boxer than anything else when the bell rings. Coach enters and Rob's the first one to speak, spewing something about his "strategy." Coach looks pissed, fiery red. If he sees Dave, who knows what will happen? I inch away from the thug.

He's talking to Marcus though, and I feel like I'm going to crawl out of my skin. This is Rob's fight. I don't need this shit. The fuck did he come here for? Who the fuck's buying meth in this crowd? Phil huddles in.

"Don't worry, yo. I got you." We pound fists as the ring girl goes round again.

"Nice, let's watch your boy get fucked up."

I pretend I don't hear, but can't help thinking that Dave may be right.

Rob dances around like before, staying out of Stetson's reach, but then Stetson rushes, arms flying, and Rob drops to one knee. Just when Stetson's over him, he fires up and catches Stetson with an uppercut to the chin. Stetson stumbles and Rob pounces. He tackles him to the mat and moves in for Stetson's neck.

Stetson's dazed but slides his knees under him. He pushes against the mat while Rob works closer to his body. Stetson stops pushing to throw a punch into the back of Rob's head, but Rob ain't feeling shit now, it's obvious. His eyes are drawn to slits, and he's got one thought in mind, which we all scream.

"Choke 'im! Make his ass tap!"

Rob perches on Stetson like a fucking monkey, drawing his entire body around the guy's head. I can't see Stetson's face anymore, but everything else is flailing and he's getting nowhere. The ref hovers, and we all stand. Rob grunts and draws tighter. Stetson's arm goes rigid and then he taps.

We burst into screams like we just won the lottery. Rob rolls off, clasps hands with Stetson, and then lets the ref declare him the winner. Coach meets him and drapes an arm across his shoulders, and as they make their way toward us I remember Dave. Fuck! I turn, to tell him to leave, to go fucking deal elsewhere, but he's gone. So is Marcus. I scan quick but don't have time to get a good look because Rob's with us now and we're all slapping his back. He pounds fists with me. "You're next, Tone. Gotta get in that ring."

I smile. "Soon as I can."

"Where we going? I got to celebrate." Amir dances around Phil, who just shrugs.

"Wherever you want." He turns to Rob and me. "You two coming?"

We're just outside the locker room, where Coach congratulated Amir and Rob and we all consoled Mike. Fights from other gyms are still going, but we're clearing out. Rob's busted a bit around the face, but no worse than he's been before. He shakes his head. "Can't go anywhere. Got shit to do."

"Like what, muthafucka? It's Friday night. You should be out. We'll get you in the clubs, don't worry. Unless . . ." Phil taps Rob's chest.

"Yo, maybe he's got some tail. Is that it, you stallion?" Amir dances some more, his energy not at all depleted by the fight. He's going to make a scene wherever he ends up.

Rob shrugs. "Something like that."

Both Phil and Amir yell, "Oh!"

"'Bout you, Tone? Or is this some kind of threesome?"

I don't look at Rob when Phil asks, but I'm sure the insult must sting. "Nah, I can't. My mom's coming home in the morning. Gotta be there for her."

"Shit, Tone, I forgot." Phil looks genuinely sad.

"It's all right. You two go nuts." I look over at Rob. He doesn't appear as if he's just won a fight, more like he's about to enter another. Every part of him is tense, and he's staring at the floor. "Ready?"

"Yeah."

We pound fists with the guys and then step out into the night. It's bone-chilling and we both pop our hoods and tuck into ourselves. We don't speak. The wind would carry our words away even if we did.

We walk on and I'm happy for Rob, but can't help thinking of Dave and how the bikers were back at the park and what the fuck that all means. Rob keeps his bent posture, striding toward his own shit. A car slows behind us, its lights resting on a stop sign.

"You two walkin'?"

Phil's voice startles me.

"Get the fuck in. I'll drive you."

Rob whips back, looks at me, the car, and then down the road. He nods to himself and crosses the street. I follow him into the back of Phil's car.

It's warm and the bass is pumping. Phil looks at us in the rearview mirror. "Where to?"

It takes Rob a second, but he answers. "Pleasant Meadows."

Phil can't hide his expression. "All right."

We drive and bullshit about the matches, wondering if Mike will come back or walk away. Then Phil cuts in. "And while you two were doing your thing, guess who showed?"

Rob and Amir look at each other.

"With some big-ass bodyguard."

Both go wide-eyed.

Phil smiles. "Muthafucking Dave."

"That bitch!" Amir burns red. "The fuck he doing there?"

"Don't know. What he say to you, Tone?"

I hesitate. If I tell these guys what Dave's into they may get even more pissed. Then again, it can't hurt to have them know. If shit gets real ugly at least someone else with be clued in. "He was there to make a deal."

"That pushing fucking bitch. What's his bag?"

Rob looks over at me, and it's a mix of shame and anger. "Meth."

"No fucking shit?" Phil slows the car and turns around in his seat. "Really? You ain't blowing smoke?"

I shake my head. They both say, "Fuck," and Phil turns back around and pulls into the park. He stops just inside. "So you weren't kidding when you said he knew people who could do what they did at Coach's?"

"No, I wasn't." I look out the window. "They live here."

Rob grabs the door handle. "Thanks for the ride." He steps out just as Phil starts yelling.

"I'll drive you to your house. Which one is it?"

I open my door and answer before getting out. "Like it matters."

Phil's got his window down. "Take it easy, son." We pound fists.

"Same to you."

He smiles and Amir yells, "Peace!" before doing a U and pulling away. Rob stands with his hands tucked into his pockets, looking toward Amy's.

"You goin' to see her?"

"Yeah. Said she wanted to see my face after the fight. Whatever that means."

I nod, even though he isn't looking at me.

"We've got an appointment tomorrow. At the doctor's."

"Yeah, for the baby?" I try to sound supportive, because he sounds so fucking hopeless.

"Kinda. She's scheduled for a, well . . . I guess she changed her mind."

I don't ask why she did because he doesn't need to tell me. Maybe they talked this afternoon? Maybe he crunched those numbers that had him so tweaked and she understood? Whatever it was, it's between them. "Oh. All right."

He turns away.

"You need help with the cash?" I don't know why I'm asking, it's not like I can help, but I just feel the need to do something. He should be happy. He won. But there's nothing happy about this moment.

Rob shakes his head. "I'll figure it out."

"All right. Good luck, then." I won't ask how because I'm sure I already know.

"Yeah. Good luck with your mom tomorrow." He shuffles his feet.

"Thanks." I laugh. "I just can't wait to see her."

He laughs and it's good to see.

"Hey, for real, nice job tonight. You are one hardcore fuck."

Rob's smile broadens. "Thanks." He steps toward Amy's but then steps back. "I meant what I said, Tone. You gotta get in there. This is gonna sound stupid, but whatever. It's like the only time in the past year I've felt fully alive." His eyes shine when he says this, and his voice is soft like it gets. He's being totally honest, and I appreciate that more than I can possibly express.

"I will."

We're about to head our separate ways when the hogs appear in the distance. They rumble in and park and the guys' shouts to one another carry over the trailers. Dave's Mustang pulls in behind them, and he pulls up to us. He cuts the engine and he and Marcus step out. I look at Rob and he sets his jaw because he knows. I match him, because it's the only way we're making it through this round.

16

"Like I said, this will be a quick one boys. Just dropping off." Dave smiles at Rob and me in his rearview mirror. I look out the window, knowing just where we're headed. Rob seems to be doing the same. He didn't say shit when Dave told us to get in. He didn't speak when Dave laid out the plan. And he didn't ask a question when Dave said we'd split the $500 for this deal.

We pull into the warehouse parking lot, and Dave parks like he did before. "Pull down the seat and grab the two boxes."

Rob and I turn at the same moment and reach for the tab. Rob shakes his head and lets me do it, and in a moment we're each holding a box.

"All right, Tony, you know the drill."

We step out of the car and when we're far enough away Rob speaks. "This what you did last time?"

"Yeah." We walk a few more steps, and then I ask the question, even though I know the answer. "We're fucked, aren't we?"

Rob looks over his shoulder, and his eyes are wide with fear. He nods once, real quick, and then turns back around. My stomach falls into my hips and we stand in front of the door.

The same shuffling comes after Rob knocks on the door and the same voice asks, "Who are you with?"

I answer, "The Agnostic Front."

The Hungarian smiles and lets us in and it's all too familiar and yet completely different because Rob's with me. We shouldn't be here. Or at least *he* shouldn't be. He just won his first fight. He's got a future. But he just keeps his back straight as the guys go through the motions of testing the drugs and then giving us a shot of vodka.

The alcohol is still boiling inside as we step out and head back to Dave's car. Rob's carrying the money, and I feel like such a bitch compared to him. He doesn't seem bothered by any of this. So why am I?

We peel out and don't speak until we're back at the park. "You two work real well together. I'll be sure to let Chaz know." Dave parks and we step out. He moves into the back, counts the money, and then emerges with two stacks. "Like I said, the busy season is here. I hope you boys are ready to work."

Dave hands over the money and as much as I don't want to take it, I like its weight. Rob's shoulders drop, and he seems to relax.

"Rob, congrats on the win, too. Even though I woulda taken your ass out. It takes the two of you to take me on." He laughs and climbs into his car and then drives over to Charity's.

Neither of us speak until Dave and Marcus are inside the trailer. "You're right, Tone, we're fucked." Rob kicks the ground.

I'm not sure what he means, because when I asked earlier I was talking about the deal, but we came out just fine. "How so?"

He shoots me a look that he keeps for the really stupid around here and I turn away. "Really, you don't get it?"

I shake my head.

"You're the smart one, right?"

"Yeah," I say, defensive that he's calling me out.

"Well, think about it. We were just dragged into that without a choice. Dave just basically said to be ready for more."

"But we got paid?"

Rob laughs. "You think this amounts to anything? You know how much they just earned?" He laughs again. "Tone, it's a joke, but we can't say no to it."

I think about what he means, how we didn't have a choice, and it's the same shit of my life in a new form. Here I am, stuck with something I don't want. But I really need this cash. So, I don't know. At least it's not all bad. "No, we can't say no, but that money should help for tomorrow."

He tilts his head, confused, but then the realization spreads across his face. "Fuck, I forgot."

I want to laugh, not because it's funny that he forgot about Amy's abortion, but because this is all so fucked up. I'm roped in with the Front, Cam's boys, the same man who put my mom in the hospital. And she'll be home tomorrow, and he'll come back around. What can I do then? I can't fight him? Not if we're on the same damn team, which there's no doubt we're on now. And Rob just won his first fight, is on the verge of becoming a trainer, but he's in the same swirl with me. And I thought we had a future.

Just goes to show when life offers something, there's always a choice to be made. Better be damn sure to pick the right hand because one will undoubtedly make you wish you never had the choice to begin with.

Camilla is huddled with my mother just inside the entrance to the hospital when the taxi pulls up. "That's her," I say, but the driver only glances over. I step out and walk through the sliding doors. She's in a wheelchair.

"Right on time, Tony." Camilla smiles and squeezes my mother's shoulder. "He's a good boy, isn't he?"

I don't know who Camilla is piling this shit on for because the last time she saw me, my mother's boyfriend was trying to kick my ass and she was bringing in security. The look on Mom's face, mouth drawn, eyes hooded, echoes how I feel.

"She all set or is there paperwork?" I continue to stand without having spoken to my mother. I don't intend to.

"No, she's all set, and all yours." Camilla gives the wheelchair a little nudge toward me. She wants me to play my part, I know, but she only fixed my mother's surface. The real damage lies much deeper.

"Thanks," I say and go and open the taxi's back door. Fortunately the hospital's got some sort of deal with the company, because they arranged the pickup and just added it to my mom's bill. Camilla shoots me a look, but then kicks out the wheelchair's brakes and rolls my mom toward the cab.

The driver watches us in the rearview mirror. I feel like punching him for not getting out to help. Camilla manipulates my mother into the backseat and buckles her in. My mother has yet to speak. Camilla closes the door and pulls back the wheelchair.

"She can walk, right?"

"Yes. She *can*. It's just procedure. Insurance."

The thought of insurance makes me think of bills and what we owe and last night, which I spent in the recliner, turning the scene over in my mind. I almost went to find Rob, to see if he had thought of a way out, but I knew I shouldn't. His plate's already full. Camilla touches my arm.

"Tony, hey, are you all right?"

"Sorry, just spaced out for a second. You know, lot on my mind."

"Is everything okay?" She looks toward the taxi. "I mean, with *everything*?"

It's nice that she cares, but honestly, if I said "No" right now, what would change? Nothing. What could she really do that would help me?

"Yeah, we're good. Thanks." I step away and climb into the other side of the cab. The driver takes off and still my mother and I have not spoken to each other.

My mom sits like a toy, immobile and eyes fixed. I know she's got pain pills and her jaw's tender, so maybe she's just out of it. Which really isn't a change, but shit, how's she going to work? Fuck, Dave knew right when to fucking strike.

The cab pulls up outside our trailer, and the driver just grips the wheel and again watches us in the rearview mirror. It's all me now, no Camilla to do my job. "Ready?" I extend my arm for her to grab. She sighs and takes hold. Her strength is for shit, and I wonder if she's really as healed as they said. I put a hand to her back, and we step away from the cab. She moves her feet in small spurts, making it to the railing and then pausing to rest. I toss her bag to the top of the landing and think about going back and shutting the cab door, but fuck that. The douche is staring at us, like we're some ugly-ass fish in a tank.

She takes the steps slowly. She heads straight for her bedroom, sits on the bed, and wrestles off her coat. I follow, slow as shit.

"Can you get my shoes?" She points at her feet and looks on the verge of passing out. It's the first she's spoken, and the words sound so formal around her locked jaw. A sarcastic remark rises up, but I bite it back and slide her shoes off. She pulls her blankets back and lies down. I'm amazed she has the strength.

"Do you need anything? Medicine?"

She shakes her head across the pillow. "Not yet. Later. I need to sleep now." With that, she's out. I step from the room and exhaustion settles over me as well. It's just after 1:00 and there's no food and nothing else to do until she wakes up and tells me her plan. If she has one.

"Tony. Tony."

I open my eyes and she's standing at my doorway, clinging to the wall. "I need to take my pills, but there's nothing to make a shake with."

I sit up and rub my face, feeling like I'm crawling out of sand. "What? What's going on?"

She frowns. "I need to make a shake so I can take my medicine."

I notice for the first time how her face has been rearranged because of her new jaw. She's different, not unrecognizable, but for a moment, not my mother. It's fucking creepy and I slide out from under my covers and don't say shit about why we have no food. "I'll be right back."

The cold air slaps and stings my skin, but I enjoy the sensation. I'm perked awake and understand what I need to do. I was headed to Rob's, to see if he could hook me up, but he's probably not there with his appointment and all, and I sure as shit don't want to talk to his parents. I turn and head the other direction, to Amy's.

Charity answers the door, and I am again put off by her

appearance. She's not the Char I remember, all round and bubbly. She's thin and hard around the eyes. "Hey, Char, Amy here?" I know she isn't, but I gotta say something normal.

Her eyes water. "No, she's at her *appointment*." She says the last word like a curse.

"Right, that's right." I pause and let her collect herself. Tears stream down her face, and she dabs at them with the backs of her wrist. Fuck she needs help, therapy or some shit. "Hey, I need to make a shake. Do you have anything you could spare?" I feel like such a pathetic asshole.

Char wipes her eyes one last time. "Why?"

"My mom just got home from the hospital and I couldn't get out shopping before. We've got nothing, and she needs her medicine."

"Hold on." Char darts from the door. Inside, I hear her clattering around. Amy's mom yells, "Who is it?" and the TV blares. Char comes back with two grocery bags. "I threw in milk, ice cream, some frozen strawberries, and yogurt." She looks up from the bag. "Some stuff for you, too." Her face is as bright as it was before, in spite of its hollowness, and I feel good for having asked her for help.

"Thanks." I can barely get the word out.

Charity nods and then her face slides back into the mask she's been wearing ever since whatever happened, happened. A knot forms in my gut when I see this, because I understand that if I work for Dave, it's truly Chaz I'm working for. The same man who did this. I wish I knew what to say, but I don't, so I turn and walk away, without the decency to say good-bye.

She's sitting on the couch staring at nothing when I return. But she sees the bags and crosses to me, more quickly than I thought possible. "What's this?"

"Groceries."

Mom eyes me with a question, but tugs at the bags and looks inside.

I offer to make it, but she has a shake blended together in no time and is sipping it carefully through a straw. I know I should eat, but I just don't have an appetite.

"My bag. It's in my room. Go get it."

I get up, happy to have something to do, even if it is to wait on her.

"A glass of water, too."

I get her bag and water and she takes her pills.

"What is it?"

"Painkiller." She puts the pill bottle away.

"Yeah, but what kind?"

She hesitates for a second but then says, "Hydrocodene."

She'll be a space ball in an hour. Better ask what's what now, while she's coherent. "So, are you all right? Going back to work? What about Cameron?"

She recoils and I feel stupid for asking, but this is shit I need to know.

"I don't know." She stares at me, looking like she's ready to fight.

"You don't know *what*?" My voice rises more than I'd like.

"Anything. Any answers to your goddamn questions!" She grabs her jaw and looks away. I feel like someone's slapped me. "I just got home. I need time to think."

I take a deep breath and wait. She's right, she does need time, but I just feel like *I* don't have any. "Fine, but we've got bills and we need food and I can't just go to Charity and expect her to take care of it."

"You got by while I was gone, didn't you?" She waits for me to respond and I nod. "All right then. You'll figure it out.

But fuck, give me time."

I don't know why I keep thinking that things will get better, that I even had the notion to believe she might have a plan for us. She never has and never will. So I *will* figure something out. Maybe with Dave and the Front? What other choice do I have?

She doesn't ask where I'm going when I throw on my coat and slide into my boots. Mom just stares at the TV like it's the only thing in the world. Maybe it is within that Swiss cheese brain of hers, eaten away by drugs and abuse.

I strap a winter hat on my head with matching gloves. No one questioned me at school, rooting around in the Lost 'n' Found. "I'll be back later."

She doesn't respond. I zip my coat and head out.

It's twenty degrees or so, but I don't care. I need some fresh air and some space to clear my head.

"Tone, that you?" Rob's voice emerges from the dark and then so does the rest of him, looking like a skeleton beneath his hoodie. "I wanted to come in, but didn't know with your mom and everything."

This may or may not be true. He looks just like I feel. In need of some air. We pound fists and then I ask, "How's Amy?"

He doesn't answer right away. "Not good. She's in bed, on meds. I think her mom's figured it out, so I bolted before she laid into me."

I kick the ground. "Char's with her though?"

"Yeah. What about your mom?"

"Same. You know. Just her jaw's wired shut and she's taking pain meds instead of her usual."

He nods and braces against the cold. "Sorry, man. Cam been by?"

"Not yet. He will, though."

Rob looks at me and seems to understand all that I mean by that. "Yeah, we'll be seeing a lot of him."

The thought makes me want to punch something. "Aren't you pissed? I mean, if we get caught, all that shit with Coach Dan, it's gone. And of course there's fucking being in jail. I can't even go there."

Rob stares out into the night. "Course I'm pissed. I want that shit more than I want anything else. A fucking way out of here, you don't turn your back on that. Unless someone makes you."

He's right, but I just hate the idea of being so powerless, even though I should be used to it. "Big O and Coach Dan. Fuck, this will kill them."

"Yeah, it will." Rob kicks the ground again. "Hey, you never told me what the big man has lined up for you. Coach Dan said something about school, but it was before the fight and I wasn't paying attention."

I laugh. "Don't sweat it. He's just got this idea that he could get me into some college. My IQ and all."

Rob stands straight up and takes a step closer to me. "So? Are you going for it? What's the deal?"

I back away, uncomfortable by his interest. "I don't know. There's strings and shit, and even Big O said it's a long shot."

Rob looks pained. "So what?" He turns away. "Tone, I don't care if it's a million to fucking one, you gotta run them odds. If it don't work out, all right. Least you tried to get the fuck out of here."

Getting out of here. Is that really a possibility? College? Can't be. If I can escape jail or getting killed, I'll get the fuck out of high school and settle in some shop. At this rate one owned by the Front. Rob's being nice, but not honest. Everything outside of here appears better, and most likely is, but no one's ever helped you figure out how to get it. But Rob already knows this. "All right. I check in with Big O. Meantime, we gotta keep our eyes open for Dave. See if we can't duck and run."

He smiles. "All right. That's what I'm talking about. We'll hide out best we can." He runs a hand over his face. "Shit, I'm beat." He looks at me like he wants to say more, but just drops his shoulders and says, "See you, Tone."

Rob walks off and I watch him go, then head up the stairs and into my trailer. The TV's on but Mom's in bed. I turn it off and check that she's still breathing. I close her door and then grab some of Charity's donation from the fridge. My mother snores in the distance, and I get up to go check on the little income I've hidden.

I sit on my bed and count the cash and tuck it away again. I look around my room and try to imagine it's a dorm room. I'd be a good roommate—clean, honest. Why not? Why shouldn't I get this chance? Other kids with fucked-up lives get to go and improve and never look the fuck back. Rob's right. We're going to pull through this shit and then make it. Because the only other option . . . fuck it, might as well go swallow Mom's bottle of pills.

17

Lance is rambling on about some shit, and I can barely keep my eyes open. Sleep at my house just isn't an option. Not since Cam's come back. I lie awake in my bed listening to their muffled conversation, waiting for him to explode. Lance just told us that George Washington had one hell of a temper as a young guy. If he was anything like Cam I'm sure people were nervous as fuck around him, for good reason.

Two weeks ago Cam showed up for Thanksgiving. Mom's onto soft solids and he brought a pumpkin pie and whipped cream. After our store-cooked chicken and instant mashed potatoes, he pulled out the pie and squirted my mother's nose with the whipped cream. He made some dirty comment then, like I wasn't even in the room. Mom laughed and wiped her nose clean and didn't say shit about how gross he is. She didn't say shit about him just coming back around, period. Because she can't remember a goddamn thing.

So he's darting in and out, but staying more often than not. He's been getting groceries and paying our regular bills and mostly avoiding me. Mostly. He said shit about my deal with Dave: "The Front's talking about you. Hope you're ready." But I didn't ask what he meant because I didn't want to give him the satisfaction of feeling smarter than me. I also thought that if I didn't acknowledge him, maybe it would go away.

I slink down into my desk, rest my head on my bicep and doodle on the paper I snagged from the kid behind me. I need to occupy myself with something other than the show at home. Hopefully Rob will be up for going back to the gym tonight. He's been spotty ever since Amy's abortion, and it's not the same without him. I haven't forgotten what he said about the gym being his out. I can't let him fuck this up.

The douche-bag janitors are moving a pallet of rock salt, stacking it next to the little four-wheeler that they rigged up with a dispenser. Franks looks at me.

"I'd make a joke but it's too easy. You look terrible."

I move toward the sweeper. Just another three weeks of this, and in the meantime, I'll just tune him out like every other fuckwad around here.

"Tony, seriously, are you okay?"

I lean against the broom. What the fuck does he care? "I'm fine. Can I go now?"

Franks tilts his head and exhales through his nose. "Yeah, you can go, but you're not sweeping."

"All right, what do I have to do, clean more graffiti?"

Franks smiles. "No, Mr. Ostrander has requested your presence. You need to report to his office."

"Now?"

"Yes, now." Franks laughs. "Funny, I didn't think you could look worse. What'd you do?"

He sounds sarcastic, like he already knows, and I shake away images of the deals, the drugs, the money. "Nothing."

Franks laughs into my back as I turn out the door. "Keep telling yourself that."

Fuck him, and fuck Big O. There's no way this is about the shit with Dave, or the fucking cops would be here. I breathe slow to calm myself and enter the office. Big O's secretary looks up from the clacking she was doing on the keyboard and gives me her did-someone-step-in-dog-shit look. "Wait there." She lifts a finger to me and picks up the phone. "Tony Antioch is here to see you." No sooner does the phone hit the base than Big O opens his door.

"Tony, come in." He extends his arm into his office and smiles. This can't be good, he's being too nice. Maybe I was wrong; maybe he's just going to hold me until the cops show. Fuck. I can't run now. Only thing to do is take whatever's coming, like a bitch. Seems to be my thing.

Last time my file was on his desk. This time he's got pamphlets and application forms. Shit.

"As you can see, I've taken the liberty to pursue the matter of your future." Big O sits and spreads his hands over the material like he's some game-show host.

"Right." I stare at the colorful pictures of kids on some campus, looking like they've all been told the same joke.

Big O sighs. "Have *you* thought any more about your future?"

I laugh, but not nearly as hard as the kids in the pics. "Yes and no." Seems the most honest answer.

The big man leans forward. "Antioch, please don't make this difficult." He waits until I make eye contact and then sits back. "I've talked to an admissions counselor and have sent over your transcript. He's interested, but you never took the SAT."

I asked Mom for the cash last spring. It seemed stupid at

the time, because no one else in Vo-Tec was taking it, but I figured *why not*? Course she didn't have the money. I shrug at Big O.

"Well, we can sign you up for the next one after the New Year. There's still time." He pauses. "That is, if you're still interested?"

I look at the pamphlets again and think of Rob and how awful he looked, telling me to go, get the fuck out. I still don't see this happening, but fuck it, what's it going to hurt to fill out a couple of forms? Besides, Big O has been good to me. Him and Coach Dan. I owe them both.

I reach across the table and grab the folder. Big O smiles. Something inside flutters and I have to take a deep breath to get steady before I stand up and leave.

The bell chimes, and the guys look up. They smile and nod and I pound fists with them, but they're looking for Rob, hoping he's behind me. Same here.

"Tony, hey." Coach Dan walks over and clasps my shoulder. "How you feeling?"

It's oddly similar to how Franks asked. I say, "All right."

He leans closer. "Rob? What about him?"

I don't know how much Coach Dan knows about that mess. "Hanging in there. You know?"

"I do, Tony, I do." He squeezes and then moves on to someone else.

I drop my gear and then stretch with Amir and Phil.

"It's gonna be a fun one tonight, Tone." Amir rolls his shoulders. "Working on striking with the head gear."

"I hate that shit. Smells like ass and you know everyone's

sweaty noggin's been in them. Just nasty." Phil makes a face and nods like I should agree with him.

"Until you're in the ring, fighting for real, you'll put that shit on and you'll like it." Amir's curled up, now, ready to pounce. Phil's not paying attention.

"Oh, I see, big man gets a fight and now he's the shit. Well, fuck that."

Amir slams into Phil, and they start grappling. It's like watching two dogs ripping into each other, but in that way they do when they're acting tough, not really trying to kill each other. I laugh along with everyone else as we watch them roll and bait and try to gain leverage. But when I look around I feel a little sad because Rob isn't here with us.

Amir forces Phil to tap and then we all clap. Coach Dan says, "That's the right kind of energy for tonight. Let's get loose and then get striking."

Coach takes us through some warm-up drills—the kind of thing I bet Rob would be doing if he were here—and then he pairs us up. I'm with Mike. He's been holding back since he lost his fight, so I'm not scared.

"Pure stand-up fighting. None of the ground game like Amir and Phil were messing with earlier." He chuckles. "And no ground and pound. If you end up on the mat, stand back up and start over."

We nod and I look at the gear. It is kind of nasty-looking, with a few rips here and there, but fuck it, what do I care?

"Remember, keep your hands up, protect your face, and never stop moving those feet. As soon as you rest on your heels, you're done." Coach looks us over and then says, "And use the gear. Focus on head shots, no body. Let yourself get hit. It's as important, if not more so, to be able to take a punch, as it is to throw one."

Mike grabs a set of head gear and straps it on. I adjust Rob's gloves and strap on my own head gear. It does reek and feels a bit slimy, but I've dealt with worse.

"You ready?" Mike speaks around his mouth guard and sounds like an idiot.

"Yeah. I'm good."

He nods, but the fire isn't there. This won't be anything like rolling with Rob.

"All right, boys, let's get to it." Coach claps and around the room jabs start snapping. I work an angle and throw some of my own.

There's so much padding with the gloves and the gear that it doesn't feel the same, like my hands are numb. I throw harder, a hook, because Mike's letting his left bob below his chin. It catches him in the temple and he staggers. The fuck? With all this shit and he's staggering?

I give him a second to regain himself and see Coach Dan watching me. He looks away, though, and Mike says, "Whoa, that's a hell of a hook, Tone."

I don't answer. I threw harder, yeah, but he hasn't felt how much force I've got.

We square up and Coach yells about moving the feet and driving through the hips. I pick up the tempo. Mike comes alive and snaps a few jabs to my cheek and forehead, but they don't feel like anything. I toy with him, purposely drop my hands, and let him go for broke. He does and I step back to brace for the fall, but it never comes. Mike hits me, but then backs off. He doesn't finish the job, doesn't follow through with the elbows and dominate. Fuck, he's a bitch.

I step up and get back into position.

Mike watches me and his eyes dart all over the fucking place. I'm moving now, bobbing low and throwing quick jabs with both hands to keep him guessing. This is easy, just like going toe-to-toe with some punk at school back in the day. Some kid who thought just because he was bigger that meant anything in a fight. I catch Coach Dan out of the corner of my eye, arms folded, cupping his chin, watching me.

The jab lands square in Mike's nose. The cross catches him on one cheek, and my hook the other. He's staggering, about to fall, trying to get his bearings, but I advance, throw an uppercut, and then rip through with the elbow, hit him with it in the back of the head as he's going down. I throw two more into his dome and that's it, he's sprawled on the mat, a sweaty rasping heap.

Coach Dan walks over. "Amir, get over here. Tony needs a challenge."

I'm scared for a second, but settle. There's no time for fear. I make eye contact with Coach so that he understands. He stares at me the entire time. "Ring his bell, Amir."

"Yes, sir."

I smile and both Coach and Amir tilt their heads.

Someone picks up Mike, and Amir and I square to each other. He throws the first punch. It's lightning fast, but has no effect. I counter and connect and we each throw a few more, feeling each other out. He's got four inches on my reach, so I know I'm in danger, but if I just keep my hands up I should be fine.

I fake a right and then nail him with a left, but he's unfazed and comes over the top and drills me in the side of the head. My vision wobbles, but only for a second. I push off him and get out of his reach and look for a target. Amir's great at everything, is probably the most athletic guy in here, so his position is perfect. He's tight, on the balls of his feet, and is rolling those hips like they're unhinged. But his wingspan is so wide that when he protects his face, there's a clear path to his chin. If only I can reach it.

I move in and back off, throw a few wild haymakers, and watch that one window. Fuck, I'm going to take a beating to get it. But like Coach said, this is where I'll prove myself.

I get low, fix my hands up around my forehead. Thankfully we aren't striking the body or this would never work. Amir cracks my ears as I advance, and while he's swinging I unleash on his chin. He covers after one hit, but can't resist reaching over top and getting my head.

The pounding echoes in my ears. It's a constant thudding that jars my vision and rattles my mouth, but it doesn't hurt. Without the gear, I'd be out cold, no doubt. Amir knows the sweet spot just behind the ear, and hits it nonstop. And I let him, and cover the top of my head. I can hear Coach screaming something, but have no clue what he's saying. It doesn't matter, though, because this feels good. Amir could drop bombs on me all night and I'd be fine. My head's been through the ringer so many times, this is nothing. But I'm not here to only take it.

I drop my hips another inch, wait for Amir's flurry and then strike. I catch him with a fierce uppercut to his unprotected chin. My hips are extended, and I've stood him up. He quickly covers, but the damage is done. I rock him back and forth with jabs and hooks and whatever the fuck else I can manage. It's just a wash of movement and then before me, nothing. Amir is on the mat.

I stop and the room comes back to me, all the noise, the yelling, the cheering, and my own heart pounding in my ears.

"Holy fucking shit!"

"Did you see that?"

"Tony dropped his ass, just laid Amir the fuck out."

I look down and immediately help Amir up. He's eyes are bugged and he's hurt, but he claps my back. "Nice work, Tone. Real nice."

Coach Dan is at my side. "Jesus, Tony. You all right? That was one pounding you gave him, but your head, aren't you scrambled?"

I pop out my mouth guard, unstrap the head gear, and hand it to Coach. "I've never had the luxury of one of these."

He looks at me and his face clouds. I know he knows about me. Sure he's talked to Big O and probably Rob, but I think this is the first time he gets it. He looks away and then back, and his words are tight. "Well, I'm glad I could give it to you. You deserve it."

I close my eyes and just let the feeling run its course. I know exactly what he means, and I know that this place has just taken on a whole new level for me. I've got to get Rob back here, because if I can feel this good in spite of all my shit, then he needs to be here with me. Like always.

I walk into the living room and my mother's staring at the screen like the janitors do with whatever's in front of them. A bowl sits on the arm of the couch, cashed but smoldering. She doesn't notice me, and I scan the room, peeking into her bedroom as well.

"Tony? Why you home so early?"

This is exactly the piece of the puzzle that Big O can't grasp. Survival first and if some of the finer shit falls away, so be it. "It's not that early."

She shrugs and looks back at the TV. I step in front of it and she shoos me, but I keep my place. "Where'd you get the pot?"

She looks at me as if I'm speaking a foreign language and doesn't answer. I reach over and grab the bowl, hold it in front of her face. "Where did you get this?"

She stares at the small black pipe as if I were showing her nothing more compelling than a button.

"Was Cameron here? Did he hook you up?" It's bad enough that he stole her pain meds and she didn't say shit, but he's replaced them with this.

She shrugs and looks away and that's all the answer I'm going to get, I know it. I set the bowl back. Least it's not meth. Not yet.

I go to the fridge and make a sandwich with the food Cam's bought and every bite is hard to swallow. I head to my room, close my door, and flip my mattress, pulling back the plastic cup around the corner. I feel for the bills. They're still there, so I set the mattress back and sit on it. I see that dorm room again and feel the same flutter when I picked up those forms. But just because I fill out the paperwork doesn't mean I'm in. And regardless, if I do get in, I'll need money. I don't want to deal, but I need to do something.

My room reeks of pot and even though all I want to do is shower and go to bed, I get up. I can't stay here right now. I need to get out. Have to see Rob.

Mom doesn't even flinch when I pass. She's completely zoned out. I shake my head and go out the door.

I never go to Rob's. His place is actually nice, but he doesn't let anyone in. His mom's just too much of a bitch, complaining every minute about shit. It's no wonder that his dad works so much.

I knock on the door and wait. The TV's on, and Rob's mom yells and in a moment the door's open. "Tone? What's wrong?" Rob's wearing pajama pants and a T-shirt.

"Nothing. But come out. We gotta talk."

Rob hesitates for a second but then reaches in, grabs his coat off the hook by the door and slides his boots on. "Be back in a minute, Ma." She doesn't answer. He closes the door behind him, and I head down his steps.

"What's up?"

"You need to come back to the gym."

Rob smiles. "You know I will. Just need some time."

I pin back my shoulders. "For what? What are you doing instead?"

Rob sets his jaw, I doubt liking my tone of voice. "You know. Handling shit."

"I'm not saying you aren't, but what good is it doing you? Besides, it's not like the guys and Coach Dan give a fuck about what happened. You think you're the only one there who's been in this spot?"

Rob looks away and works his jaw, the muscle bulging.

"Remember, Coach Dan is trying to hook you up, give you a shot? How's that going?"

Rob tightens even more. His hands are fists.

"But that's right, you're too busy *handling shit* to worry about that. Must be nice to be able to blow off the one thing that matters."

"The fuck you know about it, Tone? You wouldn't be there if it weren't for me."

"And Big O." I'm not going to let him slide, even if he's looking like he's about to take my head off.

He turns. "Exactly! And if I remember, he's got something for you, too, doesn't he?" Rob takes a step toward me. "Well, what the fuck are *you* doing about that? Huh?"

I don't answer.

"Right. Nothing." He laughs. "So don't come here and

bitch at me. I got shit in my way. This Amy thing has fucked with my head."

"Boo fucking hoo." I let the words drag out. Rob takes another step.

"What you say?"

"You fucking heard me. Don't act stupid. Unless it isn't an act, because it seems that's all you're capable of doing."

Rob is inches from me. "You stepping up, Tone? You ready to throw?"

I am. I'm ready to take on anyone or anything that comes my way, except I know I'd lose. I can't handle all this shit on my own, and I'm not about to fuck up the one relationship I have that actually works.

"No, Rob. Not like this. At the gym? Yeah. I'll fucking drop you. But not here. You get it?"

His eyes crowd and he starts to speak but doesn't. He was ready to throw, ready to hit me and probably knock me out. I don't blame him. But we're on the same fucking page. He just doesn't see it. That's what happens when your shit life gets in the way. That's what happens when you're white-trash-trailer-park-nothing. No one gives a fuck, and usually that includes you.

Rob's shoulders slump and his eyes simmer down. "Fuck." He lets out a deep sigh and we stand in the cold and I wait for him to come to his senses.

The glow from the TV is the only light and the fight is so loud it absorbs all other sound. I watch the action for a few seconds, a couple of amateur guys rolling—one bleeding from his nose and the other straddling him, throwing light jabs, just taunting him like a cat with a mouse. I'm sure Cam's loving this.

He turns and sips his beer, watching me like he's been expecting my arrival.

"What do you want, Cam?"

"Well, I already put your mom to bed, so I'm good, but thanks for asking."

Disgust and anger rise up, and I'd like to either punch him or hurl. Or both. I move to step past him, but he's on his feet and in front of me before I've even noticed he's moved.

"We need to get some shit straight between us." He reeks of beer and is too close for my comfort.

I breathe through my mouth so I don't have to smell him. "Yeah. What's that? I'm pretty sure I know where I stand with you?"

"You've got this all wrong, son. We're on the same team now."

I cock my head. Did he really just call me that?

"*The Fighter Front.* That's what they're callin' you. Your boy Rob and Dave and you." He smiles.

I hate the image, and even more, the fact that he's right. We are united. "So what?"

"I just wanted to make sure you understood that this ain't no team you can walk out on. This shit's for life. Once you're in, you're *in.*"

I stare at him, unsure of what to say. Cam holds up the pamphlets Big O gave me. "Where'd you get those?" I grab for them, but he's too fast.

"You know where, so don't fuck around." He takes one between his thumbs and rips. "Don't you go getting any ideas about trying to get out, cuz you ain't going nowhere."

I want to scream, to choke him out, to do something, but

I'm stuck. I can't move a muscle. The pamphlet falls to the floor, and I watch it for a second then look at him. Our eyes lock, and in them I see a point I've never noticed before: desperation. Maybe it's the moment, being all amped after talking to Rob, and now realizing that Cam's been in my room, rooting around with his dirty hands in my belongings. So maybe I'm wrong and it's really just anger or fear or something more pathetic. But in these shadows, as much as I don't want to admit it, I see a trace of myself.

"We need to talk, get our shit figured out. Ya hear? The Agnostics have big plans." He points to the couch with his beer. "Have a seat."

I hesitate to move and in the hesitation see myself for who I am: Just some pussy kid who thought he could fight his way out. I was wrong. Standing here, exhausted and seeing myself in this monster, I know it's time for me to give up and stop pretending. To stop fighting.

I sit on the couch and he cracks his crooked smile and I feel like a child again, and may as well be for all the control I have.

18

Amy blows smoke at Hatchet-Face, as usual, but Hatchet doesn't give her any shit. I think she might sense what I do, that's Amy's either been drinking since breakfast, or never stopped last night.

Rob and I follow her on the bus and Hatchet gives us the stink eye but doesn't say a word. We sit and I want to tell Rob about last night, about Cam and what he said, but he's focused on Amy. She's peering down the aisle, sipping on a straw she's got stuck into a soda bottle. Her eyes are dull, so much like my mom's.

"Fuck, man, what's her deal?" I elbow Rob.

He shakes his head and rests his elbows on his knees. "Ain't like I've talked to her. After her appointment, she just cut me off. Says she can't stand to look at me."

"Sorry, man." I look out the window, watch the trees whip by, and see Cameron from last night. His words were the first thoughts that ran through my head when I woke up. I turn back to Rob. "Cam was at my house last night. There's another deal coming."

Rob doesn't say shit.

I look up the aisle and Amy's sipping away, but her eyes pierce mine, as if she's been listening.

"So what's what?" Rob asks.

I lean close. "On the twenty-third we've got to help deliver a big shipment. Everyone has to be there because they don't want any problems."

"Problems?"

"You know, they got guns and shit."

"After this, Tone, we're out. All right?" Rob looks at me the same way he did last night and it hurts to know that's just not a choice.

"Yeah. All right," I say because we don't need to go into that now, not if Amy is listening. Cam's words still echo. Soon I'll tell Rob that he's fucked, even if Coach Dan does hook him up and he gets a job around here. Because they'll come calling.

For now I'm quiet. The truth set aside, until I can handle it.

I head to English, my head filled with last night and what's next, when someone grabs my arm. I pull back and spin, but the fuck doesn't let go.

"Easy, Tone, just come with me." Dave's voice is cool, but there's an electric current beneath it that I'm not fucking with. He leads me to the bathroom and once in, checks the stalls and then finds the wooden wedge for the door. He jams it in.

"We need to talk."

I back into a sink.

"You ready to go?"

How the fuck can I possibly answer his question?

"You ready to go or not? Don't give me this shrugging shit."

"I'm ready. I know it'll be different from last time, with everybody else but same place and all."

"The fuck you talkin' 'bout? We're going to Johnny B's."

The fuck is *he* talking about? "Who's Johnny B?"

"Didn't Cam talk to you?"

I nod.

"So then you know what's what. We gotta take care of this pickup so the big score goes down. No using the stash house with this size."

Now I'm completely lost. Someone rattles the door but the wedge keeps it closed. "What do you mean, this *pickup*?"

Dave cocks his head and looks me over. "You playing fucking stupid with me?"

I watch his stance. His feet are shifted just so, and his hands are no longer hanging by his sides, but tucked around his hips. He's not messing around one fucking bit.

"No, Dave. I don't know who the fuck Johnny B is or what you're talking about."

The door rattles again. Dave rushes over and kicks it, and I'm surprised his foot doesn't go through. "We're cleaning!" he shakes his head and comes back to me. "So Cam never said nuthin' 'bout tonight and me needing a little support?"

"No." Support from me? Why not Marcus, or shit, even Rob?

"Stupid fuck." The bell rings, but Dave doesn't seem to hear it. "I'll deal with his ass later." He looks up at me and his eyes search my face as if trying to make sure I'm not lying. Then he clears his throat. "Here's the deal. Johnny B's got the score we need for the twenty-third. That's how things work. But Johnny don't like the Front coming to pick up shit. He says they're too obvious and probably got police tracking 'em. So they like to send me."

I shift my weight, trying to get comfortable, because I feel like a body has been dropped on me. Another job, cops, and some guy who deals with the Front, but doesn't want to be seen with them. What the fuck am I into?

"Johnny B likes me, cuz we got the same taste in shit. But like I said, it's a big score and this is still business, so I need a guy at my side."

"What about Marcus?"

Dave laughs. "That big nigga scares the shit out of Johnny. He's not exactly welcome."

"So why me?" My voice sounds like a little girl's.

"Well, like I said, Marcus is out. I know some guys from my new gym, but don't know 'em enough yet. Ya know what I mean? Rob's a better fighter, but I trust you more." He pauses and smiles at me. "Your shit's more fucked up. You're more desperate."

The truth hits so deep that it's a struggle to breathe. I look down and nod.

"'S what I thought. You get five bills for this and whatever perks are at Johnny's."

My head swims. I don't want this, but there's nothing I can do. Getting paid doesn't matter. Not after what Cam said. What the fuck am I going to do with the money?

"I'll pick you up round ten. Johnny's shit don't go down till late."

"All right."

"Woo. Gonna be good times." Dave kicks out the doorstop and goes through the door. I head in the opposite direction to English, and can't imagine what Dave thinks is a *good time*.

I reach Myers's door and she's up front, talking away. I put my hand on the knob, but then let go. I can just skip. I don't have to deal with her bullshit, especially not now. My head's a mess. But someone in the room must have said something because she's turning now and waving me in. Fuck.

The class stares as I step through and Myers says, "Pass?"

I shake my head. "I was in gym and Jorgenson wouldn't give me one."

She looks me over and smirks. "He's a tough one. I respect that." She waits for me to respond, but I don't.

I take my seat and settle into the story we're supposed to read while she calls us up to talk about our last essay.

The story isn't that bad. This guy, Hughie Luke, is trapped by this other character, Mrs. Setliffe, and I think she might shoot his ass.

"Tony?"

I look up and Myers waves me to her. I stand and cross the room to her desk, sit and see the grade on my paper. How the fuck did I get an A?

"Tony, I have to say, this was truly amazing." She's bent forward, her words all breathy. It's creepy, and thankfully, she flips the page. "Here, where you talk about how the father chooses to hurt himself, not just his family, through his actions—no one else got that." She looks at me and tilts her head.

How the fuck the rest of the class missed that is beyond me. Myers flips the page again and looks at me. "Brilliant."

My face flushes and I want to return to my seat, but Myers inches forward in her chair. "I don't know if you are aware, but Mr. Ostrander has come to me and asked if I could write on your behalf, regarding your intelligence and potential as a student."

I feel the blood in my face drain away. I see the torn pamphlet. Knowing Big O's gone this far makes it hurt all over again.

Myers waits for me to respond, but I've got nothing.

Fortunately, she continues. "At first I wasn't sure what to say, I'd just read your *Lord of the Flies* piece, but once I read this, I knew. You can't find this kind of analysis online. *You* have potential, Tony." She looks at me, eyes wide, mouth slightly open, probably waiting for me to seem all shocked. She doesn't know that I'm already done in from a completely different angle, and that I've been told *this shit* forever. So I just nod and wait for her to finish.

"Well, I told Mr. Ostrander the same, and it seems he's got some plans for you."

I laugh. Who doesn't?

Myers tilts her head. "Something funny?"

I sit up right. "No, it's just it seems a few other people have said the same thing recently. It's just ironic, that's all."

She smiles at my use of the literary device. "I understand." She pats my paper and then asks, "So are you liking the story?"

It takes me a second, but I understand. "'To Kill a Man'?"

She nods.

"Yeah, I'm just at the ending."

Myers brightens. "Well, I won't keep you. That's the best part." I go to stand but she asks another question. "Have you decided who's the good guy and who's the villain?"

I stare at the corner of her desk for a second as the answer flashes through my head. I could just shrug and pretend like I don't know, but something inside, the small shred that wants what Big O's offering and not what Dave's forcing me into, speaks. "That's a too simplistic way of looking at it. Each has a little of both."

I'm sure she smiles and looks genuinely pleased, as if somehow she's cracked my shell and I'm now spewing forth all I've pent up. And in a way, she has. But that same part of me that spoke also reminds me of the greater reality.

Truth is, it doesn't really matter how she feels about me. Truth is, I may be smart and a bit athletic, but no praise from an English teacher or coach is going to change much in my life. Truth is, maybe not even Big O's attempts would have, either.

No matter how much I'd like any of it, for something positive, it doesn't matter what I do, it won't ever be enough. Shit's going to fall apart. Because it always does.

I hear the fight before I see it. "You never cared about me, were just worried that I'd have your baby. Didn't want to be stuck in the trailer!"

I round the corner and Amy's slouched, stumbling, but squared up with Rob. He's standing by the doorway, stiff like a mannequin, as if she's screaming at someone else.

Amy lurches. "Ha! Fool's on you. I never liked your little cock anyway." She turns to the crowd that's gathered and wiggles her pinkie. "That's it, ladies. That's all *big* Rob's packing." She laughs and snorts and some of the crowd laughs along while others pop out cells to record her. Rob stays still. I join the swell.

"Oh, look, here's the man himself, Antioch." Amy holds up her hands as if presenting me on some runway or art show. "You here to save your boy? Help him outta this hole? Jus' like you're doing with Jensen?"

My muscles tense and I search the crowd. Dave isn't here, but that doesn't mean someone else isn't listening.

"What, you think I'm stupid?" Amy pushes me and her breath is heavy with alcohol. I don't say anything, and she shoves me again before turning to Rob.

"You both think I'm stupid. That I didn't hear what you were sayin'."

Rob's eyes are dead, just like mine feel. Someone's gotta shut her up before she goes too far. There's more at stake than she can possibly comprehend. It's just not safe for her to talk about this shit out loud. I shift my weight to the balls of my feet. I hope Big O shows up first.

Amy sways, mumbling to herself. A half circle has formed around her and I can feel the other half behind me. She snaps up, looks around. "You all here for the show, huh? Well, you should come to my house sometime. See *that* show. Fucking Charity and her shit." Amy's eyes pop wide. "Any of you even remember Charity?" No one answers. "Well, she's a used-up bitch now. Any of you want her, stop by."

Someone laughs and Amy joins in. It's a disgusting sight. She's everything about the park standing amidst everyone who hates us. She has no fucking clue that they're laughing at her, not with her. Or maybe she does and just doesn't care. I don't know which is worse. I feel sorry for her because this isn't who she is. Just like Charity, something bad happened, and watching the wounds heal isn't pretty.

I check Rob and his face is a mask, no doubt feeling like I do, but covering it up better. I try to mirror him.

Amy straightens again. "But like I was saying," she looks at me, "you and your fuck buddy think I don't know. But I know." She points at her chest. "Those bikers got you. Don't they?" She steps closer and kids twist trying to figure her the fuck out. She can't do this, can't keep spilling, because if someone puts two and two together . . .

Amy stands about three feet from me. "You know what they did to Char, right? Fucked her morning, noon, and night. Everywhere." She sways while she stares me down. "And now you're gonna deal for them? You piece of fucking trailer trash shit. Might as well let yer mom's boyfriend go ahead and stick it in your ass."

I don't even think, I just plant my left foot, dip down, and whip my leg into the back of Amy's. She collapses back, eyes wide with shock, and slams to the floor. Her head hits first and her eyes immediately roll back. Then she's still, just a heap. The crowd goes dead silent and I look at Rob. His face is flat, but the tension has dropped.

Someone yells, "No shit?" and the clapping and laughter rise up. Through the crowd Big O emerges. He sees Amy and moves to her side, bending down.

"What happened?" He looks up in the vague direction of the crowd. No one answers, so I do.

"She passed out, I think. Smacked her head." I feel a mixture of relief and guilt. I can't believe I just did that, but I had to. I had no choice. Right?

Big O checks to see that she's still breathing and sees the bottle next to her. He twists the cap, sniffs, and then shakes his head. He grabs the walkie-talkie at his hip. "I need the nurse at the main entrance. Bring the wheelchair." He looks up at all of us. "Back to class or lunch or wherever you were going." No one moves. Big O's face turns red. "Go!"

I stay rooted in place while kids pass saying, "Nice job." "Sweet kick." "Shoulda blasted her nose." I wait until they're gone and cross over to Rob. We watch the nurse try to bring Amy around with smelling salts, but she only swats at the scent. Big O and the nurse pick her up and plop her into the wheelchair and the nurse wheels her away. Big O sighs and looks at us.

"Gentlemen." It feels like a question, but we don't say

anything. He walks away. Rob clears his throat.

"That was fucked up, Tone."

"I know, but you heard what she was saying. Last thing we need is Dave to hear."

"Last thing we need is any trouble." He cuts me off and stares me down. "Besides, *you* just took out a *girl*. What kind of shit is that?"

I know he's right, that what I did was fucked up. But still. "Someone needed to."

"Remember, I got something going for me now. And I've got enough problems already. I don't need any more."

If you only knew. I hate the thought, but it's true. "I fucking get it, all right? That's what I was trying to save you from." My head swells. He has no clue. No idea that I'm in just as deep as him. For all the good that he is, he can be one self-centered fuck. "Don't think I'm not looking out for you. Why you didn't wrap it up is beyond me, but don't stand there reminding me what you got on the line. I'm standing there with you."

Rob nods but doesn't say anything. We wait for the bus without another word.

19

We don't say shit to each other on the ride to Vo-Tec, while Greyson has us hook up the plow to his truck, nor on the ride home. But when we near my trailer Rob clears his throat. "So I'll swing by later? Practice?"

It's unbelievable that this is all I wanted to hear last night. That I thought him returning would set things right again. But between then and now, everything's fucking upside down. "Yeah. I'll see you at six."

He takes off and as I watch his back. I know that I have to tell him about what Cam said and about what's what with Dave, but I'll fill him in later. I head inside.

The house smells like something familiar, but so distant that the connection isn't clear. It's a fruity scent, like nail polish remover. I step into the living room, and Mom emerges from the bathroom, sees me sniffing, and smiles. The wires have been removed, and her face looks healed.

"You like? It's this new air freshener I picked up." She walks over to the outlet at the threshold from kitchen to living room, points at the thing plugged in there. We stare at it, and a fine mist shoots into the air. "Ya see, it does that, like every few minutes."

"Great," I say and notice the spray cleaner and towel in

her hand. "What's up with you?"

"Just a little cleaning. The holidays are coming, and I'd like the place to look good." She puts her hands on her hips and takes in the space. The house is in order, and I like it, but it's disturbing. First, she never cleans. Period. It's like she never learned how. Second, we don't have company. Ever. So cleaning for *them* makes no sense. Third, why not get some Christmas lights or a tree if she's feeling festive? Fuck, I know she's not buying presents.

Mom shifts her gaze from the kitchen counter to me and stares like I'm the next item on her list. I kick off my shoes and set them on the new mat by the door, in case that's the issue, but she's still watching me.

"What?" My voice cracks.

She tilts her head. "Nuthin'. It's just . . ." She closes her eyes and shakes her head.

I clear my throat and try again. "Mom, what is it?"

She keeps her eyes closed and presses her lips into a line, as if waiting for pain to pass. I don't know why I care, why it bothers me to see this after all the shit she's put me through, but I'm concerned. Something's up, and if I've learned anything, I understand that if the shit hits the fan in her life, a fucking chunk is going to splatter on me. I step to her, take the spray bottle and towel from her hands and set them on the counter.

She starts crying and then covers her eyes with one hand, tilts her head back as if she's trying to keep the tears from falling.

"Just tell me," I say, even though I'm not positive I want to hear it.

She wipes with the edge of her hand and takes a deep breath, still looking up and away from me. "It's my fault and I feel stupid."

I don't say anything.

She smiles through the tears and looks at me. "All grown up, huh? Almost eighteen? When the hell did *that* happen?"

While you were loaded and attached to your parasite boyfriends.

She pats my cheek and I jump. I can't remember the last time she's touched me. "Mom, what's up?"

Her smile fades but she laughs and wipes away another band of tears. Then she pins me with her glare. "I know. I know what you're up to, with Cam and the Front. I know you're in on the deal."

I don't know if I feel more embarrassment or shock. I look away.

"I don't know how you got tangled up in this." She sighs. "I mean, you always seemed to keep away from that shit. Kept to yourself and all. But . . ."

She doesn't finish, but I wait. I want her to continue. I need to know where she's headed with this. Because this may be advice, which she's never given. Or maybe she's worried, because she knows more than I do. Even more likely is that Cameron is using this fact to hold over her. For what, I don't even want to imagine.

She watches me and purses her lips. Her eyes cloud and her mouth moves silently. I wait. She has not been the best mother, but she has been through more than most. I can give her a moment.

"I need you to help me."

I nod and grunt, hoping that will nudge her on.

She cracks, her chest falling, and she reaches for the counter to steady herself. I don't ask what's wrong, don't offer any help. I've seen this show before. "I need you to help me." She pauses and sets her eyes on me. They are the fierce gems

I remember as a child, when she fought my father, the one person I knew was evil. This is no show. My breath catches.

"I need you to help me get rid of Cameron."

The request lies between us like a corpse and neither of us speaks. I swallow. "What do you mean?"

Mom straightens. "However you can. I just *need* him gone." Those jeweled eyes glint. "Can you do this for me?"

She's taken two steps forward, and I want to ask why, how, but don't need to. It doesn't matter. If her reasons are different from my own, so what? He'll still be gone. All I can say is, "When?"

A hint of a smile crosses her cheek, and it's as if she's zipped up the body bag. "You have some time together in a few days. A lot could happen then. Could go wrong."

I nod and run my tongue along my bottom teeth. "True." I won't say any more.

She eases back, resting her hands on her hips and sniffs the air. "You smell that? It just sprayed again."

"You doing anything for Christmas?" Rob might as well be speaking to the air in front of us.

"The fuck?"

He laughs. "Sorry. I just needed to say something. You know, after everything."

I do, but it's still a fucked-up question. "How about, 'Thanks for keeping Amy from getting us killed'?"

Rob frowns and tucks into himself. "You know she didn't mean to."

I shake my head because I don't know what the fuck I know anymore. "Anyway, I doubt she'll remember."

"Yeah." Rob steps from the sidewalk and we cross the street. "Shit musta gone down with Char or something for her to be like that."

He's right, Amy can handle her liquor. "Char isn't her problem though."

"She is until something changes."

Fuck, why's he have to say shit like that, always taking the high road. "You going to support them with all your money from training?"

Rob laughs. "Don't think so, but I might kick 'em a little of what I get from this deal."

Fuck, he's pathetic. Or nice. I can't tell the difference anymore. Damn that's sad. "Aren't you two finished? After that shit, has to be the last straw."

Rob nods but doesn't say anything.

"The fuck, man? That's why Big O is hooking you up, so you can move on." Even as I say it, I know I shouldn't have. I can't keep lying.

"Yeah, but still . . ."

I don't let him finish. "Fuck, never mind what I said. Shit. I need to tell you about what Cam said. About the shit I'm in for tonight."

Rob closes his mouth and I tell him. He takes it well, the punch that I know it is, and sighs. "I never thought of it that way. Like we got no choice. We're fucking trapped, huh?"

I nod. "Yeah."

"And who the fuck is Johnny B?"

"This shit's way bigger than just the bikers."

Rob closes his eyes. "All I wanted was a fucking chance. Why can't I have that?"

I feel his pain, through and through. But I don't have an answer that will take it away. "I don't know. But shit, let's just see how it all plays out. Who knows what could happen?" I realize that's one hell of a loaded statement considering what Mom just asked, but maybe, just maybe there is a way out of this.

"Right, right."

Rob's words are as empty as I feel. We walk on to the gym without another word.

"Hey, it's the prodigal son."

I wish I weren't standing behind Rob, because I'd like to see how wide he's smiling. Coach walks to him and wraps him up in a hug. He pats Rob's back and then holds him at arm's length.

"Good to see you again. All we've had is your protégé." Coach Dan juts his chin toward me. "And, you know, he pales in comparison."

Rob's ears flush red.

"Aww, Coach, you're gonna make him cry." Amir crosses the room and pounds fists with Rob. "Long time, man."

"Yeah, shit's been crazy." Rob finally speaks and ducks his head.

"Crazy's how we live. You know?" Phil walks over and he clasps Rob as Coach did. Then the entire room welcomes Rob back and he goes to each. I slide off my shoes and join Phil and Amir on the mat.

"So what's the deal? How'd you get him back?" Phil arches his back and pins his head to his shoulder blades.

"Some shit's changed, so . . ." I don't know how else to explain without giving the details.

Amir and Phil nod, though. They get it. It's nice to have that.

We roll and Rob's panting about halfway through. By the end he's whipped and lying in a pool of sweat, but he smiles up at me. "Thanks, Tone."

"For kicking your ass?" I help him up.

"For getting me back."

"It's what you needed."

He nods, looks around the gym and appears as if he's seeing it for the first time.

"Rob, Tony, nice work." Coach Dan walks over while the rest are packing up.

"Thanks, Coach," we say in unison.

He claps our shoulders. "Now don't be strangers, especially you." He leans close to Rob. "We've got some work to do."

Rob nods and shoots me a look. It's painful to see because I know what he's thinking: *What's the point?* Wish I knew.

"Yo, is that Dave's car?" Amir asks the room and everyone crowds the window, including Coach. My mind wipes clean, because if he's right, I'm fucked. Rob shoots me another look and we join the rest.

Sure enough, Dave's black Mustang is parked across the street. "That little dick motherfucker." Amir charges out the door. We all follow, but Coach catches him and grabs his arm. He says something and Amir nods. Then Coach Dan enters the street.

We gather on the sidewalk and steam billows up from our heads. Coach walks with his shoulders pinned, and Dave rolls down the window. Music spills out. "Well, well, Military Dan, himself."

Coach continues to Dave's car as if he hasn't heard the insult and tilts his body so that he is level with Dave's face.

Dave's laughter punctuates the air and Dan stiffens. He looks over his shoulder, toward us and my heart drops. Next to me, Rob shifts his weight from foot to foot. His eyes are bugging. Coach turns back to Dave, says something, and all I can see is the edge of Dave's head nodding. He's either confirming what Coach is saying or agreeing with his orders. Based on Dave, I'm sure it's the first. Dan walks away from the car and doesn't take his eyes off me the entire time he crosses the street.

He hits the sidewalk, and the crew shoots questions. "What's up Coach?"

"You want us to go fuck 'em up?"

I swallow and prepare to take the beating.

Coach stands before me, and as much as I want to look him in the eye, I can't. Even now, when I know what's coming, I pussy out.

"Do you want to tell me what's going on, Tony? Or do you want me to repeat what Dave just said?"

I stare at the ground and watch Rob's feet turn inward, like a child's.

"Okay, since you won't talk . . ." Coach takes a deep breath. "Gentlemen, apparently Dave is here for Tony." The statement hangs in the air and I feel the guys edge toward me. Someone murmurs, "What?"

"It seems as if they are *working* together. I'm not positive what that means, but I'm not stupid and can draw my own conclusions based on what I know of Dave."

Rob twists a toe. Fuck, I hope he's not going to say shit. So far, he's in the clear. I'll keep it that way. No need for us to both get thrown under the bus.

"We are, Coach. Dave isn't lying." I look from him to the guys. "I need the money, that's all. Not like he and I are boys." I catch Amir's eye and he winces before looking away. Coach's face is stone, completely unreadable. He uncrosses his arms from his chest.

"So, you're dealing? That's how you decided to make money? Not by getting a job, doing something honest? You've got mechanic skills! Come on, Tony!" Coach's face is a scowl.

"You don't understand. It's not like I could do that. Not with my mom and her boyfriend and their shit."

Coach waves a dismissive hand in my face. "I don't want to hear your excuses. Here I thought you were learning something from me. This place isn't just about rolling and striking. It's about pride." Coach looks up at the sky and the sadness I feel is as black. "This is how you repay me?"

My faces flushes. I'm pissed at him for not understanding, and embarrassed at getting called out in front of everyone. But mostly I'm angry because this isn't my fucking fault. Dave shouldn't have showed up. And everything I said, those aren't fucking excuses. I'd like to see Coach do any better with my piece of shit life. Who the fuck is he to say shit about what I know? Pride? I can't afford any. "I never asked you for anything."

Coach Dan's face hardens. "No, you didn't. Ostrander and Rob did." He looks over at Rob and so do I. He's on the verge of spilling, I can see it. He knows now that Dave didn't leak his name, just mine, but he knows that I could drop him in this hole with me. And his pride would make him jump before I got the chance. But I'm not like that. "You're right, Coach."

"So this is how you repay a friend, by selling drugs with the only kid I ever threw out of my gym?"

I can't argue. "Yes."

The guys murmur, but some words are clear. "Muthafucka." "Take his ass out."

Coach sighs. "There's only one option then, Tony." He pauses, looks back at Dave's car. "And I'm afraid I know what you're going to decide." He frowns but I say nothing.

"Your choice, us or Dave. Because now that I know what you're up to, I can't trust you unless you sever ties with him."

I knew he was going to make this request, and I don't blame him. Fuck, I don't blame any of the crew for wanting to beat my ass. I'm not some MMA fighter, and not some kid who goes off to college.

I look at those who will meet my eyes and say, "I'm sorry. This isn't how I wanted it to go." I swallow and look at Rob. "I'm out." I step around the group and into the street. No one tries to stop me. No one even yells my name.

Dave grins. "'Bout fucking time."

I get in and refuse to look over, and I don't look back once we've driven away.

20

Johnny B's isn't visible from the road, and Dave has to slow to a crawl to find the entrance. We turn down the driveway that's carved through the trees, and it feels like we're being swallowed. I squeeze the door handle, but the trees end and the property comes into view. The house is enormous, set on top of a hill out in the middle of farm country. "Damn."

"Exactly," Dave says, "this place is the *tits*."

He parks and I look at the cars next to us: Mercedes and a Jag. Unreal.

Dave's spraying on cologne. "Want some?"

I know I probably reek, but masking the smell isn't going make me any more appealing. But who the fuck do I need to be attractive for? "Why the fuck you need that?"

"We do our job and then party." He juts his chin toward the house and through the floor to ceiling windows are men in suits and women wearing next to nothing. A few don't even have tops on. One guy grabs a woman around the arm and pulls her close. He speaks into her ear and she shakes her head, tries to pull her arm back, but he looks at it and laughs. He lets go, but as she turns, he smacks her on the ass.

And then it clicks. This is the home of Johnny B, the Front's supplier. The same man who Charity was turned over to by her father. I'm about to walk into a whorehouse.

Dave tosses his cologne into the middle console and pops his collar. "Stay with the ugly chicks, they won't say no." He reaches back and opens the compartment in his trunk, pulls out a black bag and says, "Not like they have a choice."

It takes every shred of willpower I possess to join him, because I feel lower than I ever have. Living in the trailer sucks. Having my mom and no father blows. Losing my chance at a scholarship and getting tossed from the gym are terrible. But if I go with Dave, I'm one of them, a fucking dirt-bag dealer, white trash to the bone. If I held any shred of doubt, this will tear it away. Dave crosses the car and I watch him. Fuck, I wish the truth hurt more because it might help, might give me a way out. But another fact remains: I've got nothing to lose.

I step out and follow Dave.

We cross to the front door and Dave turns to me. "Actually, your gym gear is good. It helps. You need to look as bad-ass as you can. Stare down every fucker you see, just not Johnny. You represent the Agnostics now."

A butler opens the door and takes Dave's coat, but Dave tells him he's keeping the bag. The butler just frowns at me. People swivel to get a look and I immediately look at the floor, embarrassed by my appearance. It was one thing to see it all from outside, but up close and personal, I look downright homeless by comparison. How's that bad-ass?

"Do your fucking job, Antioch."

We move toward a bar in the corner and I pin back my shoulders, force myself to stare down every man that looks my way. A few begin to smile, but as I draw closer their lips pull into lines. They acknowledge Dave with a head nod and look away from me. Feels pretty fucking powerful.

"What you drinking, Dave?" The bartender grabs a glass and waits.

"Vodka tonic."

"All right. And for you, sir?"

It takes me a second to realize he's calling me *Sir*, but I manage to say, "The same."

The bartender nods, makes the drinks, and hands them over. Dave stuffs a twenty into his tip jar. I bite the straw in my drink and take in the crowd.

"Some hot ass here, huh?"

I can't disagree with him. The women are hot, but I can't shake loose what they really are. And I can't fathom Charity ever doing this. I look away and see Christmas decorations. How the fuck did I miss them on the way in? White lights and ribbons are draped along the bar and ceiling. Trees are propped in each corner, decorated in gold and white. It's like I'm standing in the pages of one of those magazines, except, of course, for the middle-aged men and prostitutes. Everyone's talking and touching and looking toward the stairs.

"Which one's Johnny?"

Dave takes a long swallow. "He likes to stay upstairs."

I go to ask why, but see that Dave is staring at a guy who hasn't moved from the foot of the stairs. He touches his watch and then thrusts a thumb over his shoulder. Dave smiles. "Right on time." He turns to me and again his eyes are hard. "Remember you are supposed to be my protection, so even though I could snap you with one fucking hand, you need to be one tough motherfucker."

I should just tell him to go fuck himself and let him do his business with Johnny B alone. But he'd either break me like he just said he could or leave me here and I'd have to walk home. Home. There's nothing there, either. All right, let's see how tough I can be.

I feel the heft of the glass in my hand, see all the twinkling lights and smell the intoxication of the room. I hate these people. I hate this situation. I hate Dave and I hate myself. I'm ready. I down my drink, hold out my glass and slam it to the floor.

The glass shatters on impact and causes the room to stop and look. I shake the shards off the bottom of my pants and Dave nods.

"That's what I'm talkin' 'bout."

We turn and the same guy from the stairs is moving toward us, looking between me and the glass. He wants answers or he'll bust my head. I know the look. I step to the right, to clear space and watch his body. If I time it, he'll be plating his right foot at the moment we connect. One, two, three . . . I jam my knee into his crotch and press him away from me with one hand on his neck and the other his ribs. He topples and groans. I expect someone else to take his place, but no one comes after me. Dave and I hit the stairs and my body pumps with adrenaline.

"Nice work," Dave mumbles out of the side of his mouth, and we ascend the stairs. I don't look back. What's the point?

The second floor is a series of hallways, and Dave directs me to the right. At the end of the hall stands another guy outside a door. The strap around his chest means one thing, and my heart flutters. Maybe this is why no one came after me; Dave is leading me to him. The guy reaches up, balls his fist, and knocks on the door to his right. He then touches his ear. "Go on in."

I hold my breath as I walk past and we enter an enormous office, filled with leather couches, a stone fireplace, and a huge wooden desk. Behind it sits one grizzled-looking motherfucker.

"Welcome, boys. Have a seat." Johnny B's voice is charred, like he's either smoked for a lifetime or someone tried to take out his throat. I look for the scar as I sit. He watchers us both, his eyes dancing beneath his short-cropped hair and ice-blue eyes. They settle on me. "So you're the new muscle?"

I open my mouth to answer, but cannot think of what to say, so just shrug.

Johnny B laughs, and it sounds like wood being sanded. "Nice choice, Dave. He looks like fucking Pinocchio but took out Heinrich without missing a beat."

How the fuck does he know that? But then I see the set of monitors behind him.

"I know what I'm doin'." Dave's voice is oiled and confident. It's somehow settling.

"You certainly do." Johnny smiles. "As does the rest of your organization. Word is that you're hitting record numbers this year."

"A lot of new people have found us and our charitable work. Times are hard, so we're glad to be there for them." Dave swirls the contents of his glass.

The vodka has already shot to my head. So maybe it's that, or maybe it's the tension in the room, but whichever it is, I have no fucking clue what they're talking about.

"We have one last push as the new year approaches." Dave no longer sounds like the douche he always is. He's all business, but controlled, calm. I wonder which one is the real him? Maybe neither.

"And that's all lined up?" Johnny B sits forward.

"All that's left is for me to pick up the care packages."

"Charity work is so rewarding."

My head swims again, but based on the way their faces are pulled tight, like at any moment they might slip and say the wrong thing, I understand that this must be code. "It's what keeps us going. Do you need any help with the gift baskets?"

"We've got that covered. Come, see." Johnny B stands and crosses to the windows behind his desk. As he does, Dave stands and shoots me a look and juts his chin toward the bag. I stand and position myself so I can see the door, the bag, and through the window. I'm wobbly on my feet, though. Johnny B waves over his shoulder and Dave joins him.

"The Mustang, right?" Johnny B points out the window and in the distance Dave's car is visible.

"Yeah." Dave's voice wavers. I bet he doesn't know what the fuck's going on. Shit. I look around for another door out of here.

Johnny B turns to Dave. "Something wrong?"

"No. I just don't understand."

"Watch." As he speaks two men emerge from the shadow, each carrying a box twice the size of what I held, and move to the back of Dave's car.

"It's locked." Again, Dave's voice is hollow.

Johnny B chuckles.

One of the men sets down his box, fishes in his pocket, and pulls something out. He puts it against the lock, twists, and the trunk pops open. The two then deposit their boxes into the trunk and walk away.

"And now you have the care packages." Johnny B grins, but Dave continues to stare ahead, out the window. Johnny B looks at me, and I do my best to keep my face expressionless. "Something up, Dave? Do you need to see the packages to ensure the order?"

Dave returns from wherever he was and smiles. "No,

that's not necessary. You know our motto."

Johnny B smiles a full-toothed grin, now, slaps Dave's back, and returns to his desk. "I do. But as you know, I only believe in half of it."

Dave returns to his seat and I take my own. My head's still drifting, but I'm getting used to it. Dave picks up the bag and lays it on the desk. "You don't have to agree, so long as we're both happy." He unzips the bag to reveal stacks of cash.

Johnny B runs a hand through and mutters as he touches each stack. He tilts his head. "Isn't there a bit more than we agreed?"

Dave smiles. "And?"

Johnny stares for a long moment. "*And*, why is that?"

My skin feels pinpricked. If this goes wrong, I'm grabbing the poker by the fireplace. Dave can fend for himself.

"Consider it an early Christmas gift," Dave says.

Johnny B gets up, walks around his desk, and Dave stands. I watch his body. He's ready for an attack, but Johnny's loose. He reaches out and pulls Dave into him. They embrace, but when they release, Johnny B keeps a hand around Dave's neck. "Remember, I've got a little something for you, too." Dave lowers his head and Johnny continues. "I remember what you liked the last time. You'll have to give me your impression, brand-new as she is."

Dave's smile widens and the devilish shine I'm so familiar with returns to his eyes. "Will do."

Johnny B looks at me. "Don't worry, Pinocchio, I won't leave you out." He looks me over, head to toe. "Maybe you'd like two. Could tell them some lies."

Dave and Johnny B explode with laughter and I shake my head. I fully understand him but don't want to. He can keep his gifts.

"Come." Johnny waves us along and Dave follows, no longer checking if I'm performing my duties. We walk down the hall and turn into the other at the top of the stairs. A couple of the men from the party are on their way up, each with a girl on his arm. Another is on his way down, smiling. Johnny B stops to meet the men.

"Gentlemen, so glad you could make it." He looks at the girls, and his eyes go hard. "I trust that you've got what you've come for."

The men laugh and one answers, "Almost."

Johnny B smiles and pats their backs. "You will." The couples move on and each goes into a separate room down the hall. I look behind me, and the thug from the door has taken position behind us. I never saw him move. Some muscle I am.

"Dave, you will find your present through the last door on the right. I promise not to watch."

Dave shrugs. "Don't matter to me." He sounds more like himself, and the change makes my skin crawl.

"Enjoy."

Dave heads for the door like a dog after a rabbit. He doesn't pause before going in, doesn't even knock. The door clicks shut and Johnny B turns to me. My head drifts even worse than before. Char was in one of these rooms.

"I don't know your taste, but considering who you're with, I think I have an idea." He smiles and I want to punch him so hard that he chokes on my fist. But I pin back my shoulders to look the part. "Let's have you take the room next to Dave. Hopefully you'll have as good a time as he will." Johnny B extends his hand but does not touch me, which I'm grateful for, because I don't know if I could have controlled myself. I nod and walk to the door, place my hand on the handle, and hear a rustling from within. I can also hear Dave's muffled voice. I swallow and understand just how far down I've gone. The doorknob spins and I enter the room.

A lamp in the far corner is the only light in the room, but the girl on the bed is visible. She stands and wobbles on high heels to me.

"I'm Violet." She extends her hand and I take it. Her skin is cold and I feel a tremor just under the surface. My throat knots, but she asks, "Would you like to sit down?"

I would. I'd like to sit and get my head together. Or sit and fall asleep and wake up and have never been here. My head's a mess with the million thoughts swimming through and I might spew that drink. I fall onto the bed without answering.

Through the wall I hear Dave. "Yeah! There we go!"

I cross my arms over my ears. Just like at home. Violet sits next to me. "You feelin' okay?" I roll over and she slides back. "You gonna hurl?"

I laugh. I don't know why, but something about her voice, how normal it sounds in this completely fucked-up situation is hilarious. I let go of my temples. "No, I'm not going to hurl."

She moves closer to me and opens the little silk robe she's wearing. Underneath, she's naked and her tits are perky and full. Her skin's soft and smooth and there's not a hair to be found on her pussy. I stare and my cock rises. But in the same moment I hear a hard slap through the wall, followed by Dave's voice, "Yeah, that's how you like it, right bitch?"

My face drifts from Violet to the wall and burns.

"Is that what you want?" Her voice is like a child's, and I can't bear to look at her. All I can see is home. Cameron and my mother, and all of the rest of the men who beat her. And Charity the way we found her that night. I drop my head and shake it.

"No, that's not what I want."

Violet's breath catches and a small, relieved sigh emerges. I feel her warmth next to me and can smell her perfume and know if I wanted to I could just turn and have her. She is a thousand times hotter than any girl who's given me some play, but I don't want her. Not like this. I am ashamed for her, and for who I have become.

I look up and her lips part in anticipation.

"Did you know Charity?"

Her expression stays excited, but now searches my face, maybe wondering if I'm joking. She pushes back from me. "Are you talkin' 'bout the Charity who was here?"

I nod and don't take my eyes off hers. She knows.

Violet turns. "Well, yeah, but only a little. She was Johnny's, not like us. He kept her."

The vision of Johnny B and Charity lying on a bed together clouds my vision. Was he grooming her to be one of these girls? Or was she a pet for him? My revulsion deepens.

Another slap comes through the wall and Violet and I look toward it. "You know the guy in there?"

I nod and lick my lips, which are dry and cracked. "Unfortunately."

"So why you wanna know about Charity?"

"It's hard to explain, but I know her and well . . . she's different now."

Violet sighs. "Of course she is. Who wouldn't be?" She pauses for a moment, and I'm glad the silence isn't filled with anything from the other side of the wall. "You don't sound into this, so why you here, anyway?"

I close my eyes and lean back. I would love nothing more than to unburden myself on this girl, just release all that I'm holding in, but I'm not stupid. She doesn't feel sorry for me;

she's just working an angle. Possibly so she can tell Johnny B a story about why we aren't fucking, since I'm sure he's watching. I don't blame her.

A girl's scream peals, followed by Dave's voice. "Yeah! Let me hear that again!" The girl obliges, and I open my eyes.

Violet inches closer. "It's all right, she's used to it. We all are." She runs a hand around my ear and along my jaw. Her words tickle, but I'm not soothed. I'm lying here in my sweat-dried gear, smelling like fuck, slightly drunk, and looking deranged. And this girl doesn't give a shit about any of that, just wants to get paid. Fuck that. I stand and she topples behind me.

There's more yelling next door.

I look from the wall to Violet. She's on her side, watching me like I'm playing some game she hasn't quite figured out. "I'm not down with this."

She sits up. "I can drown him out. I've got music." She goes to stand, but I move in front of her.

"No, just stay where you are."

She looks at my crotch. "Oh, so that's what you want." Her hands move to my zipper, and I swat them away. "No."

"Here it comes, bitch. Oh yeah."

I put a hand to Violet's lips to silence her, and we both listen to Dave finish.

"Is that what gets you off?"

I look at her and can't kept help but wonder how many fucked-up scenarios she's fulfilled. I want out of this room. "No, I'm just not feeling all right."

She sighs. "Fine, but I don't get paid if we don't do nuthin'."

"I'll lie, tell Johnny B that's what I wanted."

She pouts but nods.

I take a step toward the door and listen. I'm not walking

out until after Dave has left. No way I can deal with seeing him right after.

"You waitin' till he leaves?"

"Yeah."

Violet laughs. "Don't want him to think you weren't a stud, huh?"

"Something like that."

I watch the door and keep my ears open and feel Violet stand. "Charity was with Johnny."

"You said that." I turn to her.

Her face is twisted, and she's secured her robe. "I know, but Johnny's a sick fuck. I should know." She looks away. "Just thought you'd like to. Seems like you care. It's not her fault, however she is now. Whatever he did."

The door opens in the next room and then slams shut. Violet continues. "He's got some weird games, and he likes his girls to be tooted up so they'll play along."

I want to ask her to be specific, but in the same instant, don't.

"Good luck." Violet smiles, and she really is a beautiful girl. "Huh, I never got your name."

I open my mouth but hesitate. Should I be honest? Is this another angle? "Tony. I'm Tony. Johnny B's calling me Pinocchio."

Violet laughs. "Well, your nose didn't grow, so I guess I can believe you."

I smile and turn back to the door. If I could save her, I would. If I could have saved Charity, I would. Fuck, if I *can* save my mother, I will. But as of right now, I'm not even sure I can save myself. I turn the handle and walk into the hall.

It's empty but filled with the sound of muffled sex and the noise of the party below. The guard is back at the door and nods to me before I descend the stairs.

Dave's at the bar, drinking another vodka tonic, a smile plastered all the way to his neck. "There you are! Damn, son, you outlasted me." He grabs me and laughs and then turns to the bartender. "Another."

I feel like cracking him upside the head with a bottle, but instead tell myself to go dead inside. It's the only way through.

Soon I have a drink in hand and we clink glasses. "To Johnny B." Dave gulps and I take a long swallow. The crowd has thinned and is now mostly made up of bored-looking girls and too drunk men wrapped up in their own stories. I down the rest of my drink.

"Let's go. You don't want to get pulled over with the care packages."

He laughs. "You got it, Tone. Truly on top of it, son."

Dave's stopped asking about how I scored, what position I used, how hot the chick was. He's stopped telling me all the minute details of what he did with Indigo. Now we're just driving in silence, him concentrating on the road, and me, everything else beyond.

The lights to the park blossom and Dave pulls in. He parks near my trailer and reaches into a section of his door, pulls out a stack of cash. "Good work, Antioch." I take the money and stick it inside my waistband. "You ain't gonna count it."

I give him as hard a look as I can. "I trust you."

He recoils, but only slightly. "Right."

I get out and close my door before he can say any more. Dave pulls away and even though it's twenty degrees and I'm filthy and want nothing more than a hot shower, I sit on my bottom step and just breathe.

I've got two more days to figure out just what the fuck I need to do. Two days before the deal and I know I should be scared, but I'm not. It's not the alcohol or exhaustion dulling the edges, either. I know, just know that there's no point in being afraid. If something goes wrong, if the deal turns ugly, if whatever I decide with Cameron doesn't work, what have I lost? Nothing. Can't lose anything when you've got nothing.

But if it works, if I can come out the other side of this free, at least from them, well . . . I laugh and it echoes off the trailers. I try to hold it in, but can't. I laugh until I cry. And then just cry.

21

I head out the door and into the dark. I haven't been able to sleep for the past two nights, in spite of my exhaustion. There's just too much to sift through, but in the end it's pointless. I feel the same as I did when I got home from Johnny B's, empty.

I pull up my hoodie and it feels too thin for this cold, but I'll stand at the bus stop and Rob will roll up and who the fuck knows? We haven't spoken about the other night. I don't know if I can.

Rob walks up and looks everywhere but at me. Then he does and seems like he's about to cry. "Tone, we need to talk."

"Yeah? I was just thinking the same. What's up?"

He opens his mouth but the brakes on the bus squeal and Hack-Face opens the door. I watch Rob and it's obvious he's relieved. That's fine. I understand. So I hop on and grab a seat in the middle and bury my head into the notch between the window and seat. Whatever he has to say will wait. It's not like it will change anything. My eyes drift shut as the bus chugs on.

I slide into my seat in Lance's class and prop my head on my arm for the movie. He's got *Gladiator* locked and loaded, the

DVD paused and screen filled with the opening credits. A newspaper is spread on his desk. His coffee mug is filled. And he looks hungover.

The movie rolls and I grow increasingly uncomfortable with every fight scene. Nothing in real life ever goes down so smoothly. I was already on edge but now I can't stop thinking about whatever I'm going to walk into tonight. The bell rings and I head to the bathroom.

Cold water on my face helps. I stay close to the sink and cup my hands and bathe my eyes. Kids look at me, open their mouths to say something, but I stop each with a hard-ass look. It's not even difficult. In fact, they look so fucking scared that I bet I could climb into this sink naked and no one would say a fucking word.

I splash again and rub my eyes.

"'Sup, Tone? Water busted at your house?"

I glare at Dave.

"Fuck, look at you, pumped already." He steps to a urinal and unzips. "Better maintain, though; it's gonna be a long night."

I stare into the sink, watch the water spin down the drain. "Where we getting started?" My voice sounds as lifeless as my mother's.

"Chaz's. Be there around 9:00."

I dry my face. Dave zips up and crosses to the sink.

"Man, I could go back to Johnny B's right now. That girl, Indigo, I can't get her outta my head. You know?"

I grunt.

"Fuck, man, you really are in a zone. Can't even talk to you about pussy." Dave dries his hands and then puts an arm around my shoulder. "Fucking glad we got you, Antioch. I think I was wrong about you. You're one bad-ass motherfucker." Dave lets go and leaves.

I don't bother to look at myself in the mirror to see what he sees, because he doesn't know the first thing about me. There was a time when a compliment might have made me all excited, like with Coach Dan. But that shit's over. Dave thinks I'm amped because of the deal. Sure, that's part of it, but not in the way he thinks.

The bell rings and I'm off to clean and it will blow. Kids are eating candy canes and chocolates and tossing the wrappers on the ground, shredding open presents and leaving the paper, ribbon, and bows for someone else to clean up.

I turn into the janitors' office, and Mr. Franks is wearing a Santa hat. He is the most psychotic Santa I've ever seen.

"Mr. Antioch, Merry Christmas." He's leaning against the Zamboni machine they use to buff the floors. I try to respond, but it just feels like too much effort. He smiles, though and leans more of his weight against the machine. I grab a sweeper. "That won't be necessary."

I set the broom back.

"Once again, Mr. Ostrander would like to see you."

Fuck, I'd rather clean up all the goddamn wrapping paper and candy wrappers in the entire fucking school with only my hands than talk with Big O. I know what he wants.

"It's all right, Tony. I'm sure you'll screw up and we'll end up spending more time together." He laughs and his face reddens and if I weren't so fucked up right now I'd say something, bust his balls about looking like a juiced mall Santa, but I simply can't. Besides, he'd probably take it as a compliment. I turn and walk out, head down the hall to Big O's.

His secretary points to his office when I walk in. She's got Christmas music pumping out of her computer, but by the look on her face, it isn't doing much to elevate her mood. I walk into the big man's and he looks up from a stack of papers.

"Have a seat, Tony." I do and Big O turns to his computer, clicks the mouse a few times and then returns to me. "So, do you know why you're here?"

I nod. It's because of Amy, and I don't need to say it.

"So you can explain, right?" I nod again and his face darkens. "Let's see." He turns his monitor toward me and he's paused the surveillance video on the screen. It's so much like Johnny B's that my heart races and I have to shift in my seat. Amy and I are in still frame, and I know as soon as he presses play, she's going down.

The kick is solid and I'm sure Coach Dan would be proud, under different circumstances. Or, would have been. Amy falls like a clubbed seal and I look prepared to drop her ass again if she gets back up. Big O stops the footage and turns to me. He links his fingers, as if praying and watches my face. I don't look away, and up close to him I notice how dark the bags are beneath his eyes, as well as the small white scars around the corners of his mouth and eyebrows, and on his cheeks. No shit? He's been through it.

"She was drunk." The words tumble out of me.

"I know. And you weren't."

I look away. "You don't understand."

"No, I don't, so please enlighten me."

The fuck do I say? She was spilling about our deal, so she deserved it? That's gonna help. "I can't."

"Excuse me?"

I look up and his face is crawling with confusion. He's got no clue if I'm being honest or just being the trash fuck I always am. Really, it's the same. "She was . . . Amy was just a mess and talking shit—I mean smack, and, well, she needed to stop." It sounds terrible, even to me.

"What was she saying?" Big O's voice has dropped to

that comforting level he likes to use to trick you. I'm not falling for it.

"Nothing."

"Nothing? You just said she was talking 'smack.' That's not nothing, so what was it?"

I shake my head. No. I can't. I won't.

Big O leans back in his chair and gives me a moment to consider, but I'm not budging. "Who are you protecting? I've heard what the other kids said she was talking about. A couple showed it to me on their phones. Is this about Rob?"

I grab the escape. "Kinda."

Big O's face softens. "Thought so. That I can understand, but there's more." His face goes cold again. "What else?"

Motherfucker, he's good. "That's it."

He stares at me, fingertips planted beneath his nose, thinking. "You're lying."

I shrug.

"Don't, Tony. Don't do this. I know where you're headed. Remember I told you I helped someone before? Well, that was Mr. Franks."

This brings me up short. I stare at Big O and try to comprehend, but can't.

"He was in your same position. Fighting, bad home. We lost touch after I went to college. But once I got set up here, I found him. He needed the help, too." Big O pauses. "I wish I could have done more. The life he has isn't what he deserves. You understand?"

I nod, but I'm not Franks.

"I know Amy was talking about Jensen, and don't think for one second that I don't know what that means."

I'm shocked by his knowledge and try to keep my face smooth, but he must see something, because his eyebrows lift.

"Tell me you're not dealing."

I bite my tongue.

His eyes narrow. "Tell me you're not messed up with Dave and that gang."

I keep eye contact and grind my back teeth.

"Tell me, Tony, or you can forget about that scholarship. You can end up worse than you are now."

I bite my tongue and taste blood. My eyes water, but I swallow and squint.

"Don't. Don't do this, Tony." Big O's standing now.

I wipe my eyes on my sleeve and then stand as well.

Big O's on fire, face jumping, eyes popped. He's a grown-up version of me, trying to save whatever he can. Well, not this time. I'm too far gone. I step into the main office.

"Antioch!"

The secretary doesn't look up at his bellow, just keeps typing away, and like her, I pass on by as if none of this is about me.

I thought I was amped before, but now I could rip some-one's fucking face off. Who the fuck does Big O think he is? Pulling the scholarship card? That was my last fucking crumb, the only shred of hope I had, even though it was ridiculous. Even though Cam said what he did. For the past few days I've been thinking that maybe Big O could still make it happen. I'd have to get Cam out of the way, and that's monumental on its own. But I was willing to try. But now? What's the point? What will I gain? Absolutely. Fucking. Nothing.

I head toward the main lobby, and Rob juts his chin for me to come over. Like I need this now? His eyes are hard. "Tone, we need to talk."

I lean against the wall, Big O's words echoing. Rob really means that I need to listen, but I've done all of that I can.

"Really? Right fucking now? Can't it wait until tonight?"

Rob shakes his head. "Tone, I'm out."

My head throbs and I push off the wall. "What? You're what? *Out?* You can't get out."

Rob stares me down. "You heard me. I'm not doing it. I'm not going tonight." He takes a deep breath. "They can't make me."

I laugh, because he's got to be kidding, but he doesn't smile.

"They can. Or they'll make you pay. Rob, they'll fucking kill you."

He purses his lips. "No they won't. That's bullshit."

My head is ready to burst. Does this asshole really believe what he's saying? "Bullshit or not, you're fucking going. I need your fucking help!"

"No, you don't. You need to step out, Tone. Get away."

My throat tickles with laughter. "Where am I gonna go? I can't hide out at home, or at the gym, like you. Lost that fucking chance. Remember?"

He winces. "What did you want me to do? Tell Coach I'm in, too? He won't let me get mentored if I'm dealing. Then what do I do?"

"I don't know? Same shit as me. Nothing."

Kids around us are watching, probably waiting for us to throw down.

"*Nuthin'?* You've got your scholarship, you're fine. So listen to me."

Another layer of anger ignites and burns inside. "Fuck you, Rob! Don't you remember what I said about Cam?"

His eyes pop. "So what? That's just Cam talking shit like always. What's your deal?"

"That scholarship was a fucking *possibility*." I breathe to steady myself and get the words right. "It's gone now. Big O took it away." I look Rob square in the eye. "Because I kept my fucking mouth shut, again. To protect myself, yeah, but also to protect you. And because of that I lost my chance, Rob."

He opens his mouth, but nothing comes out.

"Exactly. That's all you do, watch out for your own ass. Don't even fucking think for a second about anyone else." I press close to him and kids stop and watch. "It's the same shit with Amy. You only fucking cared about how that shit was going to fuck you up. Same shit with Jensen. You haven't even asked what the fuck I went through with him the other night. And now?" I run my tongue along my teeth. "What the fuck do you think's going to happen to me when you don't show? Don't you think they'll want to know what's up? Who the fuck do you think they're going to turn to?"

"Just lie. Or tell 'em I'm at the gym. Let them swing by there, see how the crew responds."

His voice is like a little boy's and I'm repulsed. I shove him hard and he reels back. "The fuck's wrong with you? *Lie?* They'll know. Don't you remember who these mother-fuckers are?"

Rob's eyes draw down to beads. Good. Let 'em swing. The way I feel I may just take his ass out. But he stays in place, just staring.

"*Swing by the gym?* You really want to do that to Coach and Amir and Phil and everybody else?"

He looks away.

"They've been by once with that deer. Or did you forget? Don't you remember how much that fucked up Coach? Least I had the balls to take the hit and save them this shit."

Kids press in and I know soon enough Big O will be here, and I'm too hot to handle his scene. I have to get out. Plain and simple. Fuck my douche teachers. Fuck Vo-Tec and Greyson. Fuck my future. "I always think of myself as a pussy because I never stand up for my mom, or for myself." Rob tilts his head but doesn't look at me. "But now that I think of it, you're a pussy, too. I thought you were tough, but you're not. You're the same as me, hiding out when the shit hits the fan."

Rob looks up now, and his face is one hundred percent disgust.

"Good luck. You'll need it." I toss open the door, not caring that I've got nowhere to go. I'm out. All the shit I've been holding on to is gone and I just need to get through tonight. And even if I don't, not like it fucking matters.

22

Fuck, fuck, fuck. It's too cold to stay outside without a coat, so I head home. Not that I want to.

Mom's watching TV and jumps when I come in. "What's wrong?" She's wearing her pajamas still, an oversized sweatshirt, and stained sweats. It's 12:30.

I kick off my shoes. "I feel like shit."

"Oh." She hovers at the threshold, doesn't even notice that I'm shivering.

"I need to go to sleep." I move past her.

"Tony?"

I don't want to turn around, but her voice is just so pathetic. "What?"

"Tonight? Still?" She points toward her room and as cold and tired and confused as I am, I look in. Cameron's snoring away. Must be his way of prepping: get a piece, sleep, and then go score.

I look at her and she looks ancient, far older than thirty-eight. Nothing in her life has helped her stay young. Including me. Thank God she never got pregnant again. Well, at least didn't have any more kids. Maybe taking out Cam will help. Doubt it, though. I'll probably succeed in getting myself killed. Least I won't have to work so fucking hard for nothing to show. "Tonight."

She smiles. It's been a while. My insides roil, again.

Somehow I fell asleep. I don't know how with the way my mind was racing, but I managed to and now feel more calm. It's dark outside though, so I've got only a little time left, and still no plan. I guess I'll just take him out when he's not looking. Maybe get one of the Hungarians to fuck him up. But how? Fuck, I just have to see how this shit plays out. Maybe the bikers are using him. Maybe I can just get one of them to do it. Shit, what the fuck am I thinking? They might just be planning on doing the same to me.

I slide my feet to the floor and sit up. The TV's loud as fuck down the hall, so Cam must be up. Smells like something's cooking, which is good. I haven't eaten all day. I rub my face and then let my hands drop. My left touches down on my mattress. My mattress. With no sheet. Huh? I look down. The sheet's been pulled back. No. No, fuck no.

I scramble and lift the mattress and it's gone. My money's gone. I check the other corners, nothing. I look under the bed and around my closet. My room's too clean for it to be lost. It's gone and I know who took it.

I crack through my accordion door and my mom's standing at the stove, burgers frying in a pan. Cam's in front of the TV watching some sports shit. Doesn't even look at me. "Where is it?"

My mother jumps, drops the spatula, and turns to me. "Tony, you scared the shit out of me. I didn't know you were . . ."

"Where is it?"

Cameron looks up, I'm so loud.

"Where's what?" She wipes her hands on her sweats.

I step toward her. "My fucking money!"

She looks down, then at Cameron and back to me. "What are you talkin' 'bout?"

Cameron stands and shuts off the TV.

I ignore him and keep my eyes on her. "Don't fucking pretend like you don't know!"

She looks away, and I feel Cam draw closer.

"Tony, I don't. I have no idea . . ." My mom's hands fly before her.

"What, did you find it the other day when you were cleaning? Huh? What did you do with it?"

"Tony, I swear. I don't know what you're talking about." She shakes.

I know I should take it down a notch, but I can't, I've lost the capacity to control myself. "The fuck you don't." She cringes and I don't feel bad. And why should I? She's been fucking up my life ever since she gave it to me.

Cameron grunts behind me, but this isn't about him, so I focus on Mom, who cowers against the stove.

"You fuck everything up. You picked Dad, and that was a fucking disaster, had me, and we ended up *here*, in this shit hole. Then you started fucking what's his name and drinking all the time." She looks up, her face horrified. "What, you think because I was little I don't remember?" She lowers her head. "Then it was the next douche and you started getting high." I can see these men in my mind, looming, towering from my child's perspective. "What did you do with me? Nothing! I just existed and you never once acted like a mother."

Cameron grunts again. My face is in flames and I feel on the verge of tears, but I can't stop. Something's broken inside me.

My mother slouches, and I decide to finish her off. "Now you expect me to help you. Do your fucking dirty work."

She looks up and her eyes are wild. The meat crackles and pops, grease smacking the wall behind her. She stares at me like a cornered animal.

"That's right. You know I don't *have to*. And then what? What the fuck are you going to do? You'll be stuck. You'll have smoked up all the money you stole from me and where will that leave you?"

Her body trembles and she turns to the stove, shoves the pan off the burner, and then holds her temples as if keeping her head glued together. Cameron mumbles something and I turn to ask what, but in the same instant, see her flash toward the stove and turn. She charges and the frying pan's cocked like a tennis racquet. She swings and I dodge it, but she cuts with a backhand and clips my chin. Her eyes are pinned on me, and she's frothing at the mouth. I spin away and when I turn she's looking to split my head open. I dodge, again, and the momentum of the swing pitches her forward. I seize the chance and kick out her legs. She tumbles to the ground, the pan pinned by the edge of her shoulder. And without thinking, I'm on her back and have her in a rear choke.

She bucks and twists and spits. "You fuck! You little fuck! You can't do this!" But I squeeze tighter because I can, and because I have to. She stops squirming, her face shifting from red to purple, and I release some of the tension. This is beyond fucked, but all I can think about is how I'm going to get the pan. Because if she rolls once I'm off, I won't be clear, and she'll fucking wail me.

Then a hand reaches down and touches the handle. "Let it go." She shakes her head, and Cameron grabs her wrist. "Let it go before I break this."

She shakes her head again, and I just watch Cameron's hand, silently hoping he'll go through with it.

"Your choice." He hooks his fingers into the underside of her wrist and squeezes, the muscles in his arm contracting and holding, applying increasing pressure.

My mom whimpers, twitches beneath me, fighting, but ultimately screams and lets go. Cameron snatches up the pan, grips it, and shakes it as if taking aim. Beneath me I can see my mother's eye bulge and feel her body tighten. My own stomach seizes. I've all but released her and Cameron laughs, launching the pan across the room. It lands with a clatter somewhere on the counter and I sit up. My mother lies on the floor, eyes closed, breathing heavily. Cameron extends a hand to me. "Good work."

I look up and he's no different than all the boyfriends from the past, and I'm still a child, vulnerable and pathetic. But at least this time he's helping me. I take his hand. He hoists me up, and we both look down at my mother.

"We might as well get set. We can eat with the boys."

I nod and turn away, head to my room. Once inside, I sit on my bed and cup my head in my hands. What the fuck just happened?

I tuck my knees up and lock my heels into the bed frame. What did I just do? I did *that* to my own mother? I don't even know if she took the money. Why didn't I turn on Cameron? Because I'm a fucking pussy, that's why. He would have knocked me the fuck out. I should have let him, because, fuck, if there was any doubt left, it's gone now. I've become one of them.

Everything spins and I gag. Nothing comes but the sensation doesn't dissipate. I hold my shins for a moment and squeeze as hard as I can, pressing my forehead against my knees. I breathe and get calm and even though it's a lie I say to myself over and over, *You're wrong, you are not one of them.*

But it's a lie. I once thought I was different because I used fighting to keep myself safe, as protection. I never started shit, just saw it through and tried like hell to finish it. But I started that. I knew I could dominate her and I used that power. *That's* the problem. *That's* abuse. The fuck is wrong with me? I always thought I would never be like them, any of them—the boyfriends, the park trash, the Front. And him. Never like him. I told myself that. I guess I was wrong. Some things are simply beyond my reach. So much, really.

We step out into the cold, Cameron a half length ahead of me. I had to borrow one of his coats, because after I pulled myself together he looked at me and said, "You need something a little heavier." He stepped into Mom's room and came out with a jacket. She was in bed and I didn't say good-bye, just slid into Cameron's Carhartt, and off we went.

The breeze kicks up and I tuck my hands into the pockets. Something heavy and metal rests inside, but I can't figure out what it is. It's tucked in the liner. I could ask Cam, but holding whatever it is helps me get steady as we approach the steps. I know Rob wasn't bullshitting me, that what I said won't have changed his mind. In a way I'm glad, because he won't have to see the change in me. But still, I'll have to deal with his absence. The Front will take care of that, I'm sure. I follow Cam into Chaz's trailer.

Six guys sit around the kitchen table, eating. They glance up at Cameron, nod, and watch me for a moment before returning to their meals. We turn into the living room and four more guys are sitting on the couch and chairs, plates on their laps. Chaz is one of them and his eyes light up when we enter. He wipes ketchup off his beard.

"Evenin' fellas. Want some grub?" He points at his plate with his fork.

"Got enough?" Cameron asks and the four around Charity's dad laugh. Chaz takes a swig of his beer.

"Go check the stove, we got a shitload."

"Thank you." Cameron turns around and I follow. Fuck, I feel like a douche. Here I am following Cam around like a pet. If I'm one of them I'd better start acting like it.

Cameron puts a plate together and then I pile up macaroni and a couple of hot dogs on my own, grab a soda, and go sit on the couch. Fortunately, Cameron sits in a chair across the room. My stomach is squirming like a baby in the womb, but I choke down a few forkfuls of the noodles. Chaz is watching me.

"So, Vo-Tec, I hear good things 'bout you."

"Thanks," I manage. My voice is weak.

He smiles and has a wizened grandfather look about him, which is so odd considering what he is. "Not often that I hear good things from Johnny B." He turns to the group. "Fucker can't stand Marcus."

The men laugh and someone mutters, "Fuckin' nigger."

"But it's good, Vo-Tec, all good about you. That's what we need, young fellas like you and Dave and Rob. Not crusty fucks like Cam."

Again, the guys laugh, but so does Cameron. He looks up from his plate to Charity's dad. "Us crusty fucks know a whole lot more than these boys, though. Still wet behind the ears, ya know?"

"No doubt about it. But Vo-Tec here and Dave sure got something else wet over at Johnny B's."

He laughs and it's like gunshot. My throat starts to

revolt, and I clamp my mouth shut, keeping down the hot dog I was swallowing. I cannot blow chunks in this room.

"Do well tonight, Vo-Tec, and we may take a ride up to Johnny B's."

The men cheer and I feel Cameron's eyes on me. I look over, and sure enough, he's staring as if trying to see inside, figure me the fuck out. I hold his gaze for a second and then turn back to my meal, just in case he sees a glimmer of how I truly feel.

The door opens and in walks Dave and Marcus. Dave's all smiles and turns into the kitchen yelling, "It's on tonight!" Marcus hangs back and looks into the living room. He juts his chin at me, and I return the gesture. Cameron watches us but finishes what's on his plate. Chaz sips his beer but doesn't speak. Dave comes into the room, still smiling and shakes hands with him. "Tonight's the night, huh?"

Charity's dad eyes him. "Settle the fuck down, Dave, you're making me nervous."

Dave cocks his head, and the smile falls away. He turns around, sees me, and then takes a seat at the end of the couch. Marcus stands in the corner.

"Boys, clear your shit and get in here." Chaz swigs the rest of his beer and then crushes the can in his palm.

Chairs scrape and the garbage can strains from the plates being stuffed into it. I look down at my food, one hot dog and most of the macaroni left, but I don't get up to toss it because no one in this room moved an inch when Charity's dad spoke. The guys from the kitchen pile in and stand along the wall, like Marcus, arms crossed over their barrel chests. The food I've eaten feels like rocks in my stomach.

"All right, we're all here, so let's get started." Charity's dad nods.

"Where's Rob?" Dave asks.

Although the question is innocent, I close my eyes and whisper, "Fuck you."

When I open them, guys are looking around the room as if maybe Rob's in bathroom taking a shit or something. Charity's dad turns to me. "Vo-Tec, where is he?"

I swallow. I knew it would come to this, so at least I'm prepared. "I don't know, he told me he was coming." I try to sound as honest as I can, but see the question spread over Chaz's face.

"I'll go get his ass." Dave stands and I swallow.

"Sit down." Charity's dad's face has tightened. "It's not like he forgot." He pauses and that same wizened air becomes sinister. "No, something's up, and Vo-Tec is gonna let us know what."

All heads swivel as one, and I stare at the dirty carpet, worn down by the traffic of their heavy boots. I force my mind to go blank. If I can't think, then I can't throw Rob in. I just have to play stupid, something I've done so long now, I might as well be it. Besides, Rob may have pussied out, but it's not like I don't understand that.

"I said, Vo-Tec's gonna give us the answer."

I look up and the faces have all hardened. Cameron's coiled on his seat, like a dog waiting for the command to sic. My heart slams into my chest and Chaz must see something he doesn't like. He gives a short nod and before I can think to move, Cameron's cracked me one off the cheek. My food topples to the floor, but I hold my posture, do not wince or cry out, in spite of the pain. Cameron hovers over me, bouncing on his toes.

"Make this easy, Vo-Tec. You're his boy, we all know that. And you know where he is."

I don't even bother to open my mouth to answer, just brace for the next punch, which comes with the same precision to my other cheek. Cameron stands over me, but I refuse to look up at him. To think that just an hour ago, I wanted him to hurt my mother. Serves me right.

"Vo-Tec, this is not how we want this to go. Rob knows too much and if he's anywhere he shouldn't be, and you don't tell, well, you've eaten your last meal." Chaz's voice is calm, not even mildly excited, as if he's reading the facts off a label. Because of this, I know he's telling me the truth.

"He might be . . ." The words are strangled in my throat. If I tell, who knows what they'll do? If I don't . . . Fuck, is my life really worth saving? I look past Cameron to Chaz. "He's not at the cops if that's what you're thinking."

He smiles. "Good boy. Smart." He inches forward in his seat. "Now, where *is* he?"

I shake my head and wait for the third punch, but Dave yells, "At the gym! I bet he's at class now."

The room murmurs, and I look back at the floor. Out of my periphery I see Dave bounce up.

"I'll go get him, drag his ass outta there."

"Sit the fuck down!" Charity's dad's voice rumbles. "Both of you." Dave and Cameron take their seats.

My face throbs and I wait for whatever's coming.

Charity's dad strokes his beard. "So Rob's dissented? Huh? Well, what's our motto?"

The group answers in unison. "I trust you."

Hearing their deep voices speak that same fucking line at once sends chills up my spine. They don't say it like it should sound. It's evil to the core.

"Exactly. Not God, but men. Our trust extends to one another and is maintained until you break it." Chaz grunts.

"And then like gods, we break *you.*"

I pull into myself, aiming to be as small as possible. I can't save Rob now, that's obvious, and that thought alone is enough to make me want to give up, let them do whatever the fuck they're going to do. I'm fucking worthless. But for some reason, I know I don't *want* to die. It's that simple. I tremble and know that this is the most fucked-up place I have ever been, and that I want out and that I want to live.

"Can we trust Vo-Tec?"

The room murmurs again. The word "no" is clear. I wait for my fate.

"*I* believe we can."

I go lightheaded at Chaz's words and have to brace my head in my hands, elbows on knees.

More murmurs but Chaz silences them. "First, he did well with the Hungarians. They know his face, and you know how they are about that. *Drink with us, you!*" He imitates the men and the room laughs. "Second, Johnny B likes him, and Johnny B is never wrong." The room grunts agreement. "Third . . ."

The pause hangs in the air, and I release my head and look at Charity's dad. It's what he wants. It's what I'm supposed to do. And if there's any way for me to get out of this alive, I have to play along. Fuck, I know this, have lived it my entire life. There are rules and there is etiquette, and since I'm trash I'll never have the manners, but at the least I can behave like I'm supposed to.

"The boy can take a fucking hit and not spill the beans." The men nod. "You all know the fists on Cam. What Vo-Tec just did takes some willpower."

Cameron eyes me and it's a look mixed with anger and pride. It makes me want to spit in his face.

"You listen, Vo-Tec."

I give Charity's dad my full attention, face throbbing and stomach churning.

"That's one mistake. You don't get any more. Got it?"

I nod.

"Good. Now, is Dave right, is Rob at the gym?"

I hesitate a moment, short enough so that there is no question about my loyalty, but long enough for me to know that I've given up on myself. "Yeah. He'll be there until about nine."

Chaz smiles. "Thank you." He turns back to the group, and I feel like I've just turned my head while he pulled the trigger. What are they going to do to Rob?

"We'll do a drive-by, let Rob know that we miss him. The timing's perfect." Charity's dad smiles and looks around the room. "Then it's on to storage and finally the warehouse."

I don't know what he means and I don't care. All I can think about is the gym, what these fucks will do, and about Coach Dan and Rob and the rest. If there is any way, any fucking way I can make up for this, I will. No matter what it costs.

"Once we're there, you don't do shit unless I tell you." Chaz looks to each man in the room. "And when I tell you, you fucking do it."

His eyes fall to mine last, and I nod along with the rest.

"Let's roll."

We pile out and I walk with Dave, who turns to me. "Yo, you had no choice. The way it is." I have nothing to say. He clasps my shoulder. "Hop in with us." I follow him and Marcus to the Mustang and get in back. Most of the gang gets on their bikes, and the noise is overpowering. A few slip into cars, Cam one of them, and I'm relieved to be separated. I touch my cheeks, which now distend so far they're visible, and they feel as big as ant hills.

Charity's dad takes point, and the line flows in a motorcade out of the park. I sink low into the backseat and watch the streetlights whip overhead. I try to pretend this is some movie, someone else's life, but it doesn't work.

We stop and the bikes rumble in idle. I sit up and the gym is on my left; one of the bikers is crossing the street to the empty lot. I grab the door handle.

The bikes' throttles echo off the empty parking lot and the crew comes to the window. I can see all their faces, with Rob tucked behind them. Smart move, because here comes the biker from across the street, trotting, gaining speed, brick in hand. I pull the handle. Nothing. I pull again, harder. It stays shut.

The gym window glass shatters, and I duck as if I were behind it. The biker gets back on his hog, throttles it, and signals a whipping circle over his head. The caravan rolls. I hold the handle and watch the gym window until it's out of sight. I let go and fall back into the seat.

Dave and Marcus don't speak. If either of them saw me on the handle, they don't say. Dave follows the parade of bikers, and Marcus sits like a living shadow. I hope that my boys are all right and that after all of this I get the chance to explain. At least to Rob. Before they do more, because I know that was just a warning.

We follow the line to the storage facility outside town, and Charity's dad punches the code. The bikes roll in and when we pass the guard's station, I look over. He's watching a movie on a laptop. We cruise into the back corner and one of the guys motions to Dave to back up to one of the storage units. Dave almost cracks his mirror against the corner but manages to tuck it in. The same guy who signaled hops onto the hood and then the roof and above us I hear the spray from a can.

"Spray painting the cameras, just in case," Dave speaks, but keeps his eyes focused out the windshield. The guy hops off and the storage door opens. I grab a handle and Dave says, "It's still locked, Tone. You aren't going anywhere." I go to speak, to say that I was only going to help, but I understand just what he's saying. He reaches down and pops the trunk. I turn around and can barely see the black cases being placed into the car. I don't think it's meth, so what else could it be?

Guns. It's suddenly just that obvious. I burrow into Cam's coat pocket and feel the metal there. It's not a gun. I knead it into my hand, pulling it out of the liner and into the pocket. It could be a knife. No, it's only brass knuckles.

Two more raps clack off the rear panel. Dave swings a three-point turn and the bikes fire up. We leave the facility and the security guard doesn't look up, just watches the screen on his lap. It's an action movie; cars are blowing up and shit's flying everywhere. I almost laugh at the irony. Almost. I look ahead at the red lights of bikes dotting the road, headed toward the warehouse. Not one part of this is amusing.

23

The warehouse sits like a broken tooth, but this time there are more cars parked in the shadows along its edge. The bikers park next to the other, facing out. Dave pulls in behind them and no sooner does he park than the trunk is popped and the guns are being dispersed. Dave grabs his handle and looks at me. "*Now* we get out."

My face is swollen and seeing around the bruising is difficult. But one thing is clear, no one's giving me a gun. I hang by the trunk and the bikers load up, inserting clips, sliding extra magazines into their coats, and tucking handguns into their waistbands. Cam looks pleased with the nine-millimeter he's selected. Dave doesn't get a gun though, and neither does Marcus, so I feel a little better, just standing around like a tool. Dave nods for me to follow him. He pops the hidden section, revealing the boxes from Johnny B's. "Take one," he says. I fumble getting my hands around the cardboard, but pull one box out and heft it to my chest. It's five times the size of the last delivery. Dave grabs another box and Marcus does the same. Then he closes the trunk. The bikers wait for us in a half circle and Chaz steps to the middle.

"All set?"

Dave says, "Yeah," but I just nod. I don't trust my voice to work. My throat's seized up, and I feel like I might be sick.

"Good. Now, it's real simple. We've got your backs, but you must walk through those doors first. That's the deal." He looks at Marcus. "You lead them in." Marcus swallows but says nothing. "All right then, let's go."

I follow Dave. Thank God for all the time I've spent in the gym forcing my body to do things it didn't want to do, because my legs are stiff and my head's screaming *No!* But I lick my lips, try to breathe under the weight of the box, and get control of myself before we get to the door. Marcus knocks and someone inside speaks, but I have no clue if it's in Hungarian or English, my head's fucked. How did I get here? The door slides back and Marcus walks in. I follow him and Dave.

The same dim lantern burns on the table, but no one is seated at it. Instead, a group of men stands behind it. Above, on what looks like the platform to a second-floor office, another group waits, while a handful of men gather in the office behind them.

"The delivery has arrived, yes?" One of the men steps forward and smiles from beneath a thick mustache.

My heart bounces from between the box and back. I could gag on the sensation, but I watch Dave's lead and set the box on the table. The mustached man pulls a knife from his pocket and says something in Hungarian, or whatever the fuck language it is, to the men behind him. Three come around and one grabs Marcus, another Dave, and the last, me. I flinch at his touch but will myself to relax and just let him do his job. The Hungarian lifts my shirt and checks around my waistband. He bends down and checks the cuff of my jeans and then stands. Marcus and Dave are being handled the same. All three men stand and say the same word in their language.

"Very good. No record." The mustached man smiles and I get what he means: wires. They think the Agnostics would work with the pigs?

The three men resume their positions, and the Hungarian cuts into the boxes. He clicks on a flashlight, peers into both, nods, clicks his tongue, and then looks up at us. "Where is your Hammer?"

I have no idea what the fuck he's talking about, and the mention of a *hammer* makes me want to piss myself. But a voice rises. "Right here." Chaz steps forward, extends his hand. When the fuck did he come in?

"It's been a while, yes? Good to see you."

Charity's dad shrugs and looks up to the office. "The boss up there?"

The Hungarian laughs. "Yes. Of course. We go." He says something again in his tongue to his men, and the bikers form a line behind us. We all watch as Chaz and the Hungarian enter the glass-paneled room. Someone from above says, "Ah, yes, so very nice," before the door closes. Then it's just us and them.

I turn to Dave to see if we can leave, now that we've done our job, but he and Marcus are just looking ahead, sizing up the men in front of them, in spite of the fact that each has a gun strapped to his hip.

Shouts boom above us, but no one moves. There must be close to two dozen men in this room and not one coughs, sneezes, mumbles, or makes any noise whatsoever. Rushing blood fills my head, and I try to stay steady on my feet. This will be over soon, and I'll be all right. For now.

More shouts and then the door smacks open. Chaz bolts down the stairs. "Out of your fucking mind thinking I'd take that price!"

The Hungarians emerge on the steps and the two at the front have drawn their guns. As if on cue, every man in the room does the same. I'm staring down the barrel of a Glock and Chaz is still yelling. "Fuck you, István! You can fucking shoot every last one of us, you fucking pussy!" He comes off the stairs, stops, turns up to the office. "I trusted you and you fucked me like some bitch." He turns his attention to the firing squad across from us. "You go ahead and put a bullet in me you fucking scumbags. But it'll be in my back because I'm not standing here one more second."

I'm afraid to move, and afraid not to. Charity's dad goes through the doorway, not hesitating for a moment. The bikers make a show of dropping their weapons, tucking them away, and turning their backs. Dave and Marcus pick up their boxes and then fall in behind. I do the same and follow them. All I can picture is the guy behind me taking aim and my brain splattering across the wall. Again, I force my legs to move, but this time, slower than I want them to, because I'd gladly run over every fuck here to get out alive.

We shuffle out and nothing happens. In a moment the drugs are back in the trunk and I'm in Dave's car and the door is shut. Safe. My heart's still hammering, but my head hasn't been blown to pieces. Yet I seem to be the only one happy about this. The bikers all wear the same mask of anger. This isn't over.

"Back to the storage. We'll talk." Charity's dad turns away. The guys load up the guns and I let my head fall back and look up at the sky, clear and star-filled. It's almost Christmas, and the night feels as it should. Cold but energized, yet not in any way I enjoy. Dave climbs behind the wheel and we drive.

"That was some fucked-up shit, right?" Marcus's voice is

so deep that it's all bass.

"I ain't seen anything like it."

"So what you think's next?" Marcus looks back at me after Dave just shrugs.

I shrug as well. How the fuck would I know? But I get it, Marcus is fucking scared. I am too, but there's nothing I can do about it. I'm along for wherever this ride takes me. I'm just going to do what I'm told. Period. Just like the pussy I am. I stare out the window and can hear the bikes rumble. "What the fuck was the deal with the hammer?"

Dave laughs and the sound feels awkward. "*That's* what you're back there thinking about?" I nod and Dave laughs again. "Hammer is Chaz. He's old school, doesn't ever carry a gun. He likes hand-to-hand shit, and the old weapons."

"Like a hammer?"

Dave clicks his tongue. "Yeah, and bats and pipes and the rest. But he's cracked the most skulls with a ball peen. Keeps one on him at all times."

I shake that image from my mind as we pull into the storage facility. It's the same, but in reverse. The guys come and retrieve the guns and then place them inside the unit. Dave tells me to get out and I do, but no one speaks, just looks around, waiting for Chaz's plan. He goes into the unit and comes out with four gas cans and a caulk gun.

"Cameron, Marcus, Dave, Vo-Tec, get over here."

My body freezes and I wait until the others move before I do, but then I join them and Cameron shoots me a look. I can't tell what the fuck he's thinking and I truly don't care.

"We just got fucked back there and it wasn't pretty." Chaz looks each of us in the eye, and his mouth twitches beneath his beard. "So now, we need to fuck them harder. That's the way it goes. All's good till you stick it to us. Then all motherfucking hell breaks loose."

The men behind us grunt, as if listening to a preacher.

"Now, each of you has something to prove. *You* may not think so, but I do, and that's all that fucking matters." He leans closer to us. "Do this right, and we'll take care of you."

My heart gallops in my chest, my mouth goes dry, and my legs lose their strength because he didn't say what would happen if we fuck this up. I glance at Cameron and his eyes are big and bright. Dave's jumpy, but Marcus has pulled into himself, eyes hooded by the lids.

"Here's the plan. You'll get these filled." He holds up the gas cans. "Then, you'll drive back to the warehouse and park off that side road. You know the one?" Dave nods. "Good. So then you'll go in on foot and prep the place." He pauses and looks us over. "Be careful, István may be expecting something. But most likely he'll be getting piss drunk thinking about how he fucked up and how to make it right." Charity's dad laughs. "Well, too fucking late for that."

I put two and two together and do not like the results.

"Cam, you work construction, so you'll do best with this." Chaz hands over the caulk gun. Cam takes it and looks at the brand.

"What's this for?"

"To patch up the bullet holes in your ass."

Cam tries to laugh at the joke, but the sound that emerges is all wrong. Chaz stabs a finger at the caulk. "It's flammable. So after you dump the gas, caulk the door and then light the fucker." He looks up and his eyes glint. "Ain't no way out."

No one speaks. Not us and not the men around us. The *something* we have to prove involves killing a dozen men. This can't be real. This has to be some sick and twisted fucking joke because I don't feel scared, just detached. There's no way this is happening, that we're actually going to torch the warehouse. He just wants to see if we'd go through with it, a test.

Charity's dad hands each of us a gas can. "Fill 'em up at the Shell station. We got connections there, and they don't have cameras."

Dave and Cameron nod and I just stare at the empty can dangling from my fingertips. Chaz slaps my cheek playfully. "Vo-Tec's graduating tonight." He laughs the same gunshot laugh, and I come to my senses. This isn't a test. He's not fucking joking one bit. But I'm not killing anyone. There is absolutely no fucking way! I am not one of these men.

Charity's dad turns to the group. "We'll toast marshmallows back at the park to celebrate."

The men laugh and Chaz clasps Cameron's shoulder. "You've got point on this, so handle these boys. Big plans for you after."

Cameron says something I don't hear because all I'm thinking about is how this has gone so wrong. First I got roped in, and then I just wanted to make some money, help out with the bills, maybe get the fuck out of the trailer park. I didn't want to deal and go to some whorehouse. I was willing to go along because there didn't seem to be any other choice, but now? What the fuck? I'm not going to jail. What am I going to do? How am I going to get out of this?

Cameron and Marcus and Dave walk to the Mustang, and I follow.

Dave pulls into the gas station and looks back at Marcus and me. Neither of us says a word; we just get out and grab the cans. Marcus takes the nozzle. "Hold them so they don't tip." His voice is calm, but his hands are shaking.

We fill the first two and then move onto the third when Marcus coughs. "This is fucked up. What the fuck do *I* have to prove?" He looks at me like I have an answer. "I'm just a big-ass nigga to them. The fuck am I gonna gain from this?"

I wish I knew. Fuck, I don't know what this is supposed to do for me, either. Not like it's some mentor program where I get to learn how to be a wanted criminal. Not like what Rob's got. That is if they don't fuck up his world.

Marcus moves to the last can. "I don't know if I can do this, yo. I never killed nobody. Put bruthas in the hospital, sure. But . . ."

I cut him off. "You don't have a choice." Even as I speak, I know the words are for me, too.

Marcus scowls. "Yeah I do. Rob did."

He sounds like a child, and I spit on the ground, more angry with myself than anything. "You think that shit's over? You think there isn't a next step after this?"

Marcus racks the nozzle. "That's my fucking point. There's always somethin' else, and it's always more fucked up each time."

Dave's window drops. "You two bitches done, cuz I wanna get this the fuck over with." He holds a fifty out the window and I look over at Marcus, but he's already screwing on the caps. I snag the money. "Get a lighter, too."

I return with the lighter and hop in the car. It's quiet, but full of pressure, as if someone just quit screaming. I look at Marcus and he's staring down at his hands. Cam's looking out the window, jaw set hard, and Dave starts the car, but shakes his head.

"Something up?" My words spill out.

Dave edges the car out of the lot, and Cam turns around in his seat. "You thinking 'bout being a little bitch?"

"The fuck you mean?"

Cameron juts his chin at Marcus. "Fucker says he ain't down with this. Don't want to kill anybody. 'Bout you? Too much of a pussy?"

The fucking ways I could answer pack my head, but I just shift in my seat. "Marcus will be fine. Just nerves. I trust him."

Marcus shoots me a look and Cam grunts. "Better be that way."

He turns back and Dave picks up speed. A moment later Marcus nudges me with his shoulder. Then he reaches out and we pound fists. Reminds me of Phil and Amir and my insides run.

Dave pulls off to the shoulder of the side road and kills the engine, but leaves the keys in the ignition. We all step out and to the trunk.

"You heard the plan, we slip in, spill the cans, and I'll caulk. Light and run. Simple as fuck." Cam grabs a can and the caulk gun. "You think you can handle that?" He's asking all of us, but looks at Marcus real hard. Marcus grabs a can and I do the same. Dave grabs the last and closes the trunk.

"All right, Dave, Tone, start at the back wall and wrap around to the middle of each side. Marcus and me'll pick up where you leave off and wrap around the front." He stares at Marcus again. "I got my eye on you." Marcus turns away and Cam mutters "nigger" under his breath. Marcus tenses but does nothing.

"Don't leave your fucking cans. No evidence." Cam looks over at the warehouse and I do the same. It's a big goddamn building. This is gonna take a while. "Let's go."

We follow Cam, who stays along the edge of the parking lot, tucked beneath the shadows of the pine trees. All the cars are still here, and as we pass to the far corner, loud voices are clear from inside. Cameron stops abruptly, turns and points at Dave and me. He gestures us to the back and we take off.

It's slow going because the side is littered with tree roots and dead limbs. Dave steps on one, and it sounds like lightning cracking. I press against the building and feel my heart pound off the wall. No shouts come from inside, though, so we keep moving and watch our fucking feet.

We reach the back, and it's a clear field, the wall is free of obstacles. Dave and I move to the center and set down the cans.

"What a pain in the balls."

Dave keeps his voice low and I nod, but don't speak. My head's running three steps ahead of me, and I know what we have to do and am trying to believe that the result will not be my fault.

"Ready?"

His voice is a whisper, and I pretend not to hear him. He punches me in the kidney.

"You fucking ready?"

I unscrew the cap. The fumes waft out and my head spins, but Dave joins me, hefts his up, and starts pouring. He heads the way we just came. I go off to the other side, and whatever the hell is over there. Dave's crouched low and moving quickly, the gas lapping at the edge of the building. If I don't keep pace, Cameron will come looking. I pick up my can, angling it like Dave's and start pouring.

I move along the back wall with ease and when I turn the corner, half the can is empty. The far side is the same as the other, a goddamn tinder box of dead limbs and trees. Chaz must have had this planned for a while, because it's perfect. This place will go up like a torch. My head goes light at the idea, and I pause against the wall for a moment before moving on. I watch my step but notice that the can's running low. I smack into something dense. It moves and I almost scream.

"Hey, Tone."

Marcus's voice scares me so bad I close my eyes, prepared to be hit, and swallow my scream.

"We could still run. The keys are in the car. You and me. We could make it."

His voice is so genuine, it reminds me of Rob's. It takes a moment for his words to sink in and as they do I am speechless. I picture what he means, see us running. It's nice that he's willing to include me, that he's got my back, since no one seems to have his. But in the end, there's nowhere to run. At least not for me.

"Go for it. I won't say shit, promise."

"You ain't coming?"

As much as I want to say I will, I can't, and that hurts worse than any punch I've taken. "Wish I could, but I'm stuck. You know that."

Marcus looks toward the car, and I wait for him to bolt, but he just stoops down and picks up where I left off. I follow, keeping ears and eyes out, just in case.

We snake along the wall and around the front corner and there's Cam and Dave, like we fucking rehearsed this shit. Cam looks up, but quickly returns to the job, while Marcus barrels along and we all meet at the front door.

The voices inside are louder and slurred and seem angry, even though I don't know what the fuck they're saying. If they come out now, we're dead on the spot. This is it, now or never.

Cam sets down his can and reaches for the caulk gun tucked into his jeans. "Pour the rest on the door." He cuts the tip off the caulk with a knife he's pulled from his pocket.

Fucker must carry a weapon in everything he owns.

Dave, Marcus, and I look at each other, but then lift our cans and pour the remnants along the door. Cam finishes the job and puts out his hand. "The lighter!"

I dip into my pocket and start to hand it over.

He looks up at me, narrows his eyes, and then stands. "No, *you* do it!"

My insides feel as if they've fallen through my ass. I look to Dave and Marcus and they back away. Cameron joins them.

"We'll be at the car. Don't come unless this fucker's burning." He turns and they follow, and I'm left holding a can and the lighter. The noise of the drunken Hungarians and the stench of gasoline wafts around me.

I can't do this. I can't murder anyone. But if I don't do it, I might as well just walk inside and let them shoot me. I could still run, though. I'm fast and Marcus might stall them and I could get to the cops. But I reek of gas, and what if they don't buy the story? Or worse, what if one of them is working for the Agnostics?

I could run, but I'm too afraid of what would happen, because all I've ever seen is shit get worse. Fuck, it doesn't get much worse than this.

I click the lighter, and the yellow flame emerges. I watch it for a moment and then close my eyes. I see my past: all those men and my mom, and my father. I see my present: me failing, going nowhere, ending up here. I see my future: it doesn't exist. I open my eyes and touch the flame to the wet line.

A "poof" rises up, and I stand back. The fire is already climbing the walls, touching off the trees. The door is engulfed in flames, and the heat warms my face. Shouts peal from inside, and smoke billows through the broken ceiling.

I turn away but do not run. I hope someone breaks free

and sees me and knows what I've done and shoots me dead. It'd be easier than whatever I'm going have to do next: let go of my life. But that won't happen. Charity's dad's done this shit before, has planned this one to a T. There's no way out.

I reach the car and the three of them are standing on one side watching the blaze. I hand Cameron the lighter. "Careful with this." I laugh. The bubble just bursts from within and they all look at me, eyes wild. I laugh again and stare back. "What?" They don't answer and I keep laughing. Dave crosses to the trunk, and I throw my empty can at him. He takes care of it and then slides behind the wheel.

Dave starts the Mustang and Cam rolls down the window, the car already filling with our fumes. Marcus looks at the warehouse and then back at me while I try to wipe away a smile, but can't.

24

We pull into the park and the guys are outside, gathered around a metal drum, toasting marshmallows and drinking whiskey. They cheer when we stop and gather around the car like we're celebrities. Chaz breaks from the group. "Just heard the fire trucks wailing. Well done." He clasps each of us and I laugh along, no longer concerned if I do seem like a fucking lunatic. Maybe I am. Maybe something broke in my head, like it broke in my heart back at the trailer with Mom. Chaz joins me.

"Nice work, Vo-Tec. We got some shit to talk 'bout, all of us, but you done good."

"Thanks." I smile and mean it and feel the warmth of getting something right. It spreads through me and I feel like I belong. I was beginning to feel this way at the gym, but maybe this is where I was supposed to be. Maybe I've just always been fighting the inevitable.

Someone hands me a bottle. I take a long pull and warm myself by the fire. It doesn't compare to the one I set, but it feels good.

"Boys, inside. The fire was fun, but it's gotta go. Don't need the pigs driving by and seeing this. Might get wise and put two and two together."

The gang turns away from the can at Chaz's orders and one kicks it over. Another two smother the fire. We march inside, and I crash onto a couch. The men sit in every available spot, even on the floor. They pass bottles, and across from me Cameron tips one back and takes an enormous swig. My cheeks are throbbing now that I'm warmed up and part of me wants to smash the bottle over his head, and part of me thinks the guys would be fine with it, because I lit the inferno. Because it was me. I killed them. Me.

Fuck. I killed people. Thugs, yeah. But still, isn't that the way I'm headed? Would them killing me be all right?

"Boys, we got fucked but proved a point. I ain't happy 'bout it, but that's the way it goes." The men grumble and nod. "Cam, Dave, Vo-Tec, and Marcus deserve credit for what they've done." The room claps and it feels so much like being at the gym.

But this isn't Coach Dan's, and these men aren't my crew.

"Even though we taught them a lesson, it doesn't mean we can be smug. That fire will eventually get put out, and then the pigs will want answers." Chaz looks around the room and all eyes are on him. "We can't wait around for that, and we can't just take a hit on our profit."

They will come. And these bastards will throw me under the bus.

"So I've got a back-up plan. We're heading to Florida in a week anyway, so why not go now?" Chaz looks around the room, and the men look to one another. "I've got a connection in Miami willing to make the deal the Hungarians didn't. So, let's get the fuck out of Dodge."

Yeah, let *them* go, but not me. Not ever.

There's more muttering and then someone asks, "When?"

Chaz clears his throat. "Tonight. We need to move and

the holidays are in our favor. Everyone's looking to the sky for problems, not the ground. You hear me?"

The men nod and some take stiff pulls, but I relax. Shit, I couldn't have asked for more. If they go now, I'm fine, so long as the cops don't get me. And Rob's fine, and all I have to worry about is Cam. Shit, after what I just did, I think I can handle that.

Chaz sits up. "So that means Dave, you're coming. You've earned it and we need your car. Marcus, Cam, Vo-Tec, welcome aboard."

The weight of his words paralyzes me, but Dave's eyes bug and Marcus shakes his head. Cameron clenches his jaw.

Chaz looks at us and his face hardens. "I'm not asking. I trust you to make the right decision."

The tension is thick and no one speaks for a moment. My head races with excuses for me to stay, but nothing sticks, not my mother, not school, not anything about my future. Fuck, this may be my only option.

Chaz stands. "You have an hour. We roll then."

The guys stand and talk to one another and then car lights fill the room. They blink off the wall and everyone stops moving. Outside, doors click shut. And then voices call.

"Tony?"

"Hey, Tony?"

"Yo, Antioch, where you at?"

The men in the room turn to me and Chaz marches over. "Vo-Tec, what the fuck is this?"

"I . . . I don't know."

Chaz lifts me up by the collar. "Go find out and get rid of them."

He spits his words through clenched teeth and I see him, as if for the first time, as he is. This is Charity's dad. This is the same motherfucker who sold off his own daughter to sweeten his meth deal. This is the same fuck who's taken care of Cam, the one my mother asked me to kill. How can I even consider going with him? I don't want to be part of the Front. They are everything I've never wanted. Cameron made me light that fucking fire. And, now, he'll own me and will make me do whatever Chaz wants. Fuck this.

I laugh and Charity's dad lets me go. Like after lighting the fire, something has torn loose. This time, though, it feels like some veil. The world around me is painfully clear. I smooth my shirt while Chaz looks me over. "I got this." I smack his shoulder and walk to the door, head clear for the first time all night.

Phil, Amir, Coach Dan, Mike, the Blob—the entire gym—stand between their cars and the trailer, arms folded across their chests. Coach Dan steps forward. "Tony, hey, are you all right?" He touches his own face, indicating my eyes, and then looks at the trailer where, I'm sure, eyes are peering through the blinds. I shrug and tilt my head toward the horizon, where the sky is filled with smoke. Coach follows and his body tenses. "Okay."

I look through the crowd and find Rob tucked behind the Blob. My insides surge. I am not one of them. Not a murderer. I can do this.

"Tony, we came here to help. After the visit we received, we thought it best." He looks around the crew, huddled not too unlike the gang inside, and then looks back at me. "Is there anything we can do?"

I swallow because the words are screaming at my throat, but I can't use them. I need to be precise here, and if I've learned nothing else from Coach Dan and this crew, I know that you must read the situation as much as you react to it. I open my mouth just as the door behind me does.

"Well, well, well. Look what we have here." Chaz comes down the steps and places a hand along my neck and squeezes.

I watch Coach Dan. His eyes harden and he shifts his weight. He's no fool. But Chaz doesn't seem to give a shit, looks right past him, at Rob.

"Quit being a pussy and get over here, Rob."

Chaz's words rumble through me. Amir and Phil hold on to him, but Rob says, "I have to."

He steps forward, pins his shoulders back, and walks to us.

Chaz spits at his feet. "Looks like you got our message. Now let's see if you understood it?"

Rob swallows but doesn't say anything.

"We had a deal. You were part of it, and you chose to abandon us. Am I right?"

Rob nods and looks more scared than I've ever seen him. But I'm feeling all right. About to shit myself, yeah, but the crew's here. We'll be fine.

Chaz squeezes my neck again. "You left your friend as well. And he's proven great things about himself tonight." Chaz looks over his shoulder, at the smoke rising.

Coach Dan asks, "Tony? Did you?"

"That's none of your fucking business!" Chaz cuts Coach off, and he takes it, nodding once.

The crew is motionless, speechless, and I can only imagine what they are thinking. I *know* what's going on and this is fucked up. For them, shit, I would understand if they just got in their cars and went the fuck home.

"Seems like you've made a choice, Rob. But I didn't let you have that choice, so it wasn't yours to make." Chaz points at the crew. "You boys would be wise to get a move on. This has nothing to do with you."

No one moves.

Chaz nods. "Uh, huh, so it's like that." He sighs. "Well, like I said, Rob, you had no choice, yet you made one. Tony here had a choice and made the right one. So I think the only fair thing to do is ask you both to make a decision."

My heart jumps like it's trying to crawl through my ribs. I have no idea what this crazy son of a bitch is going to ask.

"Step closer." Chaz lets go of my neck and waves to Rob.

Rob looks at me, at Coach, and then back. He takes two small steps and is now striking distance away.

"Here it is. You either both come with us, or you both go with these bitches."

Rob's face darkens and I twitch. Did he really just make *that* offer?

"But it has to be both of you, whatever you decide. I trust you to make the right choice."

Fuck, fuck, fuck. There he is with that word. *Trust.* Just what the fuck does that mean in his world? It feels more like *Obey.* Well, I'm sick of obeying this bastard and I'm sure Rob feels the same. So fuck him. I go to answer but Chaz smacks my chest.

"No, Rob answers first."

Rob takes a deep breath and clears his throat. "I choose them, not you."

His words are crisp and strong and I smile.

"I agree with Rob." I step away from Chaz, and he looks between the two of us.

He's still for a moment, watching, thinking. Then he nods and speaks. "Boys you know our motto. We express it, not because we're trying to be amusing, but because it's how the world works. You gain trust and you lose trust. With some that is fine, they don't matter, they aren't made of anything strong. There is no retribution." He pauses and my neck tingles. "However, that is not the case with us. There is always a price to pay, and here it is."

Before I realize what he's doing, before I can react in any way, Chaz has lifted his arm and his fist looks like a hammer. And then I understand and move, but am stopped by the backswing of the ball peen.

It strikes Rob in the temple, and a sickening wet crack follows. A spray of blood arcs across my face as Rob falls to a heap. I freeze in place and stare. Where Chaz struck him is now a gaping hole. Blood and brains pour out. Without question, Rob is dead.

The moment freezes, and I see Chaz's face, smiling and disturbed. I'm four years old again, and there is my father with the same pleasure. He's just punched my mother and is about to backhand me. But I am no longer that boy. And now all that matters in my world is gone, and I won't let that shit happen again.

I charge Chaz like a linebacker, burying a shoulder into his stomach and driving him to the ground. Air pops out of his lungs on impact and he wheezes. I reach down, pull the hammer from him, and raise it over my head.

"Tony, no!"

Coach's voice calls from just behind me and it stops me, but only for a second, because when I look down I can still see my father's face, and I don't owe him anything but what he and Chaz have coming. I arch my back and squeeze my chest and swing.

The impact sends me sprawling on my back, and when I manage to look up, Cameron is on top of me.

25

In an instant Cameron disappears, is lifted off by Coach Dan, who punches Cameron so hard his neck snaps all the way back. I reach for the hammer, to finish the job, but it's gone, and Chaz is being pulled to his feet by the Front, who is now spilling out of the trailer, and is being met by my crew.

Fists fly, legs kick, and heads get bashed. I can barely tell who's who, but I remember what's in my pocket, slip the brass knuckles over my hand, and enter the fray.

One of the bikers sees me and hesitates and it's all I need. I step into his legs and crack him an uppercut that splits his chin in two. The blood sprays, and he grabs his face. I kick him in the stomach and he falls to the ground. Legs trample and kick him. Ahead of me Phil and Amir are holding their own. Phil takes on a biker twice his size and gets punched square in the nose. Blood gushes like a water balloon's been popped, but he manages to move away from the second punch and uses the leverage gained to toss the guy to the ground.

I charge over and kick as hard as I can, catching the fucker in the ear. My heel rips off the cartilage and the guy screams. Amir looks over and Phil looks up. I jut my chin, indicating the next asshole coming toward us. He hurls himself and I roll, taking out his legs. I hop up and see Amir send a knee into his ribs. The guy shudders like he's had a stake driven through. Someone grabs my ankle and rips me to the ground. By the time I look up for help, Phil and Amir each have another biker to contend with.

I'm being dragged across the gravel and around me boots lift and kick and it's all I can do to avoid them. I catch a glimpse of Coach Dan now tangling with Chaz. Coach's face is bleeding, but Chaz is just breathing heavy. I hope Coach kills him because this is all about revenge, and whoever the fuck is pulling me is about to find that out.

I'm whipped and crash into the side of the trailer. The impact forces the air from my lungs, but I know I can't stay down. I get up just as whoever's tossed me lunges. I throw an elbow into his face, knocking him back. He stumbles and I see that it's Cameron. Every muscle within me dances with the opportunity, and all the pain I feel dissolves, replaced by my hate.

He collects himself and I drop into my stance. He stares at the knuckles. I look down at them as well, hoping he realizes they aren't a random pair, but his, and that I'm about to pummel him with them. But then the bridge of my nose cracks and everything goes black.

Blood courses down my face, and I grab my busted nose. I can see images close to me, enough so that Cameron is visible, coming at me with a jab. I'm too slow to weave but tuck my chin and he cracks me off the top of the head. "Fuck!" he screams and shakes his hand.

I let go of my nose and catch him with a cross to the ribs. The brass connects and the bone cracks. Air rushes from him. Blood covers my chest and is dripping down my throat, but I watch his body. He's flat on his feet, rubbing his side.

The space around us is a blur, so all I can see clearly is him, but that's all I need. I charge.

He goes to kick, but I'm faster and we fall. I'm on him without thinking and pin my knees into his chest. I punch him once in the throat with my bare fist and he grabs at me, legs flailing. I drop my weight as he chokes and then let him catch his breath. I don't want this over quickly. But he spits and says, "That all you got, cunt?" I punch his forehead with the knuckles, and it splits open, blood gushing forth.

The hit doesn't stop him though. He just bucks and tries to throw me off. Blood pours from his head and I realize that this is what he did to my mother: slow, methodical torture. I'm in his place now, doing the same to him. But I don't care. Rob is dead. Nothing else matters.

I pop off Cameron and he rolls to get up. I kick him in the side. He curls but keeps scrambling. I kick again, catching his mouth, and feel teeth break. He pulls his head in between his arms, but still tries to rise. Around me all I can hear are men screaming and bones breaking. I only hope the majority of the pain is the Front's. This is one battle I'm not losing.

I turn back and Cameron's crouched, face oozing blood, a pocket where his front teeth should be, and a knife in his hand. He lunges and I step back but knock into someone and fall. On the ground is the last place I want to be. Just like in the ring.

Cameron tries to pin me with one arm, while aiming the knife. His arms are coated in blood and slide across, but his eyes are haunted, like someone possessed. If I don't find a way right now, I'm dead.

He stabs at my side, but catches my elbow. It stings but I pop my hips to roll him off. He doesn't budge, just locks his boots beneath my back, removing all of my leverage. He stabs at my face and I grab his wrist, but it's with the knuckled hand and they keep me from getting a solid grip. I slip on the blood, and he's free again.

He tucks into himself and slides down onto my thighs, but keeps his feet wedged into my spine. If he moved just a little more I could sit up, but he doesn't and I feel like I'm being snapped in half. Cameron wipes the blood from his face and grips the knife in both hands. "Should have done this sooner." Every part of my body flexes and I try with all I have to roll him, but I can't. I look behind me, to see if anyone can help, but all that's visible are legs and fists.

Cameron laughs and I turn back. He's holding the knife over his head and he smiles.

No! This is not how I want to die. Not like Rob. I cannot be another victim. I clasp my hands together and lock my arms prepared to block. Maybe he'll miss, or catch me in the ribs and I'll be able to get the knife. I just can't let him get to my neck.

"Ready?" Cameron plunges.

But a blur flashes across my eyes and I come up with the impact. I'm thrown free and when I get up I see Marcus on top of Cameron, the knife in Cam's shoulder. He's got Cam pinned though, and is squeezing his neck with the other arm, choking him out. He looks at me and neither of us speak. I want to stay and watch, but this isn't just about Cam anymore.

Chaz and Coach are locked in a hold on the ground. I step to the side, get a clean line to Chaz and kick. My toe sinks into his temple, but it's not a hammer and doesn't puncture. Coach looks up and I smile, thanking him for the opportunity. I reel back and kick again, but Coach rolls and I kick him in the back.

"The fuck, Coach? What are you doing?"

He doesn't answer, just squeezes around Chaz's neck for a moment, then slides off him. The biker is out cold and I understand. Might as well let me finish the job. I take two steps back and then charge, but Coach wraps me up, takes me to the ground.

"No, Tony. You can't."

"Fuck you, I can't." I try every move I know and don't give a fuck how much the ground eats at my face and chest. I want up and I want that man dead.

Coach is like a vice. "Tony, just look. Look at Rob." He moves my head.

In front of me, through my filtered-tunnel vision, is Rob. He's in the same position as when he dropped. I shove off the ground, and Coach lets go. I crawl to my friend.

He's surrounded by a pool of blood so wide it's incomprehensible. "Rob? Hey, Rob?"

But he does not answer, and a sickness within me rises and I hurl. I make sure to point my face away from him and retch until I'm just gagging. Then I wipe my face and turn back to him. I grab his hand. It's still warm. I move to his chest and feel for a heartbeat, check for breathing. Nothing. I lay my head on him and am too angry to cry. This hurts more than my body does. More than anything I've ever felt in my entire life.

"Tony?" Her voice is soft and feels dreamlike.

I look up at Amy. She's biting her fingers, staring at Rob. I wave her down to the ground. She kneels.

"I heard the noise and figured they were partying. But, Tony . . . what?" She loses her words into a sob. She stares at Rob and touches his cheek and loses her shit all over again.

I feel so cold, so drained of life, but I reach out to her. I put an arm around her back and whisper, "I'm sorry."

She sits up, smacks me. "You're *sorry*? That's all you can say? Rob is fucking dead and you're sorry? It's your fault, Tony! He's dead because of you. If he hadn't been looking out for your pathetic ass, he'd still be . . ." She doesn't finish. Doesn't need to. I know what she intends and I know she's right. Sorry isn't enough.

I don't want to leave his side, but I have to. This isn't over.

I stand and make my way back to Chaz. Coach blocks me. "Tony, no."

"Coach, get out of my fucking way."

"You don't want to do this."

"How the fuck do you know what I want? You have no clue, no fucking clue how life is for me. So just step out of the way and let me make one goddamn fucking choice in my life."

Coach sizes me up and I think he's about to strike, when he steps to the side. "Just make sure this is a decision you can live with."

I ignore him and move to Chaz, who is moaning, probably about to wake up. I turn and look around. The crew is broken, as are the Front. Blood flows from everyone I see, and bruises swell faces so I can't recognize most. But I see Marcus, and he's near Cameron, who's on the ground. I move to them and see the knife in Cameron's throat. I register this fact and don't feel much more than a shred of relief. I pull the knife from his neck, nod at Marcus, and make my way back to Chaz.

His eyes are open and he's sitting up, but clearly is out of it. I kick him in the head and send him right back down, straddle his chest.

"Vo-Tec. Here to finish the job?" He wheezes and smiles at me.

I don't like the smile, would like to cut it off his face. "Yes. Ready?"

"Always am."

He's calm, not even fighting, and I know it's a trick, a way for me to let my guard down. Fuck that. I lift the knife and he watches it.

"I knew you'd be one of us. Have that spirit."

"I'm nothing like you, Chaz." I spit in his face.

He laughs again. "You can tell yourself anything you want, but we both know the truth."

I don't want it to but straddling this piece of shit, it comes swift and fierce: I am one of them. But not because of how I've been raised and the shitty expectations of me, but because of this one choice. If I kill him, I am no better. He killed Rob, so he deserves it. But if I kill him, does that make it even, or does that change everything?

I look up and see the crew, Coach and the Front. In the distance Amy is crying. I stand up and throw the knife away.

"That's what I thought." Chaz gets to his feet, and the Front moves in around him.

My crew circles behind me. No one has fight left in them, except for me and possibly Chaz. I have no idea how this is going to play out.

"Answer me, Tony. Why didn't you kill me?" Chaz's voice is tight.

"Because you don't deserve it."

He laughs. "The fuck is that supposed to mean? You pussy?"

My back stiffens. "Call me whatever the fuck you want, it makes no difference. *You* make no difference."

"Stupid. Plain stupid. I just killed your friend. How can that *not* make a difference?"

I close my eyes, and for a moment wish I had killed him, and know that I still can. But I let it pass. "People die every day. Scumbags like you kill the innocent and each other. You have an effect, yeah. But you make no difference. It's all the fucking same."

"Didn't you torch that place back there? Or is that my imagination?"

"No proof of that. Of the other three who were there, one is dead. One hates you, and the other is as trustworthy as that dead trash over there." I point at Cameron and feel nothing. "Even if I did, I was forced, so say what you want, but it's only you who is listening."

"Doesn't matter what I hear, only what I know. I trust you get that now."

"I do. And I trust you know that I don't give a fuck what you know. You're going to get out of here, take that body with you, and never come back, right?"

Chaz looks around, his eyes for once, unsteady. "Maybe? Might be back. What will you do then?"

I know. I have no doubt what I'll do if this fuck ever returns. But for now that doesn't matter. For now, there is only this moment. "We'll see."

"Damn straight." Chaz circles around his head. "Clean this shit up and get packing. Our plans haven't changed." He looks back at me. "Neither have mine for you."

I don't bother to answer, just watch him go. Watch the crew support each other and drag Cameron's body into Dave's car. I watch Dave protest, give me one last look, and then slam his door shut. Marcus nods at me and then disappears into the shadows. The Front mount their bikes and then ride, the bikes searing the night with growls that match the pain swirling inside.

I turn and see who is left.

There's Coach, bloody and bruised, Amir and Phil, likewise. Mike's got a broken collarbone, and the Blob's knee is busted. The rest are equally mangled, but alive. I know I look like roadkill, but do not care. I walk and this family parts for me. I go to Rob.

Amy is still at his side. I touch her. She glares, fierce like an animal, and I'm reminded of my mother and hurt all over again. "Amy, I know you don't want to speak to me. I don't blame you. But please understand this . . ." I pull myself together. "Without Rob I'd be dead. I know that, just as much as I know you loved him. This is on me and I will never forget it. I don't know what I can do about it, but I will try. I will figure this out and make it right. Somehow."

Amy's face pulls one direction and then another. She goes to scream, to lash out, but then stops. "You'd better." Her voice is low, harsh. "You'd better because he deserves it, Tone."

I nod, grab his hand, and silently say my good-bye. "Let us"—I point at the crew—"get out of here. And if the cops don't come, call them. Tell them whatever you want. The truth, a lie. It makes no difference to me. They'll at least take care of Rob. Okay?"

She nods, her hair falling in a mess around her face. "I won't lie, Tone. I know what happened. Those fuckers killed Rob. That's all I need to say."

"Thank you." I turn from her and back to Coach. "Let's get the fuck out of here."

"I was thinking the same thing. The gym. We'll be safe there."

I'm not sure he's right, but I agree. I move toward his truck, but stop. "Give me two minutes. I need to see my mom."

"Go on."

I head to the trailer and climb the stairs.

The house is dark. "Mom?"

No answer.

"Mom, I'm home."

Nothing.

Panic spreads. "Mom!"

"What?" Her voice rips from the living room and I turn on a light. She swivels in the chair to see me and stops. "Tony! What happened? Oh my God, are you all right?" She feels me over and looks at the blood and stutters.

"I'm fine." I lean against the wall for support. "I'm going back out, to the gym, but I needed to let you know something first."

Her face clouds and she takes a step back. I see her again, from just hours before, on the floor, beneath me. I almost wish Cam had killed me.

"Mom, I'm sorry." I reach out, but she backs away. I understand. "I don't know what came over me, and I understand if you hate me forever. But I am sorry." I swallow and look directly in her eyes. "And it's done. Cameron's dead."

She falls back into the chair and her mouth moves, but the words seem to get caught in her throat. After a moment she manages to say, "Really? He's gone?"

I nod.

She puts a hand to her face. "Thank you." Tears run and I want to reach out to her, but I turn away.

"I have to go, but I'll be back in a bit. If the cops roll up, I haven't been here. I've been at practice."

She nods. I may have taken care of Cam for her, but I've got some ground to make up.

I ride in silence with Coach and when we get to the gym I collapse on the floor, in the dark, with the rest of the guys. No one speaks. No one has to.

26

've just come from Rob's funeral. It's the day after Christmas, and I've never felt so lost in my entire life. I'm numb. I have no clue if I'll ever get used to the idea that he's gone. Seeing his body didn't make it any more real than seeing him on the ground. I wish I could feel more, but I think it just hurts too much.

Rob's parents wouldn't look at me and scowled at the guys and Coach Dan. Our busted bodies told the other half of the story that everyone here is sharing, but that the cops can't prove. They questioned all of us, even yesterday, on Christmas. But the fire and Rob getting in the way of the Front's quick exit—and whatever the fuck they think happened to Cam—was just too convenient of an explanation for them to take, even if for some reason they wanted to dig deeper.

The couch squeaks beneath me as I sit, and the house is so quiet. There's no Cameron. No Front. No Rob. My mother hovers, but does not know what to say. Not that I expect her to. What can she possibly think of me now?

"You want something to drink? Hungry?"

I shake my head. "No. Maybe later."

"We should talk, Tony. When you're ready."

I turn to her. She's better than before, than when she was with Cameron, but the scars are visible and the worry in her eyes is unmistakable. "I'm ready whenever you are. I'm the one who needs to apologize."

She moves to the recliner across from me. "Go ahead."

I stare at the floor and begin. "I had no right to treat you the way I did, to think you had taken my money, and especially not to hurt you." I choke on the last words.

"I'm used to it, so don't beat yourself up."

I look up. "But that's the point. I know you're used to it and *I* used that against you. I'm terrible."

"No. No, you're not terrible. You made a mistake, but not for nothing, I think you've paid." Her statement hangs in the air. "Besides, I know you're as much a part of me as you are him. More so. It's only a matter now of how you see yourself."

She's right. For once there's real parenting coming out of her mouth and I'm amazed by it. Still, being part her is not as soothing as she might think. "All those years ago, when they tested me, and I was smart and all, why didn't you get me into the program?"

Her eyes bug and she puts up her hands. "Where is this coming from?"

"I'll explain."

She frowns and crosses her arms over her chest. "Your father was smart. Like you. Just knew shit without having to have read it or anything. Back when we got together I thought that was going to save me, was going to make up for how stupid I am. It didn't. Because regardless of how smart you are, if you drink yourself into an asshole, then that's all you are." She looks at me. Her eyes are tear-rimmed. "I didn't want you to get so smart that you saw me like he did. I didn't want you to be him."

I sigh. As fucked up as that logic is, I understand it.

"If I had the chance to use my brain, how would you feel?"

"Huh?"

I explain about Big O's offer, what could happen. How I may still have a way out. She stares and then looks away. I see the scar in her profile and feel sick for even bringing this up.

"You take it." She rushes to me, grabs my hands in hers. "You take it and you do something. I'm not smart like you. Never will be. But I know enough. Someone's willing to help, willing to get you out of here. You take it."

I pull my mother into a hug. "I'm sorry for everything. For all that I've done."

"Don't apologize anymore. You are who you are. The good. The bad. That's life."

I close my eyes and I breathe deep and am still. I don't know what will come or what I'll have to face. The Front may be back for me, but I doubt it. And if they do, I've got a family who will back me up. Coach Dan believes in me, and it has nothing to do with fighting. That's just our outlet for this fucked-up world.

Mom's right. I'm nowhere near all good. But I'll honor my promise to Amy. I'll repay all that Rob sacrificed.

On the mat, in the classroom, in the street. It's all a fight. And I'll take comfort knowing that there's no way in hell I'm ever tapping out.

ACKNOWLEDGMENTS

I must first thank my agent, Kate McKean, who has been a true champion of my work. She has guided and nudged and has helped me see my words as she does, thus providing the insight necessary to develop. Her gifts to me cannot be quantified and I thank her profusely.

My editor, Lisa Cheng, and Running Press deserve my thanks. Lisa posed questions that needed answers and pushed me to consider the depths of my story. With her help, the soul of *Tap Out* emerged. Running Press has been considerate of my ideas and supportive at every step of the process. I couldn't ask for a better relationship.

My wife, Carrie. I don't know how you have been so patient with me for all these years, but without your continued support, I would not be a writer. None of this would exist without your compassion and belief in my dream. I will continue to thank you for the rest of my life.

My daughters, Grace and Kaygan. Some day you will read this story and you will come to this page probably shocked by what your dad has written. I'm sorry, but I do hope you enjoyed the story. We'll talk when you're ready.

To my family, who has always known I'm on a different path than most, thank you for understanding, and thank you for never discouraging, and thank you for providing me the kind of life that allowed me to write Tony's and not live it.

Mark Ayotte, my first reader. Thank you for loving MMA and writing and for your willingness to be objective and read your friend's work.

MMA fighters. Your existence is so thoroughly symbolic for so many today. Please never forget the literal and figurative power you have. Fight the good fight, fully knowledgeable of the eyes on you.

Photo by Meaghan Carney

Eric Devine is currently a writer, high-school English teacher, and educational consultant. He is also the author of *This Side of Normal*. He lives in Waterford, NY, with his family and can be found online at ericdevine.org and via Twitter @eric_devine.